IT'S A WONDERFUL KNIFE

book ten of the matchmaker mysteries series

elise sax

It's a Wonderful Knife (Matchmaker Mysteries – Book 10) is a work of fiction. Names, characters, places, and incidents are the products of the author's imagination or are used fictitiously. Any resemblance to actual events, locales, or persons, living or dead, is entirely coincidental.

ISBN: 978-1719143059
Published in the United States by 13 Lakes Publishing

Cover design: Elizabeth Mackey
Edited by: Novel Needs
Formatted by: Jesse Kimmel-Freeman

Printed in the United States of America

elisesax.com
elisesax@gmail.com
http://elisesax.com/mailing-list.php
https://www.facebook.com/ei.sax.9

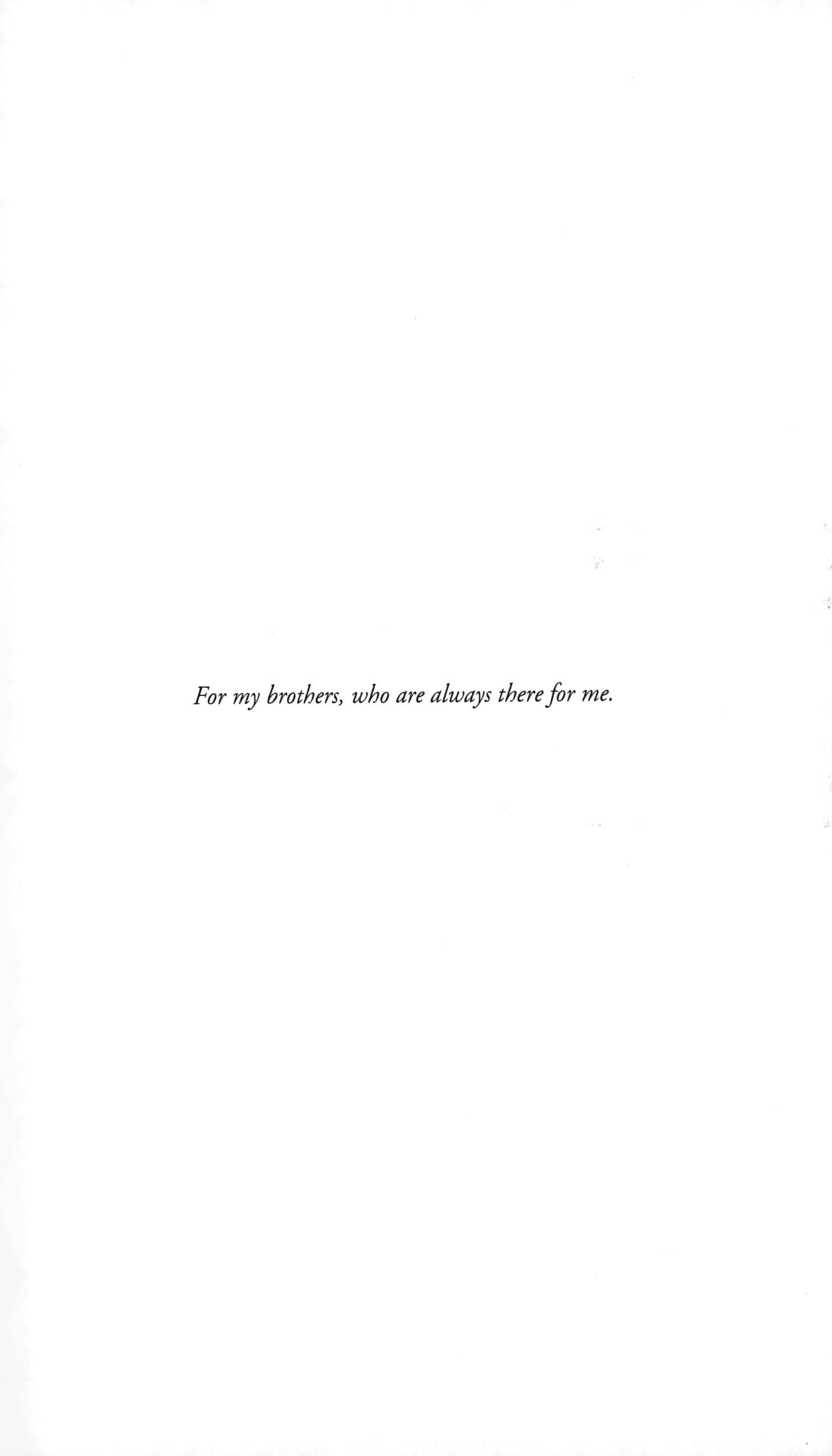

For my brothers, who are always there for me.

ALSO BY ELISE SAX

Matchmaker Mysteries Series

An Affair to Dismember
Citizen Pain
The Wizards of Saws
Field of Screams
From Fear to Eternity
West Side Gory
Scareplane
It Happened One Fright
The Big Kill
It's a Wonderful Knife
Ship of Ghouls

Matchmaker Marriage Mysteries Series

Gored of the Rings
Slay Misty for Me
Scar Wars

Goodnight Mysteries Series

Die Noon
Doom with a View
Jurassic Dark
Coal Miner's Slaughter
Wuthering Frights

Agatha Bright Mysteries Series

The Fear Hunter
Some Like It Shot
Fright Club
Beast of Eden
Creepy Hollow

Partners in Crime Thrillers

Partners in Crime
Conspiracy in Crime
Divided in Crime
Surrender in Crime

Operation Billionaire Trilogy

How to Marry a Billionaire
How to Marry Another Billionaire
How to Marry the Last Billionaire on Earth

Five Wishes Series

Going Down
Man Candy
Hot Wired
Just Sacked
Wicked Ride
Five Wishes Series

Three More Wishes Series

Blown Away
Inn & Out
Quick Bang

Standalone Books

Forever Now
Bounty
Switched

CHAPTER 1

My grandfather died when I was a little girl. I don't remember much about him, but he was a big man, and he never came downstairs before he was fully dressed in a pressed suit, tie, and pocket square. And then he was dead. The day after his funeral, I was in my grandmother's bathroom, which is my bathroom now, and there he was. Big and dressed in his best suit, he was staring back at me in the mirror. As you can imagine, I didn't say a word to him, and he didn't say a word to me. Probably because he was dead. But even when he was alive, he didn't say a word to me. So, it wasn't a big, loving reunion scene or anything, bubbeleh. He stared at me in the mirror, and after a few seconds, I turned around to see if he was in the room. Bupkes. He wasn't there. When I turned back to the mirror, he was still watching me with a blank expression on his face. He was probably as surprised to see me as I was to see him. After all, I had no business being in my Grandma's bathroom. I was pretty stoic as a little girl, but sharing a bathroom with a dead man blew through my calm demeanor. I screamed like a meshuganah. Grandma came running, and so did my mother. My grandfather disappeared before they arrived, but my mother and grandmother believed me when I told them that I had been visited by an apparition. They both spit to ward against the evil eye, and then they told me the secret of love, right there between the toilet and the tub. They explained that only love can make spirits move between worlds, because love isn't part of the physical world or the spiritual world. Love is its own world, a mystical force that adopts us or leaves us on a whim, like a cat. The more we open our hearts, the more chance we have of possessing love in our lives. There was also this, and it's probably the most important thing: The more you give, the more you get. It's the karma of love and it's not always immediate, but eventually—eventually—love comes to the loving. Be loving. Promote love. Be loved. I love you, dolly.

Lesson 3, Matchmaking advice from your Grandma Zelda

So, this was how it happened when everything was going right. Love life… right. Career… right. Hair…right. Deluxe super fancy latte maker machine in new custom-built house… right. Rockabilly band for impending wedding… right. Everything, every aspect of my life, was going right. And what normally happens in cases like this when everything a person has ever wanted—and even the things she didn't know she wanted—have come true, is that they become a serene, enlightened, sublimely happy person who can out-cool the

Dalai Lama and even give up blinking.

So funny. As if.

In reality, I had everything I wanted and everything I didn't know I wanted, and I was freaking the shit out.

It might have been because I was in charge of the Sunday Singles meeting, since my grandmother was MIA, but I was betting it was more likely worrying about Eileen the street sweeper singing Ave Maria at my wedding.

My. Wedding.

It never dawned on me that what I thought was my happily ever after was only a transition to my real happily ever after.

"Where's Zelda?" Sally Salken asked. We were sitting on folding chairs in a circle in the parlor, and I was sensing a certain amount of doubt in my abilities from Cannes' singles.

"I think she's ice skating," I said. Since Grandma had started leaving her property line, she was never home. She had been a shut-in since my father died years ago, but since we discovered the truth about his death, she was undergoing a rebirth. She had always been a social butterfly, but now the butterfly was flying all over the place.

"It's July. Who goes ice skating in July?" Sally Salken said.

"She said something about a rink in San Diego next to a churro stand," I said.

"Soon there'll be no ice skating because the earth is getting closer to the sun," Jenny Jackson explained. "That's called global warming."

"There's no such thing as global warming," Millicent Lane spat. "Everyone knows that when the earth gets closer to the sun, the sun backs up. That way the earth stays the same, temperature-wise. We're just at the time right before the sun takes a few steps backward."

"That doesn't sound right to me," Jenny said.

"I saw it on PBS," Millicent insisted.

"Since when do you watch PBS?" Sally demanded.

"Ruth Fletcher made me put it on the TV when she came in for a cleaning."

Millicent was the town's new dental hygienist, and Ruth Fletcher was the ornery tea shop owner, who would have flailed Millicent alive if she had heard her theory about global warming.

"Anyway, today's talk is about preparing for happiness," I said.

"Preparing? I'm ready," Sally announced, and everyone laughed.

"Sometimes, we don't know what happiness is, what will actually make us happy," I said. "We're trying for something, going down a path toward it, but it's not the thing that will really make us happy."

"This is depressing. Zelda never makes us depressed," Jenny complained.

My forehead broke out in sweat, and it got pretty wet between my breasts, too. Flop sweat. I knew it well. Grandma was having fun, eating churros while she ice-skated, but in her absence, I had to take up the slack and was stuck with every group meeting and volunteer organization committee. And I wasn't the best at any of it. Sure, I had gotten better since I had moved into town to help my grandmother with her matchmaking business, but I was no Zelda Burger. There was only one of her, and I wasn't it, no matter how many times she told me I had the gift.

"Sorry," I said. "I didn't mean to depress you. What I mean is that we have to prepare for happiness and really understand what's in our heart."

"How do we do that?" Sally asked.

"Vision boards," I said.

Millicent clapped her hands. "I love arts and crafts!"

I hated arts and crafts. I couldn't even draw a stick figure. But I had to make a showing with the vision boards, or nobody would come to me to be matched. I refused to be the downfall of Zelda's Matchmaking while she was having fun in San Diego. So, I had woken up early in the morning and drove to Walley's, where I bought poster boards, arts and crafts supplies, and a pile of magazines to use for pictures. Luckily, my grandmother had left me with a debit card for expenses. I had never felt so rich in my life. I even bought Crayola brand markers instead of the generic kind.

"Crayola," I announced and pointed to them, like I was wearing a spangly dress on *The Price is Right*. I laid out all the supplies on the dining room table, and the women went right to work.

"This is great," Sally said, cutting out pictures of Chris Pine from People magazine. "I know someone who did a vision board, and three weeks later she won the lottery."

"I'd love a George Clooney lottery," Millicent said. "He gets my juices flowing."

They cut and pasted. They drew little flowers and glittered everything. My vision board was blank. I didn't know what to do with it.

"Look, Gladie's board is blank," Sally said. "Of course it is. She already has the perfect man, and he's building her the perfect house."

"Yes," I said. "That's true."

But I still felt like my vision board needed something different. Something new. My grandmother had planned most of my wedding, but it was up to me to pick Spencer's wedding gift. He was the best dressed man of our town, Cannes. He had a designer wardrobe, and he now had a designer house, which was almost done. What could I get for him? What item would illustrate my love for him?

I picked up the special edition Burnt Sienna Crayola marker and drew a large question mark in the center of my board.

"Oh, that's deep, Gladie," Jenny said, studying my question mark. "What do you think about my Mercedes? Too much?"

"Not at all," I said. "I mean, if you think a Mercedes will make you happy."

She studied her glittery vision board. "It wouldn't make me *un*happy."

She had a point. I didn't think a Mercedes would make

anyone unhappy. My friend Lucy had a Mercedes with seat warmers, and she was very happy.

Fifteen minutes later, the class was over. "No class next Sunday," I announced. "I'll see you all in two weeks."

"You mean you'll see us in one week," Millicent corrected. "We've all been invited to your wedding."

"You have?" I asked, surprised. Her face dropped, and I cleared my throat. "I mean, of course you have." It was a sad attempt at covering my slight, but she accepted it.

"I'm wearing a blue and white sundress," she told me, excitedly. "I love that you're having an outside wedding. You're going to have single men there, right?"

"Of course."

I had no idea who was going to be there. I suspected the whole town was going to be there. I didn't even know it was an outside wedding.

My stomach growled. There was leftover lasagna in the refrigerator, but desperate times called for fries and a chocolate shake. "I'll walk you out," I told the women and grabbed my purse.

They left the house holding their vision boards, imbued with renewed optimism that their fantasies and wishes would come true. A blast of hot air hit us when I opened the front door.

Sally groaned. "One-hundred-two today."

"We're in a pineapple, that's why. I heard it on the news," Millicent explained.

"The pineapple is the rain. We're in a pocket," Jenny

said. "A pocket with a zipper that's closed tight, so the heat can't escape."

We were back to a scientific conversation that had no basis in reality. But one thing was certain. It was hot. I was wearing cutoffs, a tank top, and flip-flops, and I was sweating two seconds after I left my grandmother's air-conditioned house.

"It is called a pineapple," Millicent insisted. "And it's going to get worse. A super pineapple. That's what we're going to have. Sorry, Gladie. I hope your wedding won't be ruined."

Watching the Sunday Singles get in their cars and drive away, I worried that my wedding would be ruined. I pictured walking down the aisle with big fat sweat stains under my arms and my hair frizzed out, just like it was now. I had tried to tame it with a lot of product and a ponytail, but my hair had a life of its own, and it was escaping the ponytail elastic in long frizzy tendrils.

Across the street, a couple of workers were walking in and out of the house. The renovations were almost done. Spencer had pulled out all the stops to make it gorgeous, and I still couldn't believe that I was going to move into it after my wedding on Sunday. There was a Jacuzzi attached to the pool in the backyard, and there was another Jacuzzi tub and steam room in the master bath.

With all of those Jacuzzis, I would never have to worry about a sore muscle again. "How the hell did I get here?" I asked aloud and opened my car door.

Luckily, my Cutlass Supreme had killer air

conditioning. I blasted it and turned on the radio to the oldies station. I drove through the historic district on my way to Burger Boy. The town was pretty quiet, and I assumed that most of the townspeople were hiding from the heat.

Then, I saw a ruckus on the sidewalk on Main Street, next to the pharmacy. The mayor was waving his arms at a man in a military uniform. I couldn't hear them, but I could tell that it was a screaming match.

The mayor was wearing a white linen suit, and he seemed no match for the military guy with thick epaulets and a chest covered in medals. I didn't have time to wonder what the argument was about because I had a milkshake with my name on it, waiting for me.

Even though it was hotter than hell, it was a gorgeous day. There wasn't a cloud in the sky, and the mountain was lush and green. Burger Boy was by the lake, and if I had been at all athletic, I would have rented one of the paddle boats or kayaks they offered at the lake and made a day of it.

But I wasn't athletic.

I turned into the Burger Boy driveway and stopped at the large Burger Boy plastic head to order. Opening my window, I shouted into the head. "I'll have the double Burger Boy with cheese, large fries, and chocolate milkshake, no whipped cream. Oh, what the hell. Yes, I'll take the whipped cream. Hello? Hello?"

Nothing. And the window was open, bringing gusts of hot air into the car.

"Hello?" I tried again.

"The head don't work, like, you know?" a voice said. I craned my head to see a familiar-looking skateboarder.

"Oh, dude, it's you," he said. "Hey, dudes, look, it's the babe!" he shouted.

There was the sound of wheels on pavement, and then his three skateboarding friends rolled up to the car.

"Did you ever get away from that harsh killer bitch?" one of the skateboarders asked me.

They had helped me when I was running away from a killer nearly a year before. "Yes, that was almost a year ago."

"Cool."

"Yeah, cool."

"Cool, dude."

"How have you been?" I asked them.

"Like, you know," one of them answered. He was wearing board shorts and a t-shirt with *What country would Jesus bomb?* written in purple neon on it.

"Hangin'," another clarified.

"Hangin'," the others repeated.

"Can you spare a buck for a milkshake?" one asked me. Grandma's debit card burned a hole in my pocket. They were a bunch of potheads, but they weren't bad guys. It was the least I could do to buy them milkshakes.

"Sure. Let me park."

I parked by the door to the restaurant and got out. The skateboarders hopped onto the sidewalk and flipped their boards up and caught them.

"Cool," one of them said.

"Cool," the others repeated in unison.

"Cool," I said because I didn't know what else to say. They were all high, or they had smoked so much pot in their lives that they were permanently stoned.

"Oh, dude, look at that," one of them said pointing to the telephone pole over Burger Boy. There was an owl flapping its wings, but it was attached to the pole and seemed distressed. I couldn't believe my eyes.

"It's plastic," I explained.

"Cool. It's like a real kind of plastic."

"Yeah, real kind of plastic."

"You know, pot isn't good for your brain," I said.

"Weed is life. Weed is legal."

"Weed is legal."

"Like, it's a plant, dude."

"Like, a plant."

"Cool."

"Yeah, cool."

"Oh, dude, the plastic bird. Dude."

"Dude."

I looked up, again. The owl was flapping in obvious distress. "I think it's a robot," I said, gnawing at the inside of my cheek.

About a year ago, I had mistaken a plastic owl for a real one at this very spot, and the result was humiliating and life-threatening. There was no way I was going to fall for that, again.

The owl started to screech, loudly.

"Cool robot," one of the skateboarders said.

"I'm not falling for this, again," I said. "Somebody go up there and help it."

They stared at me and didn't say anything. I figured their drug-addled brains were trying to figure out what to say.

"I know. I'll call for help this time. Nine-one-one works, now." But in my hurry to get a milkshake, I had forgotten my cellphone on the kitchen table. "One of you call for help," I told them.

"My mom took my phone, dude. She said I was wasting my life."

"I lost mine at the pool."

"I took mine into the pool. Dude, phones should work in the pool."

"Dude."

"Yeah, dude."

The owl screeched and flapped its wings, as if it was panicked. If it wasn't helped soon, it would break its leg or worse.

"I cannot believe this is happening," I said and put my purse down on the sidewalk. "How is it possible to do this twice in one lifetime?" I grabbed the metal handles and pulled myself up. "Who has a life like this? Nobody, that's who." The owl screeched, again, and it sounded weaker. I stopped climbing for a second and looked up at it. Its foot had gotten tangled in some kind of wire on a metal rung. If it didn't calm down, it would snap its foot in half. "See? I'm a hero. An animal lover. Only an animal lover would do this twice in a lifetime." I had

had a run-in with an animal rights organization because of an incident with a snake, and I still got poisoned pen letters from Betty White because of it.

"I'm almost there," I called to the owl. I was huffing and puffing pretty bad, and I wondered if I should ask Bird for a diet before my wedding. She was the owner of the local beauty salon, and she was always on one diet or another. She probably had something that would work in a week. "If you're plastic, I will not finish killing you."

But it wasn't plastic. As I got to the rung underneath it, I could see that it was real. "I'm here to help you, so just keep calm," I told the bird. It screeched in reply and flapped its wings. "I'm being a hero," I reminded it.

I stretched out my arm, and as gently as I could, I tried to extricate the owl's foot from the wire.

There are times in a person's life where they realize they're doing something stupid the moment they do it. The guy who fell off a cliff while taking a selfie probably was one of them. Ditto the guy who used a match to see if he had gas in his truck's gas tank.

And then there was me, trying to save an owl on a telephone pole.

Surprisingly, the owl's foot came untangled easily, but instead of flying away, it went right for me, hell-bent on revenge. "I'm a hero," I managed right before the owl screeched and attacked me. All I saw was beak and feathers before it was on me. I waved my hands at it, trying to protect myself, clenching my thighs tight around the pole.

I stayed up for about three seconds, which felt like hours, as I battled against the bird, who obviously blamed me for getting stuck on the pole.

Life is so unfair.

I was vaguely aware of the sound of sirens coming closer, but I was focused on survival. I was looking at either death by owl or death by sidewalk. It was a tossup which was better, but my body decided for me. I grabbed the pole, wrapped my arms around it and sat my thighs on the metal rungs. Even though I had stopped swatting at the owl, it continued to fight me, dive-bombing right down my top.

"Sonofabitch!" I screamed with the owl down my shirt. It scraped and clawed at my bra, and I let go of the pole long enough to rip my shirt off and swat the owl away. Gravity took over and I fell backward until I was hanging upside down, watching the owl fly away in victory and my shirt float down to the ground.

Below me, there were a fire truck, two police cars, and one familiar-looking unmarked police car. Spencer got out of the car, holding a megaphone in his hand. He turned it on and put it in front of his mouth.

"Are you kidding me?" he shouted up at me.

CHAPTER 2

The more things change, the more they stay the same. Someone wise said that. I think it was my Uncle Morty, but it could have been Aunt Tilly. Anyway, what I'm saying is that sometimes matches seem different to you. You know what I mean? You'll think they're unsolvable, unique problems. But you'll be wrong, bubbeleh. Wrong! At times like those, think back to other matches and find the similarities. This one likes girls who giggle. That one likes girls who giggle. This one doesn't like his face touched. That one doesn't like his face touched. Start with what's the same and work out to what's different. That will give you clues about who to match them with. The same will start you on the right track.

Lesson 99, Matchmaking advice from your Grandma Zelda

The firefighters got me down in one piece, but my

Walley's purple bra had seen better days. My flip-flops had fallen somewhere, and I was now barefoot.

"I don't understand how this is possible," Spencer said when I got to the ground. He ran his fingers through his thick, wavy brown hair. "I mean, owls. Who climbs a telephone pole twice in a lifetime to catch an owl? Who? Who?"

"It's more common than you think. I heard that Queen Elizabeth did it once."

He took off his blazer and wrapped it around my shoulders. "I'm not calling you Purple, if that's what you had in mind. I'm sticking with Pinky."

"Fine with me. I probably should get a rabies shot. One of us frothing at the mouth is enough."

"I'm not frothing at the mouth," Spencer insisted, but he wiped his mouth with the back of his hand, anyway.

"I had to go up. It was in trouble, and I didn't have a phone to call for help."

"Why didn't you ask Burger Boy for help?"

"It's broken," I said, waving at the Burger Boy drive through head.

Spencer sighed. "No, I mean why didn't you walk into Burger Boy and ask them to call?"

"Oh." It was a good idea. Why hadn't I thought to do that? I stomped my foot. "That's a dumb idea. The owl needed me." I spoke fast so he wouldn't pick up the fact that I was an idiot. "I think I need a rabies shot."

"Owls don't have rabies."

"How do you know?"

"I know things, Pinky. I'm reasonably certain owls don't get rabies."

I pointed at his mouth. "What did you just do? You downgraded to 'reasonably certain.' That doesn't sound convincing."

Spencer put his arm around me and pulled me in close. "Listen, Pinky. You don't have rabies. You're not going to get rabies. You might want to take a shower to get all of the feathers out of your bra, but you don't need a shot."

"Fine, but if I go crazy in the middle of the night and bite your face off, don't come running to me."

"You can count on it, Pinky."

The firefighters found my flip-flops, but my shirt had disappeared, just like the owl. I had a few scrapes and bruises, but I had come out more or less unscathed, except for my ego, which I hadn't thought could get any smaller. But there you go. There's always room to fall further.

Spencer found me a Cannes Police Department t-shirt, and he bought me lunch inside Burger Boy. He got me large fries along with my regular order because he felt sorry for me.

"One week, Pinky," he said, softly. He put his hand on mine on the table and caressed it. Spencer had a good touch. Not too hard. Not too soft. He had the Goldilocks touch. Just right.

I put a French fry in my mouth. "One week," I repeated

and tried to smile.

The truth was that I was excited to start my life with Spencer. I felt like the luckiest woman in the world to have him with me forever.

But I didn't like to be the center of attention, and I didn't want to have to sign something and promise something and stand still while the street sweeper sang Ave Maria.

I scratched my arm. "You've got hives," Spencer pointed.

"Rabies," I breathed. "I told you."

"I'm reasonably certain rabies doesn't cause hives."

"What do you mean by 'reasonably certain?'"

"So, my parents are coming to town in a couple days. You excited?" Spencer asked, changing the subject from terrifying, deadly diseases to terrifying, deadly in-laws. Actually, I had never met Spencer's parents or even spoken to them on the phone. I was sure that they were going to meet me and tell Spencer he was crazy for choosing me.

"They're going to love you," Spencer told me, reading my mind. "As long you don't go near an owl when you're with them."

Hank Frazier, the old man who ran the fruit stand in the historic district and who was Ruth's on-again, off-again companion, walked by and hit Spencer on the back of his head with his cane. Spencer grabbed at his head in pain. He was about to let his aggressor have it, but he stopped when he saw that it was old man Hank.

"Here! You pay this!" Hank shouted at him and threw a

ticket at him, which floated down until it covered my milkshake.

"Did you get a parking ticket, Hank?" Spencer asked. "You have to get a disabled placard if you want to park in the blue spots."

Hank hit Spencer with his cane again. "It's not a parking ticket, you dolt. It's a summons to the Fussia Court for violating a sovereign nation without the proper visa."

Spencer turned to me. "It's never what you think. Never. This town is in an alternate universe." He grabbed Hank's cane before he could hit him, again. "What're you talking about, Hank? You left the country?"

"Yes!" he sputtered. "I mean, no! There's a crazy man on Main Street who's set up his own country in the old market by the pharmacy. You can't walk on the sidewalk in front of his shop without having a visa and paying a fee. Have you ever heard of such a thing?"

I once saw a donkey flying over our town, so I didn't comment about the man who had created his own country on Main Street. We lived in a crazy town. It was sort of expected that crazy things would happen. Spencer tossed me a *why me?* look.

He kissed me goodbye and headed out to overthrow the Main Street dictator. I didn't bother to tell him that the mayor had been fighting with him a moment before I was attacked by an owl.

"I think I'll go home and take a bath," I told him. He turned around.

"On Friday, we can take a bath in our Jacuzzi tub." He hopped on his heels and smiled big.

"Our Jacuzzi tub," I breathed. I couldn't believe I was living this life. I had a house with a Jacuzzi tub and a soon-to-be husband with a six-pack, a job, and limitless energy in bed. It was like I had won the life lottery. I went on my tiptoes and whispered in his ear. "Maybe we could do a trial run in our regular tub tonight."

Spencer's pupils dilated, and he arched an eyebrow. He smirked his normal little smirk. "A dry run in the bathtub. I'll try to get home early."

Spencer arrived home at the same time as my grandmother's Uber and the Chik'n Lik'n delivery man. We sat down to dinner together, and Grandma regaled us with the wonders of the world that she was re-discovering.

"Have you heard of carpool lanes?" she asked, holding a fried chicken leg. "We drove on one. It was wonderful, bubbeleh. You should try it."

Tired, Grandma went to bed early, and Spencer and I went upstairs to fool around. Three hours later, I was asleep in Spencer's arms in our bed. I was enjoying a deep sleep without dreaming when my grandmother shook me awake. It took me a moment to realize where I was and that it was the middle of the night.

"What's wrong, Grandma?" I yawned. "Do you have

heartburn again?"

"Get out of bed, dolly. I have to talk to you."

Her voice was strained and full of fear. I rolled out of bed and slipped into Spencer's sweatpants and a t-shirt. I followed Grandma out of the room, and she took my hand, pulling me into her bedroom.

"I don't know what to do," she said, pacing the floor. "This has never happened to me before. It's the end. It's terrible. It's a Krakatoa, Ten Plagues, Herbert Hoover kind of disaster." She turned around and gripped my hands, like she was holding on for dear life. "I need your help, dolly. I need you to fix this."

She was hyperventilating, and I was afraid about her health. She had suffered a heart episode recently. "Grandma, come and sit on your bed and take some deep breaths. Your face is red. Do you want water?"

She shook her head and sat down. I sat next to her and took her hand in mine. "There's no time for water. No time to breathe."

"What is it? Did someone die?" Since I had moved to Cannes, I had stumbled over one dead body after another, but my grandmother always told me that her third eye was only for love, not death.

"I made a terrible mistake. Terrible. I made a bad match, and you have to unmatch her before it's too late. Oh, what am I talking about? It's already too late. She's married to him. Married! Poor Matilda. Dolly, you have to help her."

CHAPTER 3

I have a lot of one-on-one matches, but I like to teach group classes, too, bubbeleh. There's always something to learn from another person. Never underestimate the positive energy that a stranger can offer. Even negative energy can stir emotions and spark brain juice to flow. A stranger is outside your normal circle, with different experiences, perspectives, and points of view. They may be hard to understand, but there's always something to learn from them, something to change you, even slightly, to get you on the right path, to show you what's around the corner in a neighborhood you've never visited. So, classes are important, dolly. Strangers are vital. It's like eating a short ribs dinner when all you've ever eaten is chicken and rice. Tell your matches that chicken and rice is fine, but there's nothing wrong with adding short ribs to your diet once in a while. In other words, bubbeleh, talk to a stranger.

Lesson 107, Matchmaking advice from your Grandma Zelda

Matilda Dare lived just outside of Cannes in a modest apartment complex. It turned out that my grandmother had matched her a couple months before I had moved into town. It had been a whirlwind romance, and only two days after they met, Matilda married Rockwell Dare, a salesman with a lot of charm and more than his share of teeth.

"He smiled all the time. That's what threw me off my game," Grandma told me a few hours before, downstairs in the kitchen. The sudden realization that she had made a bad match had woken her, and no amount of hot chocolate and Fig Newtons could get her back to sleep. "He had real white choppers. Just like John Gilbert."

"The guy who sharpens knives on Apple Street?"

"No, that's John Hilbert. John Gilbert was a silent movie star. He was all kinds of hubba hubba. And he had great teeth." She pointed to her teeth, which were pretty good, considering her age. Spencer had great teeth, so I knew what she was talking about. When he smiled at me—even his little smirk—my knees buckled, and it was all I could do not to drop my pants and say yes to everything he asked.

"Bad marriages happen all the time, Grandma. If you made a bad match, wouldn't they just get a divorce?"

"It's fuzzy, dolly. Fuzzy. I'm seeing the match, and with it something dark."

She locked eyes with me, as if she was searching for an answer from me. I understood the question. She had the gift for love, and there was a good chance that I had the gift for dark. I had stumbled over one dead person after another since I had moved into town, and somehow had figured out who had murdered them. My grandmother was asking me to use whatever gift I had to figure out what the dark was and to fix it.

"I don't have the gift," I whispered. "I'm just…me."

Grandma leaned forward and took my hands. "Dolly, you have the gift. I'm sure of it. You have the gift for love and for death. You know the light and the dark."

"That doesn't sound good. That sounds like the opposite of good. Like I'm a monster or something."

"No, it means that you're stronger than I am and my mother and her mother, combined. You see all of life, not just one part. Embrace your gift, Gladie."

I didn't have the heart to tell her that I didn't have the gift, but she needed to sleep, so I nodded and promised that I would help Matilda Dare. Grandma kissed me on the forehead and went back to bed. But I couldn't go back to bed. My head was filled with thoughts about gifts and bad matches, and they were keeping me up. I needed a solid nine hours to be my best and a solid seven to function. I was working on five.

"Folgers isn't going to cut it," I announced to the empty kitchen.

Ten minutes later, I was dressed and in my car, on my way to Tea Time. The owner of the shop, Ruth Fletcher made the best coffee in town, and we had struck a deal for her to give me free lattes for a year. Even though it was before opening time, I knew that Ruth was a morning person and would already be in her shop.

I parked in front and got out. Across the street, the country of Fussia, which used to be the two stores next to the pharmacy, was cordoned off and signs warning people that they needed visas to enter the country were plastered on the side of the building. I guessed that Spencer had had little luck trying to stymie the man's desire to be a dictator. Policing in Cannes was a lot different than Los Angeles, where Spencer had been a detective for many years. I bet he longed for normal gang activity instead of flying donkeys and dictators.

The store next to Tea Time was under construction. It had been the home of a short-lived coffee place, but it had gone under pretty fast. I peeked through the window to see what was moving in, now. There were shelves of bottles and jars. The store was decorated in purple and white. It was peaceful. Airy fairy. Artsy fartsy. On one wall was written, *Be Blessed.*

"What're you doing?" I heard behind me. Ruth had walked out of her shop with a dish rag in her hand. She was wearing men's gray trousers with a blue button-down shirt. Her hair was cut short. Even though she was older than dirt, she stood straight and tall, and I knew from experience that she was in better shape than I was.

"What's the new store going to be?" I asked.

"You mean the all-natural beauty product store or the dictatorship across the street?"

I hooked my thumb at the Be Blessed store. "I guess the all-natural beauty product store. It looks nice. Relaxing."

"If it is, it's the only relaxing thing in this crazy-ass town. July fourth wedding. What the hell kind of thing is that?"

I gnawed on the inside of my cheek. My first match was getting married in three days, and I was supposed to be the best man. Spencer didn't want to go because the bride, who was Ruth's grandniece, was a danger-prone Daphne, and he was sure that the combination of me, her, and fireworks was just asking to get blown up or at least burned alive.

"Fred says it's patriotic," I told Ruth.

"A patriotic wedding. What is this? The Reagan administration? Is Nancy going to be at this patriotic wedding?"

"I'm pretty sure she's dead."

"Oh, thank goodness. Now you've put me in a good mood."

"Sheesh, Ruth. That was harsh. Don't you worry about karma?"

"No. I'm pretty sure karma is dead, too."

I followed her into Tea Time. She flipped the lights on and walked behind the bar to make me a latte. The shop was empty except for Ruth and me, and there was a pile of wedding decorations in the corner.

"You're up to your neck in wedding planning, I see," I said.

"No more than you, I bet. You're down to the wire. I bet you're busy with wedding stuff all day and night."

"Oh, sure. Of course," I said and wiped at an invisible spot on the counter. Actually, I hadn't done much of anything for my wedding. My grandmother and the entire town had taken control of it, and I figured ignorance was bliss.

"I heard that you're going to be dropped out of a

helicopter onto a mountain. I heard that lions were involved. I also heard something about trained bees." She finished making the latte and plopped the cup on the bar in front of me. "I'm telling you right now, girl, I'm not coming to your wedding if any of those things are true."

I took a sip of the latte. Yum. Ruth made the best coffee in town, and it hit the spot. "You were invited? How did that happen?"

"Very funny. The whole town was invited. You're lucky I'm coming. I've got standing in this town, you know."

I let her stew in her own juices for a moment while I drank my coffee. She was right. I was lucky she was coming because at least I knew her. My wedding was going to be a circus spectacle with me the main act in the center ring. I wasn't particularly fond of being the center of attention, but at least I would have some friendly faces in the crowd. And Ruth would be there, too.

"Wait a second," I said. "What do you mean, trained bees?"

I drank a second latte and waited around until eight o'clock, when I thought it was a reasonable time to visit Matilda Dare. Outside, the man dressed as a military dictator was yelling at passersby, and there was official-sounding trumpet music blaring out onto the street from his stores / country. I got in my car and made a U-turn.

It took me about fifteen minutes to find Matilda's apartment complex. She lived near a strip mall, and her neighborhood had a very different vibe than the historic district. The apartment complex was nice, not one of the newer glass buildings, but stucco, five stories high, shaped in a square with a courtyard in the middle. Matilda lived with her husband Rockwell on the top floor. My grandmother told me to visit her without calling first. That's why she didn't know that I was coming.

She opened her door a few seconds after I rang the doorbell and greeted me with a wide smile. Matilda was about my height and weight. She had long brown hair with no sign of frizz, which filled me with envy. Her eyes matched the brown of her hair, and she was very pretty, despite a fine layer of flour all over her.

"Are you with the fire department?" she asked. "Nothing's on fire this time."

"I'm not with the fire department. I'm…"

"Oh, I have to stop Ina before she gets ahead of me. Come on in."

I followed her inside. The apartment was hotter than hell. There was no air conditioning in the apartment, but all the windows were open and there must've been ten fans going on full blast. They sucked compared to air conditioning. They moved the hot air around but nothing else. It was like a sauna, and I had no idea how Matilda could think of cooking in this kind of weather. I started sweating right away and wiped my forehead with the back of my hand.

Matilda turned off the Barefoot Contessa video on her computer. Ina Garten was paused in the making of beautiful fresh pasta, and I noticed she didn't have any flour on her. How could she? All of the flour in the world was on Matilda.

"My husband loves pasta, but it's harder to make than I thought," she explained and looked forlornly at her galley kitchen, which was part of one big room that included the living room and the dining room.

The kitchen itself looked like it had been in a war and lost. There was flour everywhere. And what I thought was a pasta machine looked like it was smoking. It could have been a pasta machine or some other kind of gadget. I didn't know. I had never tried to make pasta. I had never wanted to try to make pasta. Why do people try to make pasta? Didn't Dominos deliver? In any case, some gizmo gadget in Matilda's kitchen was smoking. There was a fifty percent chance that she really did need the fire department. I gnawed at the inside of my cheek, wondering if I should call 911 for a pasta emergency.

Then, I wondered if the pasta emergency was what Grandma had been worried about. I wasn't getting a sense that she was in danger, except maybe from fire. She didn't seem unhappy about her domestic life. There was no sign of bruises on her. She looked pretty healthy, even though she was probably ten pounds lighter than I was.

Actually, come to think of it, ten pounds lighter than I was, was the perfect weight to be. Yikes. I didn't want to focus on the fact that she was ten pounds lighter than I was because then I would have to focus on the fact that I was ten pounds heavier than she was. It wasn't a good thing to focus on when I was about to be stuffed into my great-grandmother's wedding dress and paraded around in front of thousands of people.

I clutched at my chest and tried to catch my breath. Would they point and laugh at the woman who was ten pounds overweight? What if I didn't fit into the dress? What if the dress exploded from pressure while I walked down the aisle? My heart raced, and my face was getting hot. I was in full bridal freakout mode.

"You have any tequila?" I asked, even though it wasn't even nine in the morning. I shook my head, trying to clear the anxiety away. "Sorry. Sorry. That just slipped out. I'm fine."

"You want to sit down?" she asked, concerned. "I never get any visitors. I mean, except for Fanta from across the courtyard."

"Fanta?" She pointed, and I looked through the windows across the courtyard. She had a great vantage point of her neighbors' apartments. "Did you say Fanta?"

Matilda nodded. "Funny name, but she's been very nice to me since I moved here. It's hard to make friends in a new town."

I didn't know what she was talking about. I had no shortage of new friends since I had moved to Cannes. The entire town had infiltrated my life. I was overrun with new friends. I had so many new friends that I was worried that I was going to be dropped out of a helicopter and trained bees were going to attack me during my wedding.

Matilda sat next to me on the couch. "So, you're not

with the fire department? I get a lot of interaction with the fire department."

"Me too, but not as much as I do with the police department. I'm Zelda Burger's granddaughter. I work in her matchmaking business." It was a wimpy introduction. I did more than work in her matchmaking business. I was a matchmaker. I was Grandma's partner, at least she said I was. "Actually, I'm a matchmaker. And I'm just doing a routine follow-up to see how you're doing."

It was a half lie. I was trying to find out how she was doing, but Grandma and I never did follow-up visits. If my grandmother matched them, we knew they would be fine. At least, as fine as a committed relationship could be in the modern age.

Matilda smiled wide. She was very pretty, but she was sort of hunched over on herself, like she had little or no self-confidence. I could relate. I was well below average in the self-confidence department, too, but not as much as Matilda.

"Nice to meet you, Gladie," she said, shyly. "I'm so glad you came by." Then, she slapped her cheeks, *Home Alone* style and hopped up from the couch. "Oh my God. I need to check the oven."

She ran into the kitchen and I ran after her, expecting to find a blaze. But the kitchen looked the same, and the pasta machine had stopped smoking. Matilda nervously adjusted the knobs on the stove and the oven. "I have to do this periodically because I keep forgetting and leaving the oven on. I don't know why I do it. Sometimes, I don't even remember that I ever turned the oven on. I mean, why would I turn the oven on when I'm not cooking anything? You won't tell Rockwell, will you?"

"Your husband? Of course not." Normally, this sort of confession would be a red flag. I mean, the fact that she wanted to hide something from her husband would be a red flag, not that she forgot that she turned the oven on. My grandmother regularly forgot that she turned on the sprinklers, and once I left the oven on for three days. Totally normal.

Anyway, the fact that she wanted to hide something from her husband could be a red flag for other matchmakers, but I hid pretty much everything from Spencer, so I decided to take her hiding stuff as being totally normal, too. Yup, everything looked very normal, as far as I was concerned.

"You want some chocolate milk and cookies?" she offered. "Don't worry. I didn't make them. I wouldn't do that to you."

We sat down in her living room and ate Nutter Butters and drank chocolate milk. Matilda regaled me with the tale of her whirlwind romance with Rockwell, about how it was love at first sight, at least it was for him and how he swept her off her feet. She thanked me a million times for the match, even though I had nothing to do with it and asked me to thank my grandmother, too. I liked her and even felt that she could be related to me, but in a good way. In other words, she was a lot like me.

As she spoke, her attention kept drifting toward the windows overlooking the courtyard and the other apartments.

Finally, she said, "Can you keep another secret?" I nodded. Truth was, I was lousy at keeping secrets, but I wasn't going to let that little bit of truth stop me from hearing whatever secret she had to tell. I guessed I was a lot like my grandmother. I was nosy as hell, and I would do anything for a bit of juicy gossip or the occasional secret.

Matilda opened a chest, and pulled out a couple of Afghan quilts. Underneath, she had hidden a pair of binoculars. She put them to her face and peered out the window.

"We have the only tinted windows in the apartment complex," she explained. "No one can see through to our apartment, but I can see straight through to everyone else's apartment."

I watched as Matilda spied on her neighbors. Her entire posture changed. She went from a woman with little or no self-confidence to someone totally in charge. Matilda was a snoop. Matilda was nosy. I would have judged her, if I hadn't wanted to spy on her neighbors, too.

"I'm not looking for naked people or people getting it on," she explained. "I'm not a pervert. But you learn so much about people this way." She put the binoculars down by her chest and looked at me. "I try to better myself all the time. Making homemade pasta, becoming a really good cook. It's very important when you're married to try to be the best wife and woman you can be. I've tried knitting, cooking, and the art of organization, all in attempt to better myself."

"Impressive," I noted. I'd given up on trying to be a better me. I was relieved if I could just maintain the status quo.

But faced with Matilda's determination to be a good woman and better wife, I wondered if I should have done more to prepare myself to be married to Spencer. Maybe I should've learned to knit, too. "So, you can knit and cook and organize? I should learn that, too."

Matilda looked up at the ceiling. "Well, I wouldn't say I actually know how to cook or knit or organize, but I'm trying. There's a problem with my cooking and the fire department. And the organizational thing took a nasty turn. I don't think I should talk about it." She put the binoculars back up to her face and kept spying. "But I learned so much this way. You know, to see how married people are supposed to act. Adults. It's not really spying. I mean, would you call Jane Goodall a spy?"

I had no idea who Jane Goodall was. "Of course not," I said. "Jane isn't a spy."

Some people would've thought Matilda was crazy. But I was just crazy enough to think she sounded like a genius. My grandmother seemed to know people inside out without ever seeing them. I was bombarded with people—alive and dead—and had to figure them out after the fact. But this was understanding people by studying them in the wild without them knowing they were being studied. It was truly genius. It could answer so many questions, like how many times do people really brush their teeth.

"What have you learned?" I asked with a little too much excitement in my voice.

Matilda took another pair of binoculars out of the chest and handed them to me. "Look at the apartment across from us two doors to the left." I followed her instructions. There was a woman eating a huge bowl of green beans. "She only eats green beans," Matilda explained. "I think she eats like two pounds a day. And boy does it work. She's already lost at least three sizes in two months. But she does spend a lot of time in the bathroom."

The green bean diet. It was one of the few diets that Bird the hairdresser hadn't suggested to me. I didn't know if I wanted to eat two pounds of green beans, though. Sounded like kind of a rough way to get thin.

"You should be here around noon. That's when the guy catty-corner from us does his laundry and folds his clothes. He makes Marie Kondo look like chopped liver."

I practically drooled. I wasn't much of a clothes folder. Spencer was meticulous about his clothes, but I was strictly a Walley's box store clothes shopper, and those clothes did fine, shoved into a drawer. But now I was marrying a metrosexual with a designer wardrobe, and we were moving into a custom-built house with a cedar-lined walk-in closet with at least one hundred drawers. I couldn't shove his Armani dress shirts in willy-nilly.

I had to grow up and be the wife and grown up, befitting my new position as a fancypants homeowner with a cedar-lined walk-in closet. I had to become fancypants in a hurry!

I also need to learn how to fold fancypants.

That's how I wound up spending most of the day in the stifling heat of Matilda Dare's apartment. I was supposed to be spying on her, but I wound up spying on everyone except for her. We ordered a pizza, which was delivered fifteen minutes before noon, just enough time to put away two slices of pepperoni before I got an eyeful of the art of folding.

"This is good," I breathed, soaking up the wisdom and knowledge that only comes from spying on unsuspecting neighbors. "Boy is Spencer going to be surprised when he opens his underwear drawer. Do you do this at night, too?"

"Yes, but I have to be careful not to let Rockwell see me. He would get the wrong impression and think that there's something wrong with what I'm doing. He doesn't understand about bettering myself because he's already perfect. But it's easy to get around him at night because he sleeps."

"Don't you sleep, too?" I asked.

"Oh, no. I haven't slept in fifteen years."

"Not at all?"

"Nope. I try, but I can't get beyond closing my eyes. My body and brain won't shut off."

She was speaking a different language than I was. I slept all the time. If I could have gotten away with napping twice a day, I would have and then would have gone on to get my regular ten hours at night, too.

"Aren't there pills you can take?" I asked.

"I've taken them all. Even horse tranquilizers. There's a name for what I've got, but it has a lot of syllables."

"Aren't you tired?"

"I haven't slept for fifteen years. I'm tired down to my bones."

Hours later, my phone rang, and I answered it. "I'm on my way to your place," my friend Lucy told me on the phone. "Get ready because we're going to paw-tay tonight."

"We are?"

"It's your bachelorette party. Don't you remember?"

CHAPTER 4

Drinking and drugs, bubbeleh. You know what I'm talking about. A little goes a long way. The problem is that it's hard to tell when you've passed a little and moved on to too much, oy vey, why did I do this to myself, who's in my bed. There's a lot in life that's like drinking and drugs, where a little is fine, but more than a little is a disaster and probably a big attorney bill. Now, if the attorney is single and making a good living and he's interested in you, then maybe once in a while it's good to go above the little mark, but keep that little mark in mind, dolly, for all things: Love, life, matchmaking.

Lesson 87, Matchmaking advice from your Grandma Zelda

When I arrived home, the world's longest limousine was parked on the street in front of the house. As I stepped out of my car in the driveway, my friend Lucy stepped out of the limousine in a peach organza cocktail dress and gestured to the limo, like she was pointing out a new refrigerator on *The Price is Right*.

"Don't you love it? It used to belong to a rapper. I don't know which one. But it was one of the ones with a lot of gold chains, and he may have married a Kardashian. Who knows? All I know, is that he's in jail, and his bad luck is our good luck because this bad boy is ours for the night. And I mean the whole night for our wild women bachelorette party."

I had my doubts about the bachelorette party. First of all, the only "wild women" attending were Lucy, Bridget, and me, and since Bridget was breastfeeding, I didn't think she would want to drink. Also, a couple months ago, we had given Lucy a bachelorette party, and it was pretty much a disaster. Still, I was up for riding around in the rapper's limousine and drinking until I couldn't see straight. It was the upside to the whole wedding celebration, as far as I could tell.

"Now let's get you dressed," Lucy told me, as she marched up the driveway in her peach stiletto heels.

"I'm dressed."

Lucy laughed. "That's the funniest thing I've ever heard, darlin'. We're going to really get you dressed. And by that, I mean we're going to get you dressed in not much of anything."

"What does that mean?"

Lucy knew where I hid my nice clothes, but most of them were too tight and showed too much skin.

"That's what we want, darlin'," Lucy insisted in my bedroom. "A lot of skin. This is your last night of freedom. Last night to get crazy and let loose. Shake that thang and hoochie coochie your moochie. You understand what I'm sayin', darlin'?"

"Are you drunk?"

Lucy stuck her hand out and put her thumb and forefinger about an inch apart. "Little bit," she explained. "There's a shit-ton of champagne in the limo."

Spencer was still at work, which was a good thing because I didn't want him to see me dressed like a two-dollar hooker. Not that he would have been upset about me going out on the town in a dress so short that I needed a bikini wax and cut so low that my bra showed, but he probably wouldn't have let me out of the house without throwing me into bed and doing the dirty deed, which would have made me miss the party altogether.

Grandma wasn't in the house, either. She had said something about going jet skiing. Or maybe it was a movie. Anyway, she was gone, which I was still trying to get used to. She had been a shut-in since I was a little girl, and now she was out and about every hour of the day and night. I was happy for her, but it was a big change in the house.

The limousine was more impressive inside than it was outside. There was a lot of booze inside and no shortage of psychedelic lighting. Lucy urged me to start drinking, but I didn't want to get drunk before we picked up Bridget.

Bridget was a brand-new mother, and she took her new job very seriously. In fact, I think Eisenhower had a more lackadaisical attitude about D-Day then Bridget had about raising an infant. She had brought in a professional babyproofer to her townhouse, and now every sharp edge was coated in a super safe padded, stain resistant, non-toxic, farm-to-table material. The first time I visited, she made me scrub my hands up to my elbows with surgical soap that she had pilfered from the hospital where she gave birth.

The time after that, she insisted that I not speak to baby Jonathan in a baby talk voice because it would stifle his development and prevent his brain from growing. Now, I was terrified to be near her baby, in case I made his brain stop growing. I mean, it had happened before. There were all kinds of brains out there that I had stunted, and I didn't want baby Jonathan to be the next victim.

We skipped out of the limousine, and I adjusted my boob in my itty-bitty dress. It was a losing battle. The boob had a mind of its own. I wished that I could get it to stop growing like I did with brains, because it was popping out every two seconds, but adopting my grandmother's junk food eating habits had given me a bigger cup size.

Lucy took a bottle of champagne from the limo and waved it in front of Bridget's face when she opened the door. Bridget was wearing her regular hoot owl glasses, but she was obviously ready to party because she had on a double coat of blue eyeshadow. She was wearing her shortest dress, and I was surprised that she was happily anxious to get the party going. I guessed that was normal after being stuck inside for a month with a little person who couldn't talk.

"Oh, good. Booze," Bridget said, focusing on the

champagne. "I have inverted nipples. So, I had to stop breastfeeding. I'm going to get shit-faced and three sheets to the wind. I'm going to bring down the house. I'm going to raise the roof. I'm going to blow the doors off the hinges."

I didn't know how to respond. I didn't know which was bigger news, that she had inverted nipples or that she wanted to do construction work.

Bridget waved us into the townhouse. "Come on in. I'm just giving the rundown to Jackson."

"Who's Jackson?" I asked.

"Who cares, darlin'?" Lucy said. "The good news is that Bridget has inverted nipples."

Upstairs, a woman was sitting at the dining room table, going through a stack of papers. She was a big, muscular woman in a starched white nurse's uniform. She had a thick black unibrow, which was a good thing because it distracted from her mustache.

"How far did you get?" Bridget asked Jackson. "Did you get to Addendum Part Three, Section C, Line 4, yet?"

"I think so," Jackson said scratching at her mustache. "That's the part about gender stereotypes, right?"

Bridget shook her head, obviously annoyed. "No, no, no. That's Addendum Part Two." Bridget slapped the back of her left hand on her right palm. "Pay attention, Jackson. This is serious. You're going to take care of my baby for probably the entire night."

"I thought we were not allowed to call him 'your baby' because that implies possession and ownership and would squash his identity, whatever that turns out to be," she said holding up the paper and pointing to a line.

Boy, parenting is a bitch.

I didn't know how people did it. It was so complicated. I didn't know that term papers were involved. I had to hand it to Bridget. She had organized the hell out of her first babysitting experience. She must've written seventy-five single-spaced pages of instructions in a ten-point font.

If infancy was this complicated, I didn't know what she was going do once baby Jonathan got to high school.

The baby cried in the other room, and the baby monitor on the table picked up the sound. Bridget did a little, panicked hop and ran into the baby's room to get Jonathan.

Through the monitor, I could hear her talk to her child about the history of the Teamsters Union in America as she diapered him, apologizing for crossing the boundary limits on his privacy.

Then, she walked back into the dining room with baby Jonathan in her arms. I tickled him under his chin and cooed at him. "Look at that sweet little babykins," I gushed. "What a sweetie pie. Mommy's cutie patootie lovey, little man, pooka pooka babykins. You're going to be such a good little boy when you grow up."

I felt Bridget glare at me. Uh oh. Faced with baby Jonathan's cuteness, I had forgotten the rules. I clamped my mouth closed. "I'm sorry, Bridget. He's just so cute. I don't know what came over me. It won't happen again."

"It certainly won't happen with me," Lucy said,

popping open the champagne bottle. "I don't care how cute he is. You won't get me to talk like that to anyone, no matter how much he's paying me." Lucy had been a high-priced call girl until she married the love of her life, Harry, who was a nice guy with a dubious career. "Sure, I'll be there to give him scholarship money for college, and he can call me when he gets a girl in trouble, but I'm not doing baby talk."

Bridget stomped her foot on her carpet. "Between the two of you, you've uttered at least twenty-three gender stereotypes in front of my baby. Uh…I mean, Jonathan Donovan, who is an individual and a person with his own power and abilities and self-worth, not 'my baby.'"

Oh, yeah. Parenting is a bitch.

Bridget had a last-minute crisis before we left. She burst into tears, worried that Jonathan would be traumatized by abandoning him to go to a bachelorette party. But the crisis ended pretty quickly when Lucy waved the bottle of champagne at her, again.

Bridget stuffed a bunch of gizmos and gadgets into her purse and was finally ready to go. "It's an emergency beacon and video spying equipment," she explained to Lucy in a whisper as we walked downstairs so that Jackson couldn't hear.

"Is that all? Lucy asked. "I'm not a mother, so I don't know these things, but isn't an emergency beacon and spying equipment going to extremes? Maybe a little over the top for a babysitter?"

Bridget pushed her glasses up on the bridge of her nose. "What're you talking about? I didn't get the automatic Taser option. That would have dropped Jackson to her knees if she got out of line. Boy, did I want the Taser option, but I've been a card-carrying member of the ACLU for twenty years, and I didn't think they would approve. Damn it, now I think I should have gotten the Taser option. Screw the ACLU. What if Jackson gets out of line?"

I put my arm around Bridget's shoulders and gave her a squeeze. "You're a great mom, Bridget. Really the best."

As much as Bridget had agonized and prepared for the outing, it took her about five minutes and a half a glass of champagne in the limo to all but forget that she had ever given birth.

"Yeehaw!" she shouted. "Let's get this party started!"

Lucy had planned for a pretty straightforward bachelorette party with just us three, best friends. First on the agenda was a ride through Cannes and its environs in the limo, while we drank a big chunk of the rapper's stock of alcoholic beverages. By my second glass of champagne, I was slurring my words and telling my best friends how much I loved them. I did love them, but the alcohol was making me tell them over and over. I also might've told them that I had stolen bubble gum from the pharmacy and written three bad checks since I had moved to Cannes. But like best friends, they pretended they didn't hear about my indiscretions.

"Look at us," Bridget said, wiping her mouth with the back of her hand after taking another sip of champagne. "We're all grown-ups, now. You and Lucy married, and me the mother of a child. I don't think we're doing too bad."

Lucy raised her glass. "Here's to not being too bad. Wait a minute. What am I saying? Tonight, it's all about being too bad. Lots of too bad. Gobs and gobs of too bad. Let's show Elvis how to do bad."

"Don't you mean Michael Jackson?" I asked.

"Oh, darlin', I always mean Elvis."

The limo took us through town and up further into the mountains and through the orchards and back down into the Historic District until it parked at the Bar None.

"We're going to get more shminks?" I asked, trying to focus on the Bar None sign through the limo's window. My eyes were at half-mast and I was having trouble making a fist, but I was more than happy to drink even more.

"They have nachos, too," Bridget pointed out. "I've been eating only organic whole food for the past month while I was breastfeeding and trying to get my nipples to stop inverting. I hope to God that nachos aren't organic."

"I heard the bar makes the cheese out of pork fat and Flamin' Hot Cheetos dust," I pointed out.

Bridget slapped her hands together. "Perfect."

Lucy had arranged for us to have a private room in the back of Bar None, which had a large round table and chairs. It was also the stockroom. Two orders of nachos, one order of chili cheese fries, one order of onion rings, and several margarita specials later, we were technically shitfaced.

"Do you have any she-crets to a shappy marriage?" I asked Lucy, trying to keep my head up.

"Sure thing, darlin'. Lots of money, separate bathrooms, and Viagra."

I didn't have any of those things, but I didn't panic because Spencer was his own Viagra machine, and our bathroom in our new custom-made house was bigger than my bedroom. So, I figured we could avoid each other in there, even if we used it at the same time.

"I don't believe in the paternalistic institution of marriage," Bridget said. She propped her head up with her elbow on the table. "But I think you and Spencer make a dreamy couple. You're so pretty together. And he loves you. He always looks at you like you're the steak special with an onion glaze and white truffle fries on the side!"

I perked up. "Is that true?"

"Oh darlin', oh my God, yes," Lucy said. "If he was a dog, you would be his rawhide bone. He can't wait to get to it and can't stop chewing."

I nodded, and my eyes welled up with tears. "That's so beautiful," I gushed. "I'm his rawhide bone, and he can't wait to chew me. That's poetry. That's like really nice poetry. Better than Dr. Seuss. I love you, guys." I got up and stumbled around the table, planting kisses on my friends. "This has been the nicest shime I've ever had," I said and hiccoughed.

"Me, too," Bridget said. Her eyes filled up with tears, and she wiped at them, smearing blue eyeshadow down her cheeks. "Female bonding is the best kind of bonding. My God, did I just say that? I meant that mother-son bonding is the best kind of bonding. Female bonding is the second-best kind of bonding."

I slapped Bridget's back. "We knew what you meant."

Lucy seemed soberer than Bridget and me, even though she had drunk more. The alcohol didn't even make her blotchy, whereas I looked like I got run over by a truck when I drank just one drink.

She smoothed her hair and smiled. "You two talk like this party's over. But we're just getting started. I got a big surprise for you. Hold onto your hats for a big package."

"A big package? I asked.

"Get it?" Lucy said. "Big package."

Bridget giggled. "Big package. Ha! Big package. Wait a minute. No, I don't get it."

"A stripper, honey." Lucy slapped a thick wad of five dollar bills on the table. "A gorgeous, hot body, oh Lordy, look at that, slap my mama, kind of stripper. We're going to make it rain in his big package."

"A stripper?" I asked, finally catching on.

As if on cue, the stripper walked into our private room. I wasn't sure that Lucy was right about his big package. Ditto the hot body, oh Lordy, look at that, and slap my mama. Actually, I didn't want to look to see if he was a big package. In fact, I wanted to pretend that I wasn't there and that he had never walked into the room because I knew him.

"Oh, hello there, Underwear Girl," our stripper said, greeting me.

"Fred, is that you?" I asked. I had been hoping that I was so drunk that my eyes were playing tricks on me, but they weren't playing. It was Fred Lytton.

"I'm making extra money for my honeymoon with Julie," he explained. "We're going to the monster truck rally in Fresno."

"That sounds great," I said, diplomatically.

Fred was my first match, and he was Spencer's desk sergeant. He was tall and lanky. Actually, he was a string bean with no discernable muscle mass. A telephone pole with arms. I didn't want to see him strip. I didn't want to see him strip more than I didn't want to see my accountant or an Adam Sandler movie.

If I was surprised that Fred was our stripper, Lucy was outraged. She slapped the table in anger. "Fred, what're you doing here? Where's Dapper Don? I hired Dapper Don Big Shlong for this shindig. I want my Big Shlong right this second!"

Fred put a 1980's boom box on the table and started working his shirt buttons. He didn't seem concerned that Lucy didn't want him there. "Dapper Don got a standing erection," he explained.

I shot margarita special out of my nose. "He got a what?" I croaked.

"I mean, ovation. He got a standing ovation." Fred

looked up at the ceiling for a moment. "No, that's not it. Not a standing ovation. The clap. Yes, that's it. The clap. The doctor said he has to stay in bed until the antibiotics start to work."

Fred pushed the button on the tape machine, and *I Will Survive* started to play. Fred was a nice guy, but he didn't have rhythm and very little hand-eye coordination. He was having a terrible time unbuttoning his shirt, and I hoped beyond hope that he would never be able to get his clothes off.

"I think I'm going to close my eyes for a moment," Bridget said. "I'll open them when the song is done or when he's finished. Can someone tell me when he's finished?"

"As far as I'm concerned, he's finished now," Lucy said.

The powerful Southern belle popped up from her seat and marched around the table to Fred. She hit the tape player, but it just made the music louder. She grabbed Fred's hands, ostensibly to stop him from stripping, but Fred misunderstood what she was doing and started to dance with her. At least I thought he was trying to dance with her. It had very little resemblance to dancing. It was more like professional wrestling. He turned her around, knocking her off balance, and she lunged for him in order not to fall, and as if by magic, Fred's hand got caught in Lucy's bra and Lucy's hand got wedged in Fred's sleeve, which he had been trying to remove.

The rest was fuzzy because I had reached maximum alcohol to nachos ratio and my brain was fighting with my digestive system to see which one was going to shut down or explode first.

"This is much easier than I thought it would be," Fred

said. "Beginner's luck, I guess."

"Fred, get your hand out of my brassiere," Lucy growled.

"Oh, I thought that was part of the routine."

"How about chopping off your hand? You think that's part of the routine, too? Can we make that part of the routine?"

Fred seemed to think about that for a minute, but he couldn't come up with an answer. My brain and digestive system finally let me focus on the situation, of Fred's hand in Lucy's bra, of his shirt clutched in her hand, and his bony chest on display.

"Can't we all just get along?" I asked.

Gloria Gaynor finished singing, and the tape shut off. Lucy managed to extricate herself from Fred, just as he managed to strip down to his *I love Easter* boxer shorts and a killer farmer's tan.

"Ta da!" he announced and took a seat at the table.

"Oh, for the love of Pete," Lucy grumbled.

"Is it over?" Bridget asked, cracking an eye open.

"Yes," Fred said. "Taking off my clothes was a lot easier than I expected. I thought it would be awkward."

Bridget opened her eyes and got an eyeful of Fred's bare chest, as he sat at the table. "I thought it was over," she complained.

"Make it rain," I ordered, and slapped the stack of five dollar bills on the table in front of Fred. His eyes grew enormous.

"Holy cow, Underwear Girl, it's going to be the best

monster truck rally ever."

I wondered if other bachelorette parties were like this.

The door to our private room opened again, and the mayor walked in. The last time I saw him, he was arguing with the dictator of Fussia. The mayor was a well-dressed, attractive, older African-American man with a total devotion to his job.

"Sergeant Lytton, is that the new police uniform?" he asked the mostly naked Fred without a hint of humor.

The mayor was a moron. Everyone knew that.

He pulled up a seat and sat down at the table, uninvited. Fred grabbed a remaining onion ring and a handful of nachos.

"I can't believe this is happening," the mayor moaned. "Founders Day is all but ruined."

I took another sip of my so-called margarita. Rum and Dr. Pepper "margaritas" packed a wicked punch. I blinked, but the mayor had three heads, and I couldn't decide which head to focus on. Even worse, his heads were dancing, like they were in a CrossFit class.

Perhaps I was drunker than I thought. I took another sip of my margarita.

"What's wrong with Pounders Shay?" Bridget asked, slurring her words. She had discovered the evils of margaritas and champagne, too.

Founders Day was on July fourth, which was this Thursday. The town usually put the two celebrations together, combining the country's Independence Day with honoring the town's founding, when gold was discovered in a local mine. The celebrations revolved around fireworks on the lake and picnics on its shores.

Fred and Julie were taking advantage of the day to say their vows during the fireworks. If the Founders Day celebration was nixed, Fred and Julie's wedding would be in trouble.

Fred didn't seem to understand the danger to his nuptials. He happily ate more nachos.

"It's all going to H-E-double toothpicks, as far as I'm concerned," the mayor moaned, again. "First of all, we have the wedding, which will totally distract from the celebration. And now, we have a crazy dictator who wants to take over the whole world, or at least the whole town."

I felt like I needed to defend Fred, who was my first match, and I was going to be his best man. Besides, it was totally unfair of the mayor. Fred's wedding was going to be a very modest affair. There was going to be no more than fifteen people at the ceremony and then a small picnic catered by Ruth.

"I don't think Fred's wedding will disrupt the celebrations, Mr. Mayor," I said and spilled my drink all over the table. Damn my hands. For some reason, they weren't working anymore.

The mayor pointed at me, accusatorily. "Oh yeah? Isn't Julie going to be there?"

He had a point. Julie had a way of burning down places or blowing them up or generally breaking everything she came in contact with. So, did I, for that matter, but when I did it, it wasn't my fault. With Julie, it was always her fault.

"We're putting a perimeter around Julie," Fred explained with his mouth full of our appetizers. "It's all planned out so nobody'll get hurt during the wedding. No sharp edges. Only plastic, rubber, and Styrofoam. Ruth's got it all figured out."

The mayor nodded and seemed to be okay with that plan.

"We're having a bachelorette party, you know," Lucy interrupted, clearly annoyed by the mayor's interruption.

The mayor flinched. Lucy was sweet and pretty, but terrifying when she had her full Southern going. She looked like Scarlett O'Hara, but she was all Robert E. Lee. The mayor stood and smoothed out his suit.

"I know. I know," he said, smiling. "Girls activities. Doing your nails, brushing your hair, pantyhose, and girdles. I know all about it. It's not a secret from me. I'll get out of here and let you get back to your giggling, hair curlers, slumber party People magazines." I didn't know exactly what he meant, but I decided to let it slide.

He walked to the door and turned around to me. "What is the Chief going to do about the dictator?" he asked me. The Chief was Spencer, and I knew not to get involved with his business. It was bad enough that I stumbled over dead people all the time. I wasn't going to get involved with how he dealt with an invading dictator.

I shrugged. "Beats me."

"Does he really want to take over the town?" Bridget asked.

"The man nearly got into fisticuffs with me today," the mayor said, his voice rising. "He threatened me, nearly pushed me. The chief didn't do a damn thing. Somehow that crazy dictator got the right paperwork to set up a country in my town. I say, if he has the right paperwork, we need to start changing papers, immediately."

"I hear he's organizing an army, and he has a machine that can change the weather," Fred said.

It took Fred fifteen minutes to find his clothes and get dressed, and the mayor took twenty minutes to finish complaining, but finally they left us alone. Luckily, we were still blotto. We were drunk out of our minds. But Lucy was upset that the bachelorette party had been marred by the moron mayor and the terrible stripper. I was just thankful that I was drunk when I saw Fred strip, otherwise I would've had to wash my eyes out with Clorox.

Completely drunk, our bellies filled with junk food, it was time to move the party, but to where? The town closed down at nine o'clock. Bar None was the only thing open. Even the twenty-four-hour mini-mart closed an hour before.

"I'm so sorry I let you down, Gladie, Lucy said. I put my arm around her.

"You didn't let me down, Lucy. I had a great time. I love being with my two best friends, especially when I don't have to pay for the drinks."

"But I wanted it to be better. More Shlong and less Fred."

That would have been nice, but more Shlong and less

Fred would have been out of character for Cannes and my life.

I was hit with a wave of genius. "I know what we could do," I told her. "Let's invade a country."

Funnily enough, it didn't take a lot of convincing to get Lucy and Bridget to invade a country with me. Maybe because they were both sloshed out of their minds.

I was so drunk that my boob had permanently popped out of my dress, and I didn't give a damn. Bridget and Lucy didn't care either, but every once in a while, Bridget would point at my chest and laugh.

I was excited about invading a country. I'd never been outside of America, not even a short trip to Tijuana. Sure, I wasn't really leaving the country. I was just going a few blocks away, next to the pharmacy on Main Street, but a bottle of champagne and five margaritas later, Main Street and France were pretty much the same thing in my blotto brain cells.

We piled into the limo, and the chauffeur drove us to the land of Fussia. I slapped my finger against my lips. "Shhhhh," I said, spitting in Lucy's face. "You two have never done this before, so I'm going to be in charge."

"You've done this before?" Lucy asked.

"If it gets hairy in there, I don't want anyone shooting anybody," I said.

"We have guns?" Bridget asked.

Lucy patted her peach clutch purse. "Don't worry. I'm

always packing, darlin',"

I looked down at her purse. "Maybe we should leave your purse in the limo."

We fell out of the limousine, and it took a good five minutes for us to help each other up. There was no sign of the dictator except for the signs announcing the dictator with the dictator's face on them. There was a sign threatening death to invaders. There was a sign about the visa requirements. And there were a few signs about Fussia being the greatest country in the world. But there was no actual sign of an actual person.

"Shhhh," I said again loudly, slapping my finger against my mouth. "So far so good. No barbed wire and no machine guns. This will be a snap."

"Barbed wire?" Bridget asked. "Doesn't this man know the meaning of democracy and a free country?"

"No. That's why he's a dictator," Lucy said and hiccoughed.

It was pretty easy to break in. Even drunk, I seemed to have an almost magical ability to pick a lock. It was my one great skill, and if I had just been a little less honest, I could've monetized that baby to the hilt. But as it was, I didn't use my breaking and entering ability for monetary gain, just to break into other countries.

There were more signs inside than out. There was also a cot with a couple folding chairs next to it in an otherwise mostly empty room with dictator uniforms tossed on the bed.

Oh, and there was a huge cache of weapons in the corner, too. Big weapons. Lots of them.

"I'm glad I'm drunk," Lucy said.

"I think I'm really drunk," Bridget said. "I'm seeing all kinds of crazy stuff."

There was a sound outside, and the three of us jumped a foot in the air and clutched each other.

"Oh my God. We've been found out. We're going to get mowed down and sent to Siberia," I moaned.

"I'm not going to Siberia. Organza doesn't work in the snow, Gladie," Lucy said.

"Now let's just calm down and think clearly," Bridget said.

We paused but still held on to each other. I tried to think clearly. Nope, it wasn't going to happen. My brain cells had been pushed out by the devil's evil brew. Damned margarita specials.

There was another sound, and we squeezed each other, holding on for dear life.

"I got it. I got it," Bridget said. "We run away. That's what we do. We run away."

I gave Bridget a huge kiss on her cheek. "Genius," I exclaimed. "How did you figure that out? Pure genius."

We ran through the building and out the back door. Out back, there was a large patch of dirt enclosed by a fence and beyond, was the alley.

"I'm stepping on something squishy," Lucy complained.

"Me, too." I was stepping on something squishy, and there was a pungent smell, which I couldn't place. Then, there was the noise, again. Louder, this time.

"Does the dictator have four legs and a long nose?" Bridget asked.

"I think he has a long nose, but I didn't notice four legs," I said.

"Look at that. The dictator stole the mayor's donkey," Lucy said.

The sound turned out to be the braying of a donkey. I gasped. The mayor's beloved donkey Dulcinea was trapped behind the storefront in the penned in space. The squishy substance we were stepping on was its poop.

"I know what's going on here," I said.

"Me, too," Lucy said. "Fussia is a weird, depraved sex party, donkey excuse for a country. You think you've seen it all, and then you see this."

"No. No, that's not it," Bridget countered. "This Fussia dictator guy is playing hardball with the mayor. You heard him. They had an almost fight. Didn't the mayor want this country out of here immediately? So, the dictator went ahead and stole the mayor's donkey. This is a war between Fussia and Cannes. Lucy, Gladie, we're witnessing war, and it's up to us to fix it."

There was something about Bridget's reasoning that I found troubling and not quite logical, but the margaritas and the champagne, not to mention the nachos, were blocking any clear thinking. So instead of arguing with her, I nodded.

"Sounds about right," I said.

Bridget raised her hand like she was the Statue of Liberty. "Justice!" she yelled. "Justice!"

Bridget's cries for justice were contagious. Imbued with

a sense of purpose, we decided to steal the mayor's donkey back and return it to him.

At first, the donkey fought against us, as if she liked her new home better than her old one, but we found a small supply of carrots and bribed her out of the stall and around the back of the building until we got back to Main Street and to the limo.

"This is a first," the limo driver said, staring at the donkey.

"It's the justice donkey," Bridget explained.

The driver hooked the donkey to the back of the limo with rope, and we drove through town at five miles an hour to the mayor's house. It was touch and go in a few places because the donkey wasn't too keen on being tugged by a limo. It fought against the rope, and I was starting to get worried for its well-being.

A few months before, I had had a run-in with an animal rights group, and I didn't want word getting out that I had hurt a donkey. I opened the sunroof and stuck my head out.

"You're okay, Dulcinea," I cooed at her. "You're okay. Who's Mommy's little girl? Who's Mommy's little girl?"

Despite Bridget's warnings that I was hurting the donkey's brain, it worked. The donkey calmed down, and we rode like that with the donkey behind us and my head sticking out of the sunroof cooing at it until we got to the mayor's house.

By the time the mayor opened the door, I was all in on the justice plan. Like heroes, we had managed to right a wrong. We managed to find justice for the mayor and his beloved donkey. Score one for democracy and down with dictatorship. I had never felt so patriotic.

When the mayor opened the door, I shouted "Justice!" And I lost my balance and stumbled. Lucy caught me.

The mayor was wearing silk pajamas, which were crisply ironed. He wiped his eyes. "What's this? What's this? Has the town burned down?"

"We have returned your beloved Dulcinea," I announced.

"That evil dictator stole her, but we got her back for you," Bridget said.

"I stepped in donkey droppings, darlin', but I guess it's okay in the name of truth, justice, and the American way," Lucy said and hiccoughed again.

"Where?" the mayor asked, looking around in a panic. "Where is my beloved Dulcinea? What do you mean that evil man stole her?"

"He's right in front of your eyes," I said tugging at the donkey.

"That's not my Dulcinea," the mayor said. There was a sound of sirens in the background, but I ignored them. Since I was already seeing three mayor heads, I figured that hearing things would be next.

"Just a minute. Just what do you mean by that's not your Dulcinea?" Bridget asked.

"I know Dulcinea," the mayor said. "This isn't Dulcinea. Dulcinea is beautiful. Dulcinea is the world's smartest donkey. And besides, Dulcinea is female."

Lucy, Bridget, and I froze and then in unison, bent down and looked under the donkey. "How the hell did that get there?" Lucy asked.

"I didn't see that, either," Bridget said.

Dulcinea had grown a huge donkey penis.

And the sirens were getting closer. A bit of common sense and logic were starting to invade my senses.

"Mayor, I swear that penis wasn't there when we stole the donkey," Bridget said. But I noticed that she crossed her fingers behind her back.

"So, who is this donkey?" The mayor asked. The sirens were very loud and getting louder.

"Beats me," I said. "Never seen it before in my life."

"I've never seen it before, either," Lucy said.

"What do you mean?" Bridget asked. "It's the donkey we sto..." Lucy kicked her with her poop covered shoes, shutting her up.

"Oh, geez. The fuzz. I think we should beat it," I urged, turning around. One squad car and one unmarked police car that was very familiar to me parked next to us. The sirens stopped, but the lights continued to flash.

Spencer stepped out of the unmarked car and took a look at the three of us, the limo, and the donkey. He approached me, and he wasn't happy.

"Are you kidding me?" he said.

"It wasn't my fault. Bridget wanted justice."

Spencer started to respond, but I threw up all over his Armani suit and passed out cold into his strong arms.

CHAPTER 5

The grass is always greener on the other side of the fence, bubbeleh. We always want what we can't have. And most of the time, we don't realize what we actually have in the first place. It's hard to make a match when they don't know what they got and think they want what they wouldn't want if they knew what it was. The Dalai Lama calls it the mindfulness of matchmaking. At least that's what he said to me on the phone a couple months ago. He might've just been pulling my leg. Anyway, make them focus on what they got. Never mind the schmuck next door.

Lesson 49, Matchmaking advice from your Grandma Zelda

Thank goodness Bird's hair salon had a great air-conditioner. Our heatwave was getting worse. If we continued like this, I would be sweating through my wedding dress on Sunday.

"Is business bad?" Grandma asked Bird, as she sat in one of the hairdresser's chairs. It was her day to get her hair done. We were the only ones there except for Bird and the pedicurist.

"No, Zelda. I usually block off Mondays to come to your house to give you the royal treatment. Now, you come here. So, you're my only customer. Although, we should start work on Gladie. There's a lot to do to get her ready for her wedding."

"No offense, Bird," I said. "But your voice sounds like a jackhammer. Can you turn it down? And could you turn off the Frank Sinatra? I'm not going to let you do anything to me today. I have days before my wedding."

"What's with her?" Bird asked. She draped a cloth around my grandmother's neck and snapped it together.

"Gladie has a hangover," Grandma explained. "She and her friends had a little party last night and over-imbibed."

"I heard you stole a donkey and started an international incident," Bird said, putting rollers in my grandmother's hair.

"It wasn't an international incident. It was Main Street," I insisted. I had insisted the same thing to Spencer when he had also accused me of inciting an international incident.

"Only you can turn a bachelorette party into an international incident," he had complained. The country of Fussia next to the pharmacy wasn't a real country, but breaking and entering and grand theft donkey were real charges.

And the dictator was pressing charges.

The night before, Spencer arrested us. Lucy, Bridget, and I were all fingerprinted and let go. I didn't remember much because I had been unconscious for most of it.

"Gladie, I have a whole plan for you leading up to your wedding," Bird explained, happily. "And it's all on me. That's my wedding present for you. Finally, I'm going to do exactly what I want to you. From soup to nuts. You'll be totally under my control."

"Is it going to hurt?" I asked. "My head already feels like it's a cantaloupe that was dropped at the grocery store."

"Gladie, you have to suffer to be beautiful," Bird said, wisely.

"Bird, you need to send her to Muffy & Dicks," the pedicurist said. She was going at my grandmother's heels with a cheese grater. "They wax everything off in no time flat. You'll be bald as a billiard ball. Clean as a baby. Spencer will have no trouble finding the forest for the trees during your honeymoon."

I self-consciously put my hands in my lap. "Spencer doesn't have a problem finding my forest even with trees," I said. "What's Muffy & Dicks?"

"He could get bald as a billiard ball, too," the pedicurist suggested. "That's the Dicks part of Muffy & Dicks."

Bird pointed at the pedicurist. "That's a good idea for Gladie. We'll do the hair, makeup, and Mani-Pedi. But we'll get Muffy & Dicks to wax it all off and give you a facial peel. When was the last time you had a facial peel? You look ten years older than you are."

Was that true? Did I look ten years older? Was Spencer going to take one look at me in my wedding dress and tell me he couldn't marry such an old bag?

"You look beautiful, dolly," Grandma said. "She looks just as old as she's supposed to look, Bird."

"See?" Bird said. "Nobody wants to look as old as they're supposed to."

"My head," I moaned. All the talk of how old I looked was making my hangover worse.

"You should try the raw food diet." Bird suggested. "You know, people aren't supposed to eat cooked food."

"I'm reasonably sure people are supposed to cook their food. Didn't cavemen cook their food?" I asked.

"All I know is that I've lost fifteen pounds in ten days," Bird said. "And look at my skin. I don't look as old as I'm supposed to." She harrumphed and farted. "That's the only drawback to the raw food. The fiber. I haven't stopped farting. But who cares? What's a little farting when you lose fifteen pounds in ten days and your skin is clear?"

She had a point. If I looked old and fat, how could I get married on Sunday? It was already Tuesday.

Tuesday, Wednesday, Thursday, Friday, and Saturday. That was five days. According to Bird's diet numbers, I could lose seven-and-a-half pounds by my wedding.

"You have any celery sticks?" I asked.

"Dolly, you look perfectly fine," my grandmother insisted. "You don't need celery sticks. None of us needs celery sticks."

"At least get the facial peel and waxing at Muffy & Dicks," the pedicurist urged, like I was an emergency.

"But what's Muffy & Dicks?" I asked. "I never heard of it."

"It's the place that just opened next to Ruth's."

"The natural beauty supply store?" I asked.

"Natural beauty supply store and butcher shop," the pedicurist said. "It just opened. I got a Brazilian wax and six lamb chops. The lamb chops were delicious."

"I got my eyebrows done, but no lamb chops for me," Bird explained. "You can't eat raw lamb chops."

"Maybe I do need some sprucing up," I said.

"Thank you. Thank you," Bird said, obviously relieved that I wouldn't be an old, fat mess at my wedding. "I mean, don't you have Bridget's baby's christening tomorrow and then the wedding on Thursday? This is not a week where you should be looking like that," she said, pointing at my old-looking, cooked food-eating face.

She was right. I was going to be on display all week. It was going to be hell. But I was also going to eat cake all week, I realized. A week of cake was pretty good, even with all of my freaking out.

Cake was definitely an upside to hell.

With my beauty plan set up to start tomorrow, the pedicurist went quiet while she worked on Grandma's feet, and Bird finished with the curlers and squeezed permanent solution onto my grandmother's hair.

"How's it going with Matilda?" Grandma asked me. "Did you unmatch them?"

Drat. I'd forgotten all about Matilda. "I went there, but

didn't have enough time to really figure out the situation. But she looked fine to me. Really happy with her husband and married life."

Grandma scratched her chin. "I don't know. Maybe my radar is wonky. I could've sworn that she needed help and that her husband was all wrong. Maybe I didn't make a mistake with my match? I don't know. I keep getting signals. I keep seeing things."

"You want a cup of coffee, Zelda?" Bird asked her. "A glass of water? A Danish? You look a little pale."

"Yes, I'd like all of those things. And a bagel. You got a bagel? I just feel a little off kilter. Maybe my eyesight isn't as good as it used to be."

"Are you kidding me?" Bird said. "You're more reliable than the six o'clock news. Your sight is never fuzzy. Your radar's never wonky."

She was right. Grandma's radar was never wonky. She'd always been right except on a blind day. And this wasn't a blind day.

"I have some time today," I said. "I'll give her another visit."

After Grandma was finished at the hair salon, we ate lunch at Saladz. I was still hungover, and the food hit the spot. My grandmother got a lot of attention in the restaurant, since it had been delivering to her for years, and this was the first time she had gone to eat there. We had chicken and waffles with brownie à la mode for dessert.

"I guess I'll start my raw food diet tomorrow," I said,

looking at my empty plate.

Afterward, Grandma went off to do something exciting, and I picked up my car and drove back to Matilda's apartment.

She opened the door with a smile, happy to see me. "Two visits in two days. This is great. The only other person who visits me is Fanta. How are you, Gladie?"

She let me into the apartment, which was even hotter than the day before. The windows were closed and the fans were on. This time, she wasn't alone. There was a man in the living room watching TV. He was about five-foot eight, balding with a little paunch. He stood up and greeted me in surprise. Matilda introduced me, and he smiled, warmly and gestured for me to take a seat on the couch.

"The granddaughter of the woman who's responsible for my happy ending," he said, smiling. "I'm so glad you came to visit."

"I dropped by yesterday and I figured I'd come back," I said, not thinking of an excuse about why I was coming back.

Rockwell smiled. "Matilda didn't tell me she had a visitor. Matilda, you should've shared that with me. I would've loved to know you had a visitor."

"Rockwell likes me to share my days with him," Matilda explained. "It slipped my mind, honey."

Rockwell put his arm around her and gave her a squeeze and a kiss on her temple. "My absent-minded girl. I couldn't love you any more if you never forgot a thing. Did you remember to lock the door? She always forgets to lock the door."

"Oh!" she exclaimed. "I'll check."

While she was gone, Rockwell offered me a glass of lemonade, which I gladly took, since I was sweating bullets and was already dehydrated from spending two minutes in their sweltering apartment. Rockwell was very welcoming and hospitable, and when Matilda returned, he asked me a lot of questions about my work and how my grandmother was doing. Every chance he got, he touched Matilda, drawing her into an embrace, giving her pecks on her cheek and her neck. They were so obviously in love that I wondered if Spencer and I were not.

Spencer was a play big or go home kind of guy. He was all in or not at all. He never gave me pecks on my cheek. Sure, he jumped my bones every chance he got, but was that romantic? Was that a death-do-us-part relationship?

Where were my pecks?

"I have to go off to work," Rockwell announced, as if he was disappointed to leave his wife. He gazed lovingly into her eyes and gave her face a series of little kisses. "No rest for the weary. Off on the road again to bring home the bacon. You girls stay here and have fun. But, Matilda, don't tire yourself out. You know how you get when you're tired."

"He's right. When I get tired, I get forgetful and a little airy," Matilda explained.

"She just does things like leaves the stove on or the water in the bathroom sink. Stuff like that. Nothing dramatic. Listen, sweetheart," he told her, clutching her in an embrace. "When I get back, how about we go out for a candlelit dinner and then a bubble bath and I give you a massage?"

He had such a romantic way of speaking. Spencer would've told me he wanted to do me with me on top, without any mention of bubbles. At most, he would have brought a box of Oreos to eat after he bonked my brains out. It wasn't exactly a massage and a candlelit dinner.

I guessed Grandma's radar was wonky. These two were the most romantic couple I had ever met.

After Rockwell left to go to work, Matilda made a beeline for the chest and took out the two pairs of binoculars. She handed me one. "Lots of stuff happening," she explained. We looked out the window to the apartment directly opposite. "That's Fanta," she explained. There was a woman with red hair just like orange soda having an argument with her husband. The man gripped Fanta's arms tightly and shook her. "They don't have the best marriage," Matilda said. "They argue all the time. Rockwell and I never argue."

I gnawed the inside of my cheek. Spencer and I argued all the time. We constantly argued. I didn't think we communicated in any other way than arguing. Still, he had never grabbed me and shook me. He had never gotten angry like this man was with Fanta. The argument stopped pretty quickly, and the woman ran into the bedroom, locking herself in. I felt dirty, spying on someone's private moment, but I couldn't bring myself to look away.

"Yesterday, you were saying that you are new in town. Where do you come from?" I asked Matilda.

"Orange County. I've moved around a lot. No family.

I've been kind of like a searcher, not knowing what I wanted to do when I grew up."

I understood completely. I had gone from one job to the next until I came to Cannes to help my grandmother with her matchmaking business.

"I studied a lot," Matilda continued. "I have three PhD's, two Masters, and four Bachelor's degrees." Yowza. I didn't know why someone would want more than one degree, but I wasn't exactly an expert on the world of higher learning. I had dropped out of high school, and I never watched PBS.

But I didn't think I needed to tell Matilda that.

I put my binoculars down. "Wow, you're smart."

"But that doesn't stop me from being airy. I also have a little OCD problem lately. Don't tell Rockwell, but I check the door locks twenty times a day. I don't trust myself anymore, Gladie."

"Have you tried the raw food diet? I hear that's pretty good except for the farting."

My phone rang. It was Spencer. "Pinky, if you're not out stealing more beasts of burden, you need to come home immediately. It's an emergency," he said and clicked off. There was no, "I love you" or offers of a bubble bath and champagne and romantic candlelit dinners. Spencer was nothing like Rockwell. Was our marriage doomed to fail? I said goodbye to Matilda and left.

CHAPTER 6

These days, the news is sixty percent about what could happen instead of talking about what's happening now. I'm sort of known for talking about what will happen. But emes my hand to God, bubbeleh, what will happen is not nearly as important as what's happening right this second. While you're wondering if your house will flood, it's already on fire. You understand? Make sure your house isn't on fire. There those are wise words from your grandma.

Lesson 119, Matchmaking advice from your Grandma Zelda

Spencer had sounded completely panicked on the phone, which wasn't his go-to emotion. His normal go to emotions were irritation and annoyance. I was used to that. But never panic. I couldn't imagine what would make him so scared.

I parked my Oldsmobile Cutlass Supreme in my grandmother's driveway, and before I could even turn off the engine, Spencer ran out of the house and opened my car door.

It was a very romantic gesture, something he had never done before. All at once, I felt better about my worries that our relationship wasn't as romantic as Matilda and Rockwell's. Spencer did love me. Here he was running outside, opening my car door, very excited to see me. That was as romantic as Matilda and Rockwell's pecks and bubbles and candlelit dinners.

Besides, Rockwell was a dumpy guy, and Spencer looked sexy as hell today. He was wearing one of his nicest suits, and he obviously had taken extra care with his hair and his personal grooming. He was the sexiest man I have ever known, but today, he had outdone himself.

And it was all for me. He had made himself look as attractive as he could because he loved me and wanted me to be happy. That was the definition of romance.

I couldn't believe we were about to be husband and wife and live together forever. I was such a lucky woman to have him.

I got out of the car and wrapped my arms around him. Hugging him, I felt thankful for my loving romantic Spencer.

Then, he picked me up and put me down an arm's-length away from him. In other words, he pushed me away.

"We don't have time for that," he growled.

"Huh? Wha…?" I stammered.

Spencer ran his fingers through his hair and looked past

me. “Don’t panic,” he ordered.

“I’m not panicking. Should I be panicking? Are you panicking? Why shouldn’t I panic?”

I took a step forward, and he pushed me back, again. “I told you not to panic. Please don’t panic. And for God’s sake, don’t be you. I mean you know, don’t be…” Spencer ran his finger up and down over his lips, in the international insane gesture.

“I’m pretty sure I should resent that,” I said.

“Well, you know it’s true. But listen. You need to take a breath and brace yourself. My mother is here. I mean, my parents are here.”

I gasped. “But it’s not the wedding, yet.”

“For the rehearsal dinner.”

“There’s a rehearsal dinner?”

“Focus, Pinky. This is serious. My mother’s here. You need to remain calm.”

“I’m calm.”

“No, you’re not. You can’t be calm. Just be calm. Be calm!” Spencer said, his voice a half-octave higher than usual.

“Okay, I might not be calm,” I said. “Not now. Not the way you’re acting. Why are you acting like this? Does your mother have three heads? Does she breathe fire?”

“Yes! I thought I made that clear to you.”

“Oh, geez. Oh, geez. Your mother. Your mother.”

“My mother. My mother.”

“Your mother. Your mother.” We were in a panic loop without a way of getting off.

"Stay calm."

"I'm calm."

"No, you're not. You're hyperventilating, Pinky. Stop it."

I huffed and puffed. "I can't stop breathing. Wow, I'm breathing a lot. Why am I breathing so much? Now, I'm lightheaded. Why do I keep breathing like this?"

Spencer's eyes were huge, and his perfectly groomed hair was standing up because he kept running his fingers through it. "Because my mother is on her way. I mean she's here. She's sitting with my father in the parlor. Stop breathing."

"Okay, I'll stop breathing."

We walked inside. I had never met Spencer's parents before. I had never even spoken to them on the phone. For some reason, Spencer had kept them under wraps. I had met his brother, Peter, when he had come to town to visit. But never his parents. Spencer was very close to his mother. He talked to her all the time and gave her updates, but I wasn't sure he gave her all the updates about me.

That would have been a whole crap-ton of updates.

As I walked into the house, I wondered why he had kept me all but a secret. Perhaps he was ashamed of me. Since puberty, Spencer had only dated supermodels, actresses, and the occasional cheerleader. I wasn't a supermodel. I wasn't any of those things.

But supermodels weren't good with parents. Nobody wanted to introduce a supermodel girlfriend to their mother. Skinny, tall girls in designer outfits weren't true wife material. I was wife material. I was a girlfriend to introduce to parents. I was…

I was crazy.

I was wrong.

I wasn't girlfriend material or wife material. I wasn't fit to be introduced to anyone's mother. I was a wreck. I was wearing Walley's cutoff jeans and a tank top with a coffee stain on my chest.

And according to Bird, I looked my age. No. Older than my age. And I needed a facial and a wax from Muffy & Dick's. And now I was going to meet Spencer's mother, and I didn't look anything like a supermodel.

I didn't even look anything like a cheerleader.

I looked more like a homeless person.

Spencer took my hand, and we walked into the parlor. Spencer's father stood and smiled at me. His parents were breathtakingly beautiful people in their sixties. I was surprised that they were so good looking, even though they had made two beautiful people and would have of course been beautiful.

Spencer's father was even taller than him and his brother. He was well-built and fit with a thick head of dark hair and a straight back.

"Isn't she lovely, Mother?" Spencer's father said.

He wrapped me in a warm embrace, and my hyperventilating stopped. This isn't so bad, I thought. It didn't matter that my shirt was stained. It didn't matter that I looked my age or older.

Then, Spencer's mother stood and clasped her hands in

front of her. Beautiful, her thick dark hair was jaw-length. She wore a Chanel suit, and despite our heatwave, there wasn't a sweat stain anywhere on it. She looked me up and down, pausing at my little paunch and my coffee stain. I forced myself not to cover my body with my hands. And not to run away.

"Yes, isn't she precious? Bless her heart," Spencer's mother said.

"She's not southern," Spencer whispered to me. "Beware the southern accent. It's deadly."

Spencer's mother embraced me, but it was the kind where she didn't actually touch me. She was cold as ice, at least to me. To Spencer, she was warm and bubbly and extremely maternal. She kept touching his face and telling him how wonderful he was.

Spencer's mother definitely didn't subscribe to Bridget's rules of motherhood. Spencer was still getting cooed at, and he was in his thirties.

But there was no cooing for her future daughter-in-law.

The afternoon moved at a snail's pace. Spencer's mother insulted me every chance she got in a very nice way. She made references to my poverty, my lack of education, and the people I kept company with. She mentioned Spencer's old girlfriends, who were extremely accomplished and nothing at all like me.

She was so nice while she insulted me that I didn't realize my feelings were hurt until after she had insulted me and had moved on to the next insult. I couldn't catch up. She had a never-ending supply of criticisms of who I was, and by definition, why I wasn't good enough for her son.

Normally, my grandmother would've been there, acting like a buffer, but she was out on the town, marveling at the world's new technologies that had been created during the time that she had been a shut-in. The last I heard, she was at the pharmacy putting her debit card in and out of the machine over and over and giggling. For his part, Spencer regaled them with my successes in matchmaking, pointing out Fred's wedding this week. He avoided talking about owls and donkeys. It didn't matter. No amount of compliments could have competed with the bad vibes coming in waves from his mother.

Finally, it was time to go upstairs and get dressed for dinner. Spencer followed me. "Why do you keep calling them Mr. and Mrs. Bolton?" he demanded. "Call them James and Lily."

"I can't. Every time I try to, I start hyperventilating again. Mr. and Mrs. Bolton makes me calm."

"Call them James and Lily, Pinky. The Mrs. Bolton crap just makes her sense your fear. What did I tell you about her smelling fear?"

It turned out that Spencer's mother could smell fear like a lion or a tiger. "I'll try. I'll try. Maybe I need a Xanax. Or a horse tranquilizer. Where can I get a horse tranquilizer?"

Spencer supervised my getting dressed for dinner. He made sure that I wore the least objectionable dress with no stains.

"Just try to be normal. Not Pinky-normal. You know what I mean. Normal people normal," he said, adjusting his tie in the mirror.

It had been a long time since I had known anybody who was normal-normal. I didn't know what normal was for normal people. I only knew what normal was for weirdo people from our weirdo town. If he wanted me to act like normal people, we shouldn't have lived in this town.

"We have to move," I said. "We have to move somewhere normal to be normal. Let's go right now. Hop in the car. We can get to Los Angeles in a couple hours. Los Angeles is normal."

"Pinky, get ahold of yourself."

"Kiss me to relax me," I commanded.

Spencer took a step backward. "Are you crazy? My mother would know if there was any hanky-panky happening anywhere near her, and then she would go ballistic. It would be off the charts nuclear war passive aggressiveness. You know what that means?"

I had no idea what that meant. "Of course, I know what that means. I'm not stupid."

"Besides, I can't kiss you. I have no spit. My saliva glands stopped working."

We walked downstairs and Spencer's mother handed me my cellphone. "I put my contact information in your phone," she said.

"How did you get my code?" I asked.

"Oh, my dear. You're so funny. Isn't she funny,

Father?"

"Now that you have my contact information," she continued, not bothering to explain how she broke into my phone, "there's no excuse for not contacting me. You can give me regular updates. Let me know what's happening. Let me know how you're taking care of my Poopykins."

I looked over at her Poopykins. Sweat had popped out on his forehead, and he was looking up at the ceiling.

Spencer drove us up into the mountains to a fancy restaurant with a great view. The conversation in the car somehow got focused on the fact that I had shown my underpants to the town and that I had killed numerous people.

"She just found them, Mom," Spencer told his mother. "She didn't actually kill them."

His mother wasn't convinced. At the restaurant, we were seated at a table for four in the center. I made a mental breakdown of the evening so far, and I realized that I hadn't actually made any major faux pas. I was doing pretty well. Yes, Spencer's mother hated me and thought I was worthless and a murderer who showed her underpants to everyone, but I hadn't yet belched or passed out or threw up on her. So, I was taking the night as a win.

But my heart sank when the waiter approached our table. I recognized him immediately. The last time I'd seen him, he was in the hospital after he ate a gun. And that wasn't the worst thing I had ever seen him do.

I wasn't a religious person, but I prayed right there and then that he wouldn't recognize me, or at the very least wouldn't introduce himself.

Of course, my prayers weren't answered.

"Hey there," he said to me. "Do you remember me? It's me, Tim."

I noticed the moment that Spencer recognized our waiter. He gripped the side of the table so hard that I thought the table would break off in his hands.

"Yeah, sure, Tim. What's the special today? Any good soups?" I asked, trying to get him off the topic of exactly who he was.

"Why don't you introduce us to your friend?" Spencer's mother suggested, as if she had internal radar on how to prove that I was unfit to marry her Poopykins.

"We know each other," Spencer interrupted. "I'd also like to hear about the specials. How about steak? You make a good steak here?"

"I've never eaten it," Tim said. "You know, I like to eat odd things." He turned to Spencer's mother. "I once ate five lightbulbs and a gun. But the gun thing was a mistake." He rubbed his stomach. "I'm still paying for that one. Remember that, Gladie? Remember when I ate the gun?"

Spencer's mother glared at me, as if I had stuffed the gun down Tim's throat.

"I like steak, too. I'm not one of those vegan girlfriends," I told Spencer's mother. "Those kinds of girlfriends are irritating. I'm a meat eater. Lots and lots of meat. Meat, meat, meat, meat, meat. Can't get enough meat. Yum. Go meat. Love me some steak."

Spencer's mother glared at me. "I'm a vegan," she said through clenched teeth.

"Eaten anything interesting lately, Tim?" I asked, changing the subject.

"They got me in some kind of therapy program. A thing for folks with different appetites. So, I've been off metals for a while. I'm trying to get off glass, but it's a hard addiction to break. You got any addictions?" he asked Spencer's mother. She ignored him and continued to glare at me, as if I was Satan and about to fly over the table and take Spencer straight to hell.

"Oh, God. Kill me now," Spencer moaned, slapping his forehead.

Thankfully, Tim finally took our orders. But before he left, he couldn't leave well enough alone. "Remember when we met?" he asked me and laughed. "That was funny. My penis in a pipe? I'll never forget how they had to cut me out. Boy, that pipe was tight. I thought my fun days were way behind me. But it turned out fine. Everything works just fine down there. You want to see?"

Spencer stood before Tim could show us how he was still intact below the belt. Spencer's face was bright red, and he looked like he was going to explode. "Tim, go get us our food, or I'll take this fork and jam it into your digestive system, but it won't go down your throat. It'll go in the opposite way. All the way up. You get me?"

Tim blanched. He probably would have been more than happy to eat the fork, but he didn't want any part of a fork enema.

Our appetizers arrived, and I was thrilled that our mouths were full so we couldn't talk. But it didn't last.

"Mom, Dad, I can't wait to show you our new house on Friday," Spencer said. "You're going to love it. It's a dream come true. And of course, there's a guestroom for you whenever you want to visit."

I choked on a stuffed mushroom cap. "There is?" I managed.

Truth be told, I hadn't been all that involved with the house. I let Spencer do what he wanted with it. I had never owned property before, and I was still thinking it wasn't quite real, like I was never actually going to move into a gorgeous, custom-built home for me and my gorgeous, hot-stuff guy.

"Is the house in your name, dear, or in both of yours?" Spencer's mother asked, sweetly.

I got the impression that there was only one good answer. The table got quiet, as we waited for Spencer to respond.

"Just mine, Mom," Spencer said quietly and slipped a stuffed mushroom cap into his mouth.

I didn't know how to feel about the fact that my new home was only in my husband's name. I mean, it was totally fair. Spencer had bought it with his own money. I hadn't given anything to the project.

But those were the logical reasons why it was fair for the house to only be in Spencer's name. And logical reasons never matter. Spencer's confession made me feel even more like our new house wasn't really my home.

Spencer's mother was delighted, however. It was the first time that I saw her smile a completely genuine smile. Relief. I recognized it. It was the first crack in the terrifying reality that her son was going to leave her forever for a woman that didn't deserve him.

"I can't wait to see your house," she said, happily. "By the way, I took the liberty of setting up an appointment for you two with my friend, tomorrow. One o'clock. Be there on time. No need to thank me."

She handed a business card to Spencer. I leaned over and looked at it.

"Marriage counselor?" Spencer asked.

"You don't buy a car without it being inspected first," his mother said, as if that answered everything. She touched her arm and gasped. "Where the hell is my bracelet?" We searched the table and under it, but there was no sign of her expensive bracelet.

Tim came to the table with our main courses. "Are you looking for your bracelet?" he asked. "I couldn't help myself. It was so shiny. But don't worry. I'll give it back to you in about twenty-four hours. Two days, tops."

Thankfully, Spencer's parents were staying at a bed and breakfast just outside of town. They picked up their car at my grandmother's house and said goodbye without coming in. Spencer and I waved goodbye and walked inside. Grandma was already in bed. We trudged up the stairs, like the defeated Napoleon at Waterloo.

"I can't believe you told my mother that your mother is a farmer," Spencer said, closing my bedroom door behind us.

"Well, she's on a farm," I said. "You didn't want me to tell her that she was in a prison farm because she ran a mobile meth lab on her moped. Did you?"

"Good point. The best thing about your mother being in prison is that she'll never meet my mother. I don't know how we could ever get through that."

"We're not going to this marriage counselor, are we?" I asked.

"What can it hurt? My mother wants us to go, and maybe it would be good for us to talk to someone before we got married."

My feeling of panic welled up in me again. Wanting to go to marriage counseling before we got married wasn't a good sign. First no romance and now Spencer was having second thoughts? I had been right that my relationship with Spencer was nothing compared to Matilda and Rockwell's. I felt like our relationship was running through my fingers like sand. What if this was all a mistake? What if it was going to blow up before we actually got married?

Somehow, I had to fix things. Fix us. I needed to spice things up. While Spencer laid in bed, watching The Simpsons on television, it was up to me to put a little heat into our relationship and save it from dying.

In the bathroom, I took off my clothes and took a series

of smutty, naked selfies. Sexting. I had never done it before. I had never taken a naked picture of myself. But desperate times called for desperate measures. I knew it would put a little heat back into our relationship. From everything I heard, sexting worked like gangbusters.

Click. Click. Click. I took the pictures and texted them to Spencer.

I walked back into the bedroom. Spencer was in bed, still watching TV. He raised an eyebrow when he saw me walk in, naked. There was some movement under the sheets, as if a part of him was growing.

There. That worked. He patted the bed next to him. “Come on over here, Pinky. Let’s get it on, do the nasty, rumble in the sheets, bump uglies.”

Men are so easy, when you think about it.

“You’re not worried about your mother?” I asked.

“She’s outside of city limits. So, we’re safe. And please, Pinky, don’t talk about my mother. Not now.”

“You know, tomorrow morning’s Bridget’s baby’s christening. I’m going to have to wear a suit and look respectable.”

I got into bed and Spencer moved himself on top of me, lifting my knees up over his hips. “Then, let’s work out all of the disrespectful out of you tonight, Pinky.”

CHAPTER 7

How the hell did I get here? Who are you, and why are you in my bed? No, I'm not getting dementia, dolly. No, I'm not absent-minded. I'm just trying to explain a little about true love. Sometimes, it's not what your match had in mind. They thought that love would be a beautiful silk scarf, but suddenly they're sharing a bathroom with an old shmata and they're as happy as Sally Field at the Oscars. Tell your matches to embrace their shmata and don't second guess it. One person's shmata is another person's silk scarf. It's just the way of love. It's full of dirty rags.

Lesson 55, Matchmaking advice from your Grandma Zelda

I woke up happy. Even though I had a mean mother-in-law to be, no romance in my marriage-to-be, and my name wasn't on the deed to my new, fancy house, I still had been made love to all night long, as if I lived in a romance novel, but only the good bits.

I was woken at five by my phone, which was buzzing off the nightstand. It was Matilda. I took my phone into the bathroom and called her back.

"Something happened, Gladie." she said, breathlessly. "Something bad. Can you come over?"

"What kind of bad? A fire?"

"No. Worse. It might be a matter of life and death."

I sighed. If I had a penny for every time it was a matter of life and death, I would have a shitload of pennies. I would be the queen of pennies. The lord and master of the universe of pennies.

"I can come after my friend's christening," I told her.

Matilda was fine with that. She thanked me and explained that she didn't bat for the other side before she hung up. I didn't understand what she meant by that, but I said okay and hung up, too.

I got a couple more hours of sleep, and then Spencer and I got dressed for the christening. I wore a long skirt and a light blouse. It was an outfit that was hopefully church-acceptable but would hopefully not make me sweat bullets in the continuing heatwave. The small Catholic church in the Historic District was as old as the town and considered a historical structure. Therefore, there was no air conditioning or any other non-historical conveniences except for a toilet that backed up, regularly. So, it would be a sauna during the ceremony.

Spencer and I met my grandmother downstairs, who

had also dressed up for the christening. She was wearing a red, knockoff Oscar de la Renta ball gown, which was at least two sizes too small. Grandma believed that clothes should suffocate you, or they didn't really fit. She also didn't seem to worry about sweating because her ball gown was so voluminous, it was like a portable sweat box.

We filed into Spencer's car. Grandma sat in the passenger seat in the front, and I sat in the back. "I hope there're bagels at this christening. I've got a hankering for a bialy with butter."

"I don't think there's a lot of bialys at christenings, Zelda," Spencer said, driving down the street. "I think this is the cherry danish kind of shindig."

"Cherry danish!" Grandma and I exclaimed together. There was little we wouldn't do for a fresh danish.

At the church, there was a good gathering for the christening. There were about ten of Bridget's friends and about twenty-five of her bookkeeping clients. We did the rounds, saying hello as we made our way to Bridget. Perhaps it was the solemnity of the moment or the power of the historic church, but nobody made eye contact with me, and at least half made eye contact with my boobs, which were politely covered by my conservative shirt.

"People are weird," I noted to Spencer.

"You just noticed?"

Bridget was standing at the front of the church with baby Jonathan in her arms and her babysitter Jackson by her side. Lucy came dressed like Scarlett O'Hara with her husband,

Uncle Harry, who was dressed like Al Capone and smoking a thick cigar. His arm was wrapped around Lucy's small waist, and he gave her a peck on her cheek as they walked up to the front of the church. Lucy blushed, and I was happy to see that she was still thrilled to be married to Harry.

"Hey there, Legs," Harry greeted me and kissed my cheek. "Or should I call you boobs?"

"Huh?" I asked, but he and Lucy moved into the crowd.

My grandmother mixed and mingled, cornering Sister Cyril to tell her not to eat potato salad next week. "It'll be bad," she told the nun.

Bridget didn't seem all that happy, and it didn't take me long to figure out why. Baby Jonathan was being assaulted with baby talk by guest after guest.

"Isn't Sweetiekums the sweetest sweetie of all the sweeties in the world?" one person said, making Bridget red with anger.

"I don't argue that he's sweet," Bridget said, trying to keep her temper even. "But we don't speak to him in those terms, because it degrades his intelligence and makes him believe that he's not a fully formed person. But he is a fully formed person, even if he's a baby and doesn't yet know how to speak."

The person stared at Bridget as if she had three heads and walked away, carefully.

Even though Bridget had managed to fend off one baby lover, there was a steady stream of other people ready to dose Bridget's baby with an onslaught of baby talk. Bridget gave her spiel to each one of them, but it was like pushing back the tide or eating just one potato chip.

Impossible.

Poor Bridget. It was hard to be her. Grandma gave her a big hug, and so did I.

"Beautiful day," Grandma said, carefully avoiding the topic of her baby.

"If I believed in fate or God, I would say that he was shining down on Jonathan, giving him a perfect day for a pivotal moment in his life," Bridget said.

She gazed adoringly at her baby in her arms. Bridget didn't only love her son; she was in love with him. Seeing how attached she was to him made my heart full, and I choked up, swallowing my tears before they had a chance to fall.

Spencer gave Bridget a kiss on her cheek, too. I guessed a lot of kissing was normal for a christening. "Congratulations, Bridget," he said. Spencer was a tall, muscular man and leaning over the baby, he dwarfed him, completely. Spencer seemed almost mesmerized by baby Jonathan. Slowly, he touched the baby's hand with the tip of his index finger, and baby Jonathan gripped on tight.

Spencer's eye grew wide, and he smiled wide. He took a deep breath and proceeded to shower the baby with the longest string of baby talk cooing that I had ever heard.

"What a sweetie babykins, lovey-dovey cutie pie," he gushed. "Does baby waby love his blanky wanky?" His eyes were only for Baby Jonathan, kind of like the love that Matilda and Rockwell showed each other.

He caught me staring at him, and he stopped cooing. A slight tinge of a blush appeared on his cheeks, and I wondered how much he liked kids. I had never figured him as a fan of children.

Or a guy who wanted children.

"There's a lot of bedrooms in your new house," my grandmother whispered in my ear. "Like he's planning for a big family."

My mouth dropped open, and I stopped blinking. Grandma had dropped a big bomb in my ear. I stared at her, as she slipped away to find the danishes in the back room. I followed her, hoping she would explain what she had just said.

I double-timed it to catch up, but my grandmother was fast when she was on the scent of breakfast pastries. But without her explaining, I already knew that she was probably right. Spencer wanted a big family. He wanted to have children. That's why he custom-made a gigantic house with a pool and enough rooms to house the Brady Bunch.

But did I want children? I didn't know. What did I want? I didn't know. When would I know? I didn't know.

Besides a cherry danish, I didn't know what I wanted. It was another question about the foundations on which our marriage was going to be built. Chemistry was great, but was it enough to build a life together on? And what if he wanted children and I didn't? What would happen then? Would that leave us with a life of resentments?

Oh, yes. I needed a cherry danish.

After two cherry danishes, it was time for the

christening. Spencer and I stood next to Bridget in our place as Jonathan's godparents. I took baby Jonathan in my arms after I wiped my sweaty hands on my skirt, remembering not to coo at him. I was terrified that I was going to drop him because I was sweating so badly, but I managed to hold on tight.

All eyes were on me and the baby. I wasn't good about being the center of attention, but I loved showing off baby Jonathan. There was a smattering of laughter from the pews and then there was a wave of photo-taking by the guests with their phones. After the picture-taking, half of the church studied their phones and there was a wave of mumbles and murmuring. With the eyes off of me, I instantly relaxed.

The christening ceremony was short. We said a couple of prayers before I handed the baby to the priest, who sprinkled Jonathan with holy water and oil. A few minutes later, the baby was officially named for my father. Success. Bridget held her baby, looking at him with so much love that I was sure he could feel the love through her gaze.

"I just want to say a few words," Bridget announced before the guests had a chance to get up. "Religion is evil. It's the downfall of society, and this country was founded on the principles of the Enlightenment and the Age of Reason and there wasn't one of our founding fathers who really gave a shit about religion. Sure, they read the Bible, but they didn't believe in the mythological hocus-pocus of religion."

There was an audible gasp, and Sister Cyril grabbed the priest before he could pass out. I looked up, expecting to be hit by lightning. Spencer smirked his normal little smirk. About half of the guests were looking at their phones and shooting looks at me, seemingly unconcerned by Bridget's blasphemy in church. In fact, they didn't seem to be paying attention to her. They only had eyes for their phones. And for me.

"Even though religion is medieval," Bridget continued. "I'm so happy that my son got christened in the church today. I love this church, and I love our new priest, who never killed anybody, which is a plus."

She turned around and smiled at the priest, whose face had completely drained of color, and he kept shifting his feet as if he wanted to escape or leap into the air and pulverize Bridget.

"Well, I'm assuming you never killed anybody. What are the odds, right?" she asked him.

About a year ago, we had issues with a priest who had shot at Bridget. Since then, Bridget had been walking a thin line between being a devout Catholic and a staunch atheist.

"Keep it rolling along, Bridget," Sister Cyril said sweetly. "The lox and bagels are waiting."

Bridget nodded. "So anyway, if I believed in God and believed in religion, I would say that this is a perfect moment and that I'm so happy that my son has a good start and is one with the Lord. I would also say, peace of the Lord be with you always."

The guests put their phones down long enough to respond, "and with your spirit."

Spencer put his arm around me and kissed me behind my ear. "You're crying, Pinky," he whispered. He wiped the tears off my face with his thumb. "My beautiful, sensitive almost-wife. Have I told you recently that I love you?"

I sniffed. "No, you haven't. You told me that I have a great ass."

"You do have a great ass. And I love you, too. It was an oversight on my part not to tell you, Pinky. I love you more than Bridget loves the Lord."

I didn't know how to take that.

Lox and bagels were served out back in the church's small courtyard. The fresh air was welcome, even though it was hotter than hell. Bridget, Jackson, Lucy, Harry, Spencer, Grandma, Sister Cyril, and I sat at a table with two of Bridget's bookkeeping clients, Kevin and Chloe. The priest chose to sit at another table, far away from the blaspheming Bridget.

"I don't want to put undue pressure on Jonathan regarding his potential," Bridget said while she chewed on an onion bagel. "But did you notice how aware he was during the ceremony? He understood what was going on. That's why he was so calm. He *knew*. He *knew*."

"Gladie, I'm so glad you have all of your pubic hair," Chloe announced out of nowhere. "All these women today waxing it all off in order to look like little girls. But you're all there. Real big bush."

Everything bagel shot out of my mouth and landed on Sister Cyril's face right between her eyes, and a wad of cream cheese flew out of my nose and landed with a splat onto Spencer's plate.

"I like your pubic hair, too," Kevin said.

"No comment," Harry said. "But you're very

photogenic, Legs. And generous."

"Uh," I said.

"What's going on?" Spencer asked. "It's like I came in late."

I had no idea what was going on. One minute we were christening a baby, and the next minute we were focused on my hoohah.

"There's nothing wrong with a woman expressing herself," Bridget insisted. "Women have been objectified since the beginning of time. Gladie's just taking her power back. Don't worry, Gladie. You can send me all the nudie pics of you, you want. I think that Bella Abzug would've approved."

Spencer looked at me and arched an eyebrow.

"I thought the pictures had something to do with fashion and sizing for new clothes," Lucy said. "Very fashion forward, Gladie. I mean, except for the backward fashion down there."

Spencer arched his other eyebrow.

"Wait a second. Wait a second," I said. The nonsense was starting to make sense. "Wait a second. Wait a second!" Rummaging through my purse, I took my cellphone out and studied my texts. Somehow, instead of sending my sexting pictures to Spencer, I had sent them to the entire guest list for my wedding.

The entire town was coming to my wedding.

I sexted the entire town.

The world spun around, and I saw stars.

The entire town saw me naked. That was so much

worse than seeing my pink underpants.

Spencer took my cellphone out of my hands. "Holy shit, Pinky," he said, smirking his little smirk. "Did you send out a new wedding invitation?"

I yanked the phone away from him. "Technology sucks!" I yelled. "I was sending it to, to, to…you."

I stood up, as if I had gotten stung by a bee.

"Oh. Now the text from my mother makes sense," Spencer said, slapping his forehead. "I knew she thought you were ditzy, but the whole floozy thing came as a surprise to me."

"What?" I said, clutching my purse to my chest.

"Danger, darlin'," Lucy told Spencer, dabbing at her lips with her napkin.

"She thinks I'm ditzy?" I asked Spencer. Of course she thought I was ditzy. How could she not think I was ditzy? But a floozy? A floozy?

"She'll get used to you," Spencer insisted. "And you'll show her eventually that you're not after my money."

"Oh, damn," Sister Cyril said. "He went there. And they say nuns are crazy for never getting married."

"Your mother saw me naked," I said, finally understanding the ramifications of trying to lay on the sexy for Spencer. "The whole town saw me naked."

"With your leg lifted on the rim of the bathtub," Kevin said. "That was my favorite picture."

"I gotta go," I said to no one in particular. I spun around, trying to figure out where the exit was. "There's a matter of life or death. So, you know, I have to go."

"Don't go, darlin'," Lucy said. "Nobody cares about a photo or two."

"I do," Kevin said. "I have a new screensaver thanks to Gladie."

My grandmother squeezed my arm. "If I were your age and looked like you, I would never put on clothes," she told me.

I gave Bridget a hug goodbye. "Congratulations, Bridget. It was a beautiful ceremony. I have a life or death thing I have to deal with."

"Someone's dead?" Lucy asked, hopefully. "You need help?"

"No, you stay with Bridget. Nobody's dead," I said.

Humiliation was my middle name. I had gone through a lot. But I couldn't deal with this at Bridget's christening breakfast. I mean, my foot up on the rim of the bathtub, and they all saw that.

I stumbled toward the fence and found a gate. After a few tries, I got it open and walked into the alley behind the church. I didn't have a car, and it was sweltering outside. I would have to walk home and get my car and hope that I didn't melt on the way.

A hand touched my shoulder, making me jump in surprise. It was Spencer, and he turned me around. "Pinky, where're you going?"

"It's a work thing. I have to…"

My voice drifted off, and I couldn't make eye contact. "Oh, Pinky. You're breaking my heart." Spencer wrapped me in his arms and pulled me close. I rested the side of my head on his chest and inhaled sharply. He smelled so good. Like expensive cologne, lox, and Spencer. He ran his fingers through my hair, and held me tight with his other hand.

"We're about to be married," he said. "Christening on Wednesday, Fred's wedding on Thursday, and our wedding on Sunday. Four days until it's you and me forever. Some people would be nervous. Some people would be getting wedding jitters."

"Second thoughts."

"Second thoughts. Is that what you're feeling?" His voice was smooth and soft, as if he was talking to a mustang that was debating whether to be tamed or continue being wild. Like a horse ready to bolt out of its paddock.

"No, I'm not having second thoughts. But I bet some people would be." I wasn't having second thoughts about marrying Spencer. Just the idea of losing him made me feel indescribably sad. "There's a lot of rooms in the house."

"And you're worried about my mother visiting and using one of them. I swear to you that with her Mahjong group and her furniture-making class and making my father crazy, she'll be too busy to stay with us. She'll never visit. Twice a year, tops."

I wasn't thinking about his mother. But he had a point. "What if you won't love me because your mother doesn't love me?"

"My mother's crazy about you. She just doesn't know it, yet. It's a territory thing, Pinky. You crossed the DMZ. You're not a skanky model. You're a skanky matchmaker. You're the real deal. You're under my skin. It's got her worried."

"I'm not skanky."

"C'mon, Pinky. Let a guy dream, will ya?"

"Okay. I'm skanky."

He kissed the top of my head. "Thank you. Listen, I don't give a fuck about what anybody thinks about you. I'm set in my ways, Pinky. Nobody can sway me. I love you. I'm crazy about you, and I'm locking this thing down on Sunday and nothing's going to stop that. Till death do us part, Pinky, and unless you kill me, that won't be for a long time. I've got the cholesterol level of a twenty-year old triathlete."

I wiggled my arms around him and squeezed him tight. I didn't correct him about my concerns about the extra bedrooms. There was time later to talk about babies, and for now, I was happy to know that Spencer loved me for more than my ass.

CHAPTER 8

Isn't the word MATCHMAKER the most beautiful word in the world? Matchmaking is matching one soul with another soul, with the express goal of creating love for eternity. How could anything be more beautiful than that? You'll have matches who will kvetch. You'll have matches who are real putzes. At those moments, you'll wonder if I lied to you about the beauty of matchmaking. But I'm not lying. Keep your eye on the happy ending. Keep your eye on the match, their two souls bound together in love. A good match is everything.

Lesson 4, Matchmaking advice from your Grandma Zelda

After Spencer drove me home to pick up my car, I drove to Matilda's. Her apartment was as hot as usual. She opened the door before I had a chance to ring the doorbell.

"I was watching through the peep hole," she said and

pulled me into the apartment. The fans were going, but the windows were still closed so that Matilda's neighbors couldn't spy on her while she spied on them. "Would you like a sandwich?"

"No, thank you. I just ate. What's wrong? What happened?"

Matilda handed me a pair of binoculars. "I was up all night. Well, you know, I'm up all night every night. But last night I was up all night watching Fanta and her husband."

My giddy enthusiasm for voyeurism had dissipated, now that the entire town had seen naked pictures of me. It was one thing to spy on others, but it was a totally different thing to be spied on.

I was about to give her a lesson about privacy, but Matilda was hell-bent on telling me all about Fanta and her husband, Chris. "They were arguing on and off. That's nothing new, but this time she gave as good as she got."

Despite my recent humiliation, my ears perked up. Nosiness was my biggest talent.

"I watched them for hours," Matilda continued. "There was some yelling, some knick-knack throwing, and a bunch of passive-aggressiveness. And then it happened."

I scooted forward in my seat. "What happened?"

"I went to the bathroom."

"You went to the bathroom?"

Matilda nodded. She had a far-off expression, like she was reliving going to the bathroom in her mind. "My bladder was ready to burst. I couldn't hold it. So, I went to the bathroom." She pointed toward the bathroom. "When I came back, I checked the oven in the kitchen to make sure I hadn't left it on. Yesterday, I discovered that I had opened all of the mail and then put it back into the mailbox. I don't remember ever opening it, though. Rockwell says I have too much on my mind and that's why I'm having these episodes."

She seemed to think about that for a moment. She chewed on her lip, and I realized how worried she was about her so-called episodes. Matilda shook her head and looked at a vase of roses on the dining room table.

"Rockwell sent me flowers," she said, smiling. "He's always thinking of me."

"I like roses," I said. Spencer hadn't given me a lot of flowers during our relationship, but he liked to bring me home chips and root beer about three times a week.

"Anyway," Matilda began again. She was very pretty, and I was happy to see that her eyes, which had been cloudy with worry, were now bright with excitement. "I was in the kitchen, checking the oven knobs. That's when I heard the noise."

"What kind of noise?"

"A boom. No, it wasn't quite a boom. It was more like a whap. A loud whap."

"What was it? What made the whap noise?"

"I don't know. I didn't know. So, I ran out of the kitchen and spied on Fanta and her husband again. That's when I saw it."

"What?" I asked.

Matilda pointed at my binoculars and urged me to look through them at Fanta's apartment. "It looks the same," I said.

"No, it doesn't. Don't you see the difference?"

"No. There's their living room and kitchen. It's exactly the same as it was before."

"Look again. Look at the bedroom," Matilda urged.

"I can't see the bedroom. The shades are down in the bedroom."

Matilda touched my back. "Exactly. The shades are down."

"The shades are down," I repeated in a whisper. "The shades…"

"Are down. Yes. For the first time since I moved here, their bedroom shades are down. It happened after the whap."

I studied the bedroom shades through the binoculars. "It happened after the whap?"

"Listen, Gladie," Matilda said. "You're going to think that I'm crazy, but I think that man killed Fanta. I think she's lying dead in their bedroom."

"The whap was a murder?"

I had a lot of experience with murder, but I had never heard one before. I usually came around after the murder already happened.

"I'm ninety-percent sure the whap was a murder," Matilda said. "Actually, I'm a hundred percent sure that Fanta has been snuffed out by her brutish husband. She's in there, dead, dead, dead."

I sat down and took a deep breath. This was so typical. I

was getting married in four days, and now a woman was murdered. "And we have to get justice for her, I'm assuming?" I asked Matilda.

"Well, yes. Don't you think so? I mean, she was killed. We have to bring her killer to justice."

I sighed. "Yeah. Yeah. Justice. I guess we have to. You got any cookies? I like a nice chocolate chip cookie before I get justice."

"I have Nutter Butters. Would that work?"

"I like milk with Nutter Butters. Do you have milk?"

"I have lowfat. Is that okay?"

"I guess so."

I ate ten Nutter Butters and two glasses of milk. After, I still wasn't ready to help poor dead Fanta, but Matilda was raring to go. As I was eating, she gathered a bunch of rope, a crowbar, and a roll of duct tape.

"Do we need anything else?" she asked.

"It depends. What're we doing?"

"We have to break into their apartment while Chris is out. Then, we find Fanta's body, take pictures for proof, and go to the cops."

"Okay. I'm still a little fuzzy about the duct tape, but let's do it. Let's find justice for Fanta."

Matilda gathered her supplies together in a Trader Joe's reusable shopping bag, and we walked to her front door. Right before she put her hand on the doorknob, Matilda stopped and turned toward me.

"I've never felt so full of life," she said. "Is that horrible?

A woman is dead, and I'm giddy with excitement. That's probably bad karma, right?"

Matilda and I had been separated at birth. I had gotten giddy in the face of a poor unfortunate's murder at least nine times in the past year. I had a whole lot of bad karma that I had to work against or I would wind up a cockroach in my next life. But as much as I tried to push down the giddiness and just feel a swell of empathy and horror, the sleuthing bug had bitten me big time, and I couldn't wait to discover poor Fanta and get her husband on death row.

"It's bad karma," I agreed. "You shouldn't be excited about a murder. That's low, Matilda. Real low."

"You're right. I don't know why I feel this way. There's something about discovering something horrible that nobody else knows that gets my heart pumping. Think about it, Gladie. If I hadn't been watching, no one would have ever discovered that Fanta was murdered."

"That's true."

"I'm like a murder genius. I, alone, know that Fanta's husband killed her. I feel like I have purpose, that I'm special. I'm the Albert Einstein of death. I'm the Stephen Hawking of murder."

"You're special," I told her. "And not just because you figured out about Fanta. That was genius."

"Poor Fanta," she said and turned the door knob.

As she opened it, we gasped in surprise. Fanta was there on the other side of the door, about to knock. It turned out that Fanta wasn't poor. She wasn't even dead. She was at Matilda's door, dressed in khakis and a blue button-down shirt.

"Did I catch you going out?" she asked. "Do you have an egg? I'm making brownies."

Matilda gurgled, and she had stopped blinking. She was like a robot that had wound down. I elbowed her to restart her. "I wasn't going out, Fanta," she said, finally. "I was just saying goodbye to Gladie."

Fanta smiled at me. "Oh, good. I'm dying for brownies."

She walked past me toward the kitchen. I shrugged at Matilda, and she shrugged back at me. I had never seen anyone so disappointed to see that someone was alive before.

"Matilda, you left the oven on again," Fanta called from the kitchen.

"I'm sorry," I whispered to Matilda.

"It's okay. Rockwell comes home tomorrow. He always makes me feel better. But we don't need to tell him about this, right?"

"Right," I said and left.

I felt no guilt about eating half of a package of Nutter Butters because I had sweated away at least five pounds in Matilda's apartment. I was grateful for my car's air conditioning, but I was even more grateful that I had a bathtub at home, because I was planning on filling it with cold water and soaking in it for an hour.

What a day. I had become a godmother and the town's porn star all at the same time. That had to be some kind of record. Despite the heat, I craved a latte. Church coffee wasn't cutting it. I parked down the block from Tea Time because the parking spaces in front were full. It didn't take me long to figure out why. Muffy & Dicks had opened and was doing bang-up business.

Meanwhile, across the street, the dictator of Fussia was pacing back and forth, as if he was preparing for an attack.

"Look at that maniac," the mayor told me, coming out of Tea Time. "Tourism is down four percent. Did you know that?"

"It is?"

"Four percent, and it's his fault. Nobody wants to eat pie and buy antiques in a town where there's a maniac dictator. I'm the mayor! We're not supposed to have dictators. Nobody would let Mussolini move in, so why are we letting that nutcase in?"

I didn't know what to say. The maniac dictator was pressing charges against me for stealing his donkey. "You're sure he's a maniac?"

"He's setting up his own post office, Gladie. He's going to offer discount stamps. The maniac is going to put our post office out of business. Benjamin Franklin started the postal service. One of our founding fathers! Now he thinks he can do a better job? Better than Benjamin Franklin? That's treason! He should be shot. We need to put him up against a wall and shoot his treasonous self."

I hadn't used a stamp in five years, so I wasn't very worried about his post office. "Did he say anything about his donkey?"

The mayor adjusted his tie. "I have to remain neutral, Gladie. It wouldn't be good for me to interfere in an ongoing criminal investigation."

"Criminal?" I gulped.

"I'm not talking to her about her criminal behavior!" the mayor announced loudly. He looked across the street at the dictator and then hightailed it to his Cadillac.

The Tea Time door opened, again, and Ruth's two sisters walked out. "Look, Naomi, it's Zelda's granddaughter. How's it going, Gladie?"

"Just fine." It was the first time I had seen them at Ruth's tea shop. Normally, they stayed busy in their house and neighborhood. They were ninety-three years old, but they were as active as Ruth. Naomi was dressed in a Jackie Kennedy lookalike pink suit, and Sarah was wearing her usual overalls and frilly shirt.

"We're helping out with tomorrow's wedding. Ruth's about to blow. She doesn't believe in barbecues," Sarah explained.

"She won't let us help, so we were just giving her moral support," Naomi explained.

"She didn't want that, either," Sarah said. "She told us to go to hell."

"No, she didn't, Sarah. She told us to go fuck ourselves," Naomi said.

"Oh, yes. That's right. Fuck ourselves. I must have had a little senior moment. Are you going over to Muffy & Dicks, Gladie? Going to get your vagina modernized?"

"I like her vagina, Sarah," Naomi said, coming to the defense of my private parts. "It's lovely, dear. I especially liked your picture with your tush sticking out. That was nice of you to send it to us. Don't let peer pressure change your vagina."

"It's 2018, Naomi. It's time to modernize and keep up with the times," Sarah insisted. "We don't have hair down there, and neither should she."

"Don't let her bully you, Gladie. Our hair stopped growing down there twenty years ago."

"The thing is…" I started and then clamped my mouth closed. I didn't want to have to defend my personal grooming habits. The truth was that waxing hurt, and Spencer didn't mind that I looked like a real woman. At least I didn't think he did. But maybe Ruth's sisters and Bird were right. I was going to get married in four days, and I needed a little spit and polish. And maybe some waxing.

I said goodbye to Ruth's sisters and walked into Tea Time. The tea shop was packed to the rafters. Pushing my way to the bar, I tried to get Ruth's attention, but she was distracted, brewing pots of tea as fast as she could.

"Ruth, latte," I called.

"Don't you see that I'm busy with every meat-eating, waxed person in Cannes?" she sneered.

I looked around. She was right. The shop was filled with the spin off from Muffy & Dicks, the organic beauty products, waxing, butcher shop. Men and women with little to no body hair, all carrying butcher packages had filled Tea Time. Suddenly, I craved a steak.

"Sorry," I said.

Ruth whipped around and studied me. "What did you say?"

"Sorry."

"Sorry?"

"Sorry."

"You never say sorry," Ruth noted. "You give as good as you get. What's the matter, girl? You having second thoughts about the cop, or is it the fact that the whole town has seen your puff that's got you cowering in a corner?"

"Ruth, don't say puff."

"Hey, I'm not the one who sent nudie pictures to hell and gone. When Stieglitz wanted to take nude photos of me, I told him to shove off. Then, he took them of Georgia O'Keeffe and she got rich. So, maybe I'm the dumb one and you and Georgia are the smart ones."

I leaned forward. "Ruth, I didn't mean to send those photos to the town."

"So what happened? Was it the Russians? Was it the maniac across the street? The Fussians? Did they hack your phone?"

I wanted to say yes so bad.

"It was dark. The buttons were small."

"I never push those damned buttons," Ruth told me. "Those small buttons can kiss my ass. Fine. I'll get you a latte.'

I sat down at one of the few empty tables and got halfway through my latte when Ruth sat next to me, bringing a pot of tea and plate of scones with her. The shop had died down by then, with most of the customers rushing home to put their meat in the refrigerator.

"Did you know that men get their scrotums waxed?" Ruth asked. "Their actual testicles. I can't imagine the staggering level of stupidity it takes to get your balls waxed. That's the Dicks in Muffy & Dicks. Did you know that? I've been learning all kinds of new things today. Stuff that I never wanted to learn, Gladie."

I was relieved that we had gotten off my genitalia, but I wasn't sure I wanted to talk about my neighbors' balls.

"Are you ready for Julie's wedding?" I asked, changing the subject.

"Barbecue. Blech. I'm going to be manning the grill right there at the lake."

"I love barbecue."

"I wanted to do an English tea, but no. Pork ribs instead of clotted cream."

My mouth watered, and I grabbed one of Ruth's scones. Pork ribs sounded delicious. I hadn't eaten much at the christening, and Nutter Butters weren't filling. I decided to surprise Spencer and Grandma by bringing home ribs for dinner.

The door opened, and Spencer walked in. He marched up to our table. "Good. You're here," he said. "We're running late. We gotta go."

"Where?"

"The marriage counselor. Don't you remember that my mother made an appointment for us?"

I put my hand out to Ruth. "Help," I mouthed.

CHAPTER 9

Faces, bubbeleh. Love is about faces. Private faces and public faces. What a person is at the PTA meeting is nothing like he is when he's watching the football game at home in his undershorts. It's up to us to figure out all of the faces. One fakakta punim that's private when it should be public can throw a wrench into our works.

Lesson 127, Matchmaking advice from your Grandma Zelda

Spencer knew.

I didn't have to complain. He just knew.

"It's just an hour, and then my mother will be off our backs," he told me as he drove us to the marriage counselor's office, which turned out to be near Matilda's apartment building. "We'll just shine her on. I'll give her the big spiel about us being in love. It won't hurt a bit. We'll get out of there with a glowing report on our future happiness. My mother will be happy. You'll be happy."

"Let's get ribs on the way home," I said. "We're eating barbecue at Fred's wedding tomorrow, but I could go for some tonight, too."

"I'm proud of you for focusing on pork instead of the marriage counselor, Pinky. I know you're upset about the counselor. And you know, my mother."

"I'm okay. Weddings are stressful. The bridezilla thing is a reality for a reason." But I had done nothing for my wedding. My grandmother and her posse had made all of the arrangements. Besides going to my bachelorette party and going to Bird's salon on Saturday, all I had to do was show up to my wedding.

"It's almost over. Sunday we're married, and we can move into our house and live happily ever after with our double-sized refrigerator and Jacuzzi tub."

In other words, I had four days to grow up. It was time. Most people grew up when they turned eighteen. I was way behind in the growing up department.

Spencer put his hand on my knee. "And you know we can't have barbecue tonight. My mom's vegetarian, and we have to get on her good side."

"Your mom's coming over for dinner?"

"Yeah. I guess I forgot to tell you. My folks are coming over. Zelda is ordering vegetarian."

"Did you explain to my grandmother what vegetarian is? She might think it means extra ketchup on her hamburger."

"I mentioned beans and salad."

Blech. "Sounds good. Did you explain to your mother about the pictures?"

His fingers danced up my thigh. "I never said thank you for the pictures. I'm a lucky man, Pinky. Not a lot of guys get pics like that from a woman."

Actually, every guy in Cannes had gotten pics like that from a woman, but I decided not to remind Spencer of that.

"I was trying to inject some romance into our relationship," I explained.

Spencer put his hand back on the steering wheel and grew quiet. We rode the rest of the way in silence, which led me to believe that maybe we really did need to see a marriage counselor before we took our vows.

Spencer had not let go of my hand since the moment we walked into Dr. Tiffany's Love Happiness Factory. Her office was housed in an old H&R Block in a strip mall. I looked around for her diploma, but all I saw were signs on the walls with affirmations written on them in pastel-colored cursive handwriting.

"*Beauty begins the moment you decide to be yourself*," read one of them. "*Complainers are doomed to live longer*," read another one.

"This doesn't look so bad," I told Spencer while we were sitting in the waiting room, but he didn't respond. It dawned on me that he liked this counseling idea less than I did. Spencer was an alpha male who was used to giving orders. I didn't get the impression that he was in a hurry to spend an hour in Dr. Tiffany's Love Happiness Factory and have Dr. Tiffany tell him what to do in his marriage.

A side door opened, and a cloud of lavender and bergamot wafted out, followed by a woman, who I assumed was Dr. Tiffany. She was wearing a tailored, red suit. She was about my age, and she was very attractive.

"Spencer and Gladys?" she asked with a smile. She waved us into her office, and we walked in as if we were on our way to our execution.

"I've never done this before," I said, taking a seat on a sofa. Spencer sat next to me, still holding tight to my hand.

"That's good," Dr. Tiffany said. "You haven't been polluted by bad advice and diagnoses. Here at Dr. Tiffany's Love Happiness Factory, we do things differently. We do things the right way. What we do works. We don't talk."

"You don't talk?" Spencer asked with more than a tinge of hope in his voice.

"This is 2018, Spencer. We've moved beyond talking. Talking is the old way. We're the new way. The better way. The only way."

Danger, Will Robinson. Be afraid. Be very afraid. My interior warning lights turned on and were blinking like they were on speed.

"That sounds great," Spencer said, relieved. Fool. He didn't know that we had walked into a trap. A new way only way meant bad news for us. But Spencer didn't have warning lights. That might have been why he was going to marry me. Poor Spencer.

"After speaking to your mother and seeing you together, I can say with utter certainty that your marriage is doomed to fail," Dr. Tiffany said, matter-of-factly.

Spencer dropped my hand. "Excuse me?" he asked.

"That is, if you don't implement my therapy immediately."

"What do you mean, doomed to fail. Why?" Spencer persisted.

Dr. Tiffany glanced at me and lifted her eyebrows before she returned her focus to Spencer. "The question is, why not. Not why. Doomed. Do I really need to list the reasons?"

I squirmed in my seat and hoped that Spencer wouldn't ask her to list the reasons because I was sure the reasons would revolve around me. But he didn't ask. His face had turned red, and he was pursing his lips. The hand that had been holding mine was now tightly clenched in a fist.

I never loved Spencer more than I did at that very minute, realizing that he wanted to punch a woman in the face for saying that our marriage was doomed to fail. It was the most romantic thing he had ever almost done for me.

"Am I right to assume that you'll agree to the protocol?" Dr. Tiffany asked.

"Uh," I said.

Dr. Tiffany ignored me and gave Spencer her undivided attention. "Your mother assured me that you would agree to the protocol. Should I tell her that she was wrong?"

On the bright side, Spencer let me pick up pork ribs on the way home, since he had agreed to the protocol, against my wishes. I wanted no part of the protocol. The protocol was nutso. It was loopdy-doo. It was insulting and a royal pain in the ass.

"We're not actually going to do the protocol," Spencer assured me.

"Let's talk about this after I eat the ribs."

"I mean, I'm not crazy."

"And potato salad."

"I just said we would do it to avoid any problems. We want smooth sailing until the wedding. Right?"

"I'm ordering ribs for the dinner and extra for the car ride home," I said. "Give me your wallet."

He parked. I took his wallet and went into the store.

On the ride home, I ate a half rack of ribs and a pint of potato salad. If money can't buy happiness, barbecue sure could. I wasn't exactly angry at Spencer. I understood the need to pacify annoying family members. Besides, he really loved his mother. And truth be told, I would probably see me as the enemy, too, if Spencer were my son.

Spencer would be hard to give up.

So, I wasn't angry. I was tired and stressed. The ribs and potato salad went a long way toward sedating me, though. By the time we got home, I felt much better. Spencer parked in the driveway and turned off the motor.

"Just a second," I said and put my hand on his leg.

He turned toward me. "Okay. Give it to me. Lay on the abuse. I deserve it."

"I love you."

"You do?"

"Yes. I love you. I'm sure of it. We're not doing the protocol. I'm not going to eat beans and salad for dinner. Tell your mother that I'm wonderful. There. I'm glad I got that off my chest. Now, come closer and kiss me."

"Your face is covered with barbecue sauce."

"What's your point?" I asked and grabbed his tie and pulled him in close until I captured his mouth with mine. Our tongues crashed together.

Spencer was a great kisser. Either that, or he had toxic saliva, because every time I kissed him, I got dizzy, and my body heated up to serious fever level. It was like his lips were the plague, but in a good way.

He unhooked my seat belt and dragged me over, lifting me onto his lap. His hands were everywhere, and my body moved to meet him. The kiss went on and on. It occurred to me that the marriage counselor was wonderful because I never loved Spencer more than I did at that very second.

Or it could have been his hand on my breast that made me love him so much. It was a toss-up.

But all good things must come to an end, and even in my fever state, I knew that we couldn't get down and dirty and naked in the car when Spencer's parents were ten feet away in the house and could come out any second to see what the ditzy floozy was doing to their perfect son.

I broke the kiss and opened my eyes. Spencer's eyes were still closed, and the lower half of his face was covered in barbecue sauce.

"Did you fall asleep?" I asked.

"I was just trying to keep the moment going for a little while longer. Sex mixed with barbecue sauce. It was the crossroads of my two favorite things. It was like the Bermuda Triangle of ecstasy." Spencer opened his eyes. "Pinky, if we bottle this, we'll be billionaires. Meat and booty. Nothing better than that."

We wiped our faces clean and walked inside. Grandma and Spencer's parents were in the kitchen. My grandmother had drafted Lily into setting the table and drafted James into fixing a cabinet door.

"Hello, dolly," Grandma said, as we walked into the kitchen. "Do you feel better? That was so kind of you to bring extra food. We have lots of beans. Lily added apple cider vinegar to them. Wasn't that clever? She says that they prevent cancer. That's so handy, Lily. Nobody likes cancer. James, I love what you did to my cabinet door."

"It was nothing, Zelda. Just a tight screw."

"You did it very well," Zelda said. She had them eating out of the palm of her hand. It was great to have her on my side. It was like LeBron James getting off the bench to help a team in trouble. "But stay away from saws until September," she told James.

"Excuse me?" he asked.

Spencer slapped his back. "You should probably listen to her, Dad. No saws." He kissed his mother hello and then excused himself, in order to change his clothes, since he was still wearing what he wore to the christening. So was I, but it was my most respectable outfit, and I figured I should keep it on to give me an edge.

"Hello, Lily," I said, giving her an awkward hug after I put the food down on the table. "James, how have you been? Did you have a chance to see the town?"

"There was a crazy man who wouldn't let me walk on the sidewalk because I didn't have a visa," she said, looking me up and down, as if she expected me to be naked again. "You look nice," she told me, not making eye contact.

"Thank you. You do, too."

"Let's sit," Grandma said, sitting. I sat down next to her, and Spencer's parents sat, too. "Pass the beans, please, Lily, even though I'm not going to get cancer."

Spencer walked in, wearing sweats, a skin-tight white t-shirt, and no shoes. "I'm starved," he said.

"How was your day, dear?" Spencer's mother asked him.

"We saw your counselor. She said we're a wonderful couple, and we have to do a protocol."

Lily arched an eyebrow, just like Spencer did twenty times a day. "She said that? Did she use those words? Wonderful?"

"I remember those words," I said. "Especially protocol.

We have to do that."

"What's the protocol? Does Gladie have to fill out a questionnaire? Are you going to do a compatibility test? How about financial records?"

Lily was huffing and puffing, running out of breath.

Spencer shook his head. "The doctor is sending over some kind of device we're supposed to use to help us smooth over conflict. I don't know what it is. It's supposed to come with directions. Happy? We went to your doctor. Now, let's eat."

"A device?" Spencer's mother asked. "How can a device help you?"

"It's 2018," I explained. "Counselors don't talk anymore."

"What about the murder thing? Didn't she say something about the murder thing?" Lily asked, in a panic about the marriage counselor's lack of talking.

"Gladie's over the murder thing." Spencer stuffed a forkful of food into his mouth to cover up his lie.

"I haven't seen a dead person in weeks," I told her. She flinched, and her right eye spasmed. "Cannes is a very nice town. I'm sure we're done with murders. I probably won't stumble over another dead person for a long time," I added to assuage her fears. It didn't work. Her left eye started to spasm, too. "Probably forever. I mean, what are the odds, right?"

My grandmother touched Lily's hand. "Don't worry about the murders. Gladie has the gift." Spencer's mother didn't look convinced that the gift was a positive. As usual, my grandmother didn't care about doubters and naysayers. "And as for Gladie and Spencer, they're perfectly matched. I knew it the first moment I met Spencer. He was made for her, and she was made for him. Like a tea cup and a saucer. They're going to be married for many years, and I wouldn't worry about Gladie's financials. She's going to be running my matchmaker business, and she'll have enough money to put her kids through college."

"I will?" I asked.

"Kids?" Spencer asked.

"Everything in good time," Grandma told him. "Lily, I've been matchmaking my whole life, and I know a love match when I see it. I know best friends when I see them. I've never been wrong about a match. Never…"

My grandmother drifted off and stared into space. "Grandma?" I said, concerned. She had recently had a heart episode, and I was worried about her health. "Grandma, are you okay?"

Finally, after a terrifying moment, she blinked and came back to herself. "Bubbeleh, Matilda was a bad match. I let her down. We must help her. We must."

I put my arm around her. "We will, Grandma. I will. I'll help Matilda."

As far as I could tell, Matilda and Rockwell were a normal, happy couple, and there was no need to break them up. But I wasn't going to argue with my grandmother. I would do anything to alleviate her worry and make her feel better.

"I'm not hungry, dolly," she said.

"You're what?" Spencer asked. It was the first time my

grandmother had refused a meal since I was born.

"Would you help me up to my room?" she asked me.

I helped her up from her chair and walked with her out of the kitchen. "What did that mean?" I heard Spencer's mother say in the kitchen, as we walked down the hallway. "So, does she know about married couples or not? What does that mean for you?"

Her voice drifted off, as Grandma and I walked up the stairs. "She'll come around," my grandmother whispered to me. "Kill her with kindness. Then, she'll be yours forever."

I put my grandmother to bed and sat with her until she fell asleep. I closed her door, gently and went to my bedroom, where Spencer was waiting for me.

"I sent my parents to their hotel," he told me. "What do you need?"

"Can you give me a lift to my car? I left it at Tea Time. I have to visit one of my grandmother's old clients."

"Do you want me to go with you? Is it dangerous?"

"Of course, it's not dangerous," I said, telling the truth for once. The life or death thing had passed, and Fanta was found alive. Matilda was just a nosy, bored housewife, but I owed it to my grandmother to double check that she was all right.

"You said that without blinking," Spencer pointed out. "Either you're not lying, or you've crossed the psycho line."

"It's a matchmaking visit. I promise. It's as safe as staying here and watching *Family Guy* in bed, like I know you're going to do. Believe me, nothing's going to happen at

Matilda Dare's apartment."

CHAPTER 10

Men are not mind readers. None of them. The Amazing Kreskin? Not a mind reader. There's not a man on this earth who can read minds. That's why a woman needs to tell a man that she's interested. Otherwise, he has no idea. Sure, he can guess, but men are bad at guessing, too. So, tell your matches to speak up! Tell them that it's not a shanda to say how they feel. Telling a man that they're interested is the first step to a simcha. It's the first step to happiness. Because you know what steps are, don't you, dolly? Steps are about moving forward.

Lesson 86, Matchmaking advice from your Grandma Zelda

I had a feeling that it was going to be a long night at Matilda's, so I told Spencer not to wait up. He promised to look in on my grandmother while I was away and make sure she was fine and didn't need anything.

I knocked softy on Matilda's door, and she opened it. She had changed her clothes into shorts and a tank top, and her hair was wet. Her apartment was still an oven, but a slightly cooler oven than it had been in the afternoon.

"Oh my God," she said, welcoming me in. "I'm so glad it's you. There's so much going on."

"There is? That's sort of why I came." It wasn't easy to tell a woman that she married the wrong man, especially because I thought she was perfectly happy with Rockwell. But my grandmother was never wrong about love.

"After you left, Fanta stayed around for a couple hours," she explained. "She's never done that before. Usually, she comes for fifteen minutes, tops. She acted strange, like she was relieved to be in my apartment. As soon as she left, I went back to watching her place, and I've been doing it ever since. Gladie, there hasn't been a sign of her husband, Chris. I think we got it all backward. I think Chris was the one who was murdered."

Matilda turned off the lights in the apartment so we could spy easier. The blinds in Fanta's bedroom were still closed. The television was on in her living room.

"She's lying on the couch, but we can't see her from here," Matilda explained. "Normally we can see the bedroom and the living room, but there's a hallway that connects the two and leads to the front door that we can't see. So, there's a lot we're not seeing. But I saw her lie down on the couch, so I know she's there. No sign of her husband."

"Holy shitballs," I breathed. "The husband's missing."

A familiar feeling of irresistible nosiness crept up my

spine until it took over me.

"Rockwell's still out on the road, working. He comes back tomorrow. I was going to stake out Fanta's place from here. You want to stake it out with me?"

Yes, I did.

God help me, I did.

Whatever it said about me, I preferred to spy in order to find out if someone was murdered than to talk about marriage and relationships. My grandmother said that I had the gift, but she was so wrong.

A couple hours later, we were still sitting on the couch in Matilda's dark living room, spying on Fanta's apartment. We both had super large plastic cups of Diet Coke and ice and a bag of Flamin' Hot Cheetos.

"They have nice furniture," I noted.

"Chris smashes cars. He owns Cannes Smiley Auto Wrecking. There's a lot of money in car smashing. That's how come Fanta has that sofa. I looked it up online. Seven thousand dollars. My couch cost six hundred dollars."

I didn't have a couch. I didn't own anything. Then, I remembered that I had all kinds of furniture waiting for me in my new house. "I don't know how much my couch cost," I told her. In fact, I didn't know how much my house cost. I had left the whole thing in Spencer's hands. He had tried to get me involved, asking my opinion about wainscoting and other things I knew nothing about, but something inside me didn't believe that the house was mine, let alone the fancy couch.

"You live at Zelda's house, right? I love that house. I

love old things. Her house is so cozy. I feel safe there. Is that crazy?" Matilda asked.

"No, I feel safe there, too. Really safe." My grandmother's house was a sprawling Victorian, which was built during the early days of Cannes, soon after gold was discovered in the local mine. The furniture was all ancient. The kitchen was the most modern room of the house, and it was stuck in the 1950s.

"I always wanted to live in an old house with a lot of history in it," Matilda said. "That way, you're living with your family and all the families that lived there before you. That's a real home. Once Rockwell gets a promotion, we're going to move into a house."

It was a perfect segue to talk about her marriage. "So, everything's good between…" I started, but Matilda wasn't listening. She had bolted up from the couch and put the binoculars up to her face.

"She's on the move," Matilda breathed. "What does she have? What is that?"

I looked through my pair of binoculars. Fanta was wearing a green jumpsuit, and she was lifting boxes onto a dolly. "Boxes," I said. "Is she moving?"

"Those are metal boxes, Gladie. Who has metal boxes? Nobody. Why isn't she using cardboard boxes? Because cardboard boxes aren't waterproof. They aren't goo-proof."

"Goo-proof," I repeated. I knew exactly what she meant. Even if Fanta had air conditioning, her poor husband would be gooey by now. Dead people got gooey. I knew that from experience, unfortunately. "Those are small boxes," I said.

"Holy shitballs. The bitch cut him up," Matilda breathed.

"The bitch cut him up," I repeated. I put my binoculars down. "Wait a second. Wait a second. We're jumping to conclusions. We don't know there's a cut up husband in those boxes."

Matilda pointed. "Look."

I looked through my binoculars, again. Fanta was carrying an empty box into the bedroom. "There you go," Matilda said. "She's going back in for some more body parts."

With Fanta in the bedroom, we couldn't see any action, so we sat back on the couch and ate some more Cheetos. "What's our plan?" Matilda asked me. "We need to stop her before she hides the evidence. We need to tie her up and force her to tell the truth. Right?"

"Yes. That sounds like a good plan." But somehow, I couldn't let Spencer's mother find out anything about it. If she heard about me being involved in another murder, she would never let me marry her son. Or at the very least, she would make my life even more miserable. "But we'll do it quietly. How can we do it quietly?"

"I could stuff a kitchen towel in her mouth."

Suddenly, Matilda's front door opened, and we jumped a mile in the air. Matilda threw her binoculars at the intruder, like she was pitching at the World Series. With amazing accuracy, she hit him square in the gut. He grunted, loudly, and went down like a sack of potatoes.

I turned on the light, and Matilda ran to see who her victim was.

"Rockwell? What are you doing here?" she asked. "I mean, are you okay?"

I leaned over her shoulder. Rockwell was lying on the floor in a fetal position. His suitcase was in the doorway. It looked like Rockwell had returned early.

"Oh my God, I killed the man I love," Matilda cried.

"He's not dead. You just stunned him a little. I've done it a million times. He'll forgive you. Spencer's always forgiven me."

"Are you sure he's alive?"

Rockwell clutched at his stomach and moaned.

"See? Alive," I said, pointing at him. "In these cases, I like to say it's not my fault. We should blame someone else."

But Matilda was more honest than I was. She fessed up immediately. "I'm so sorry, sweetie. I thought someone was breaking in. I didn't know it was you. You came home early. Not that I'm upset that you came home early. I'm so happy you came home early. Early is good. Early is really good. I'm so glad you're home."

I put my hand on Matilda's shoulder. "I think he gets it. You're happy he's home."

We helped Rockwell up and sat him down on the couch. "Why is it dark in here?" he asked after a while, when he could breathe again. "Am I blind? Did I go blind?"

Matilda and I exchanged a look, and I knew right there and then that she was going to tell him everything. She was going to tell him that the lights were off so we could spy better. She was going to tell him about Fanta and Chris. Stupid woman. She didn't know a thing about the importance of lying and keeping secrets. Sure, she had tried, but she was a real amateur.

So, she told him everything. About watching Fanta and her husband. About Fanta killing her husband, and about metal boxes and the dolly.

Rockwell was quiet for a long time, as he took in all of the new information. Then, he shook his head, sadly, as if he was upset about the sad state of affairs in politics today.

"Not this, again," he moaned.

"What do you mean?" I asked. "Has Fanta killed before?"

"No, of course she hasn't. Nobody's been murdered. This is just Matilda's newest thing. I don't know why she's had all of these troubles. But she obviously needs help. Matilda, I've been begging you for a long time that you need professional help, and now it's urgent. Please say you'll get help."

This was a new one for me. I was used to Spencer being angry and upset at me, but he always believed me. Even if he thought I would be better off taking antipsychotic medications and making a visit to the rubber room, he never once mentioned it.

But there was no anger in Rockwell. He wasn't yelling or getting upset. He was sad. Sad that the woman he loved had gone off the deep end. I felt like I needed to come to her defense and help him out at the same time.

"There really is something suspicious going on over there," I told him.

"Did you actually see something?" He asked me.

"There are boxes. And the shades are drawn." I realized immediately how stupid I sounded. Boxes? The shades are drawn? That wasn't very suspicious. Was Rockwell right about Matilda, and had I gotten sucked into her delusions?

"Please, Rockwell. Go check. If I'm wrong, then I'll go see whoever you want. Promise," Matilda urged him. Rockwell gave her a sweet kiss on her lips.

"I love you, Matilda," he said. "Okay. I'll check for you. I'll go to Fanta's and find out what happened to Chris. I'll get to the bottom of this."

We watched the window, waiting for Rockwell's entrance into Fanta's apartment. We saw Fanta walk out of the living room, but we couldn't see the actual conversation between her and Rockwell since the hallway and the front door were out of our line of sight.

"This is frustrating," I noted.

"Rockwell will get to the bottom of it," Matilda said. "He's very good with people and knows what questions to ask."

About fifteen minutes later, Rockwell returned. He sat down on the couch next to Matilda and took her hands in his.

"Matilda, Chris is fine. He's at his mother's house in Phoenix. Fanta even let me talk to him on the phone."

"But…" Matilda started.

"What about the boxes?" I asked.

"Books. She's donating them to the library."

"Are you sure it was really Chris on the phone?" Matilda asked.

"Yes. I recognized his voice, and frankly, why would he lie? Now, my sweet dear, will you get the help you need?"

A tear ran down Matilda's cheek. "Yes. I'll go to anyone you say. I'll be the best patient, ever. I promise."

Rockwell turned to me. "Matilda always tries her best at everything. Whatever she takes up, she works the hardest at it. I know she'll get better soon and come back to me."

They held each other in a loving embrace, and I realized that it was my time to leave and give them some privacy. By the time I got home, I was completely exhausted. I checked on my grandmother, and she was sleeping soundly in her bed. Spencer was in our bed in a deep sleep, snoring softly. He had fallen asleep with the TV on. I turned it off, went to pee, and dropped into bed with my clothes on. I was asleep the second my head hit the pillow.

The next morning, I woke up to my grandmother sitting on the bed and nudging my shoulder. "How'd it go with Matilda?" Grandma asked.

"They looked really happy to me, Grandma. In love. But Matilda is going to get some therapy. That's probably what you felt. She turns on the oven and forgets about it," I explained.

My grandmother nodded, but she didn't look entirely convinced. "I think my third eye is on the fritz. I'm getting all kinds of weird signals today. I can't make heads or tails of them. Like, I keep seeing you in the army. You're not planning on joining the army, are you?"

"No, the army makes you get up too early in the morning. Speaking of that, what time is it?"

"Early. Six-thirty. The mayor's downstairs talking to Spencer. Something about the dictator. Actually, now I understand about the army thing. I'll go down and make coffee while you talk to them."

"They want to talk to me?" I asked, but my grandmother had already left the room and was heading downstairs.

I hadn't gotten much sleep, and I felt like hell. Today I was supposed to be the best man at Fred's wedding and I was going to be puffy. Just my luck.

I found Spencer and the mayor standing in the entranceway. Spencer was barefoot, wearing sweatpants and no shirt. His hands were on his hips and his head was cocked to the side, as if he was trying to make out what the moron mayor was trying to say.

The mayor, on the other hand, was wearing a dapper suit. He smiled when he saw me and greeted me with a bear hug.

"Oops," he said, pushing me away. "I didn't mean to hug you. Me, too. Me, too. Right? Me, too. Anyway, I'm so glad you're here and looking great, Gladie. You know, today's Founders Day."

"It's July Fourth," I said.

"And Founders Day. You know how important Founders Day is, right?"

"Do you mind if we move this into the kitchen, Mayor? My grandmother's making coffee, and I probably need some before I hear about Founders Day."

"Coffee sounds great. You know, our founders loved coffee."

Grandma was toasting bagels in the kitchen. I poured myself a cup of coffee and opened the refrigerator to take out the milk.

"The founders weren't too crazy about milk, though," the mayor said. "Just coffee. But even though it's Founders Day and I'm the most patriotic Cannes citizen, I think that I'll take a little milk in my coffee this morning, Gladie."

I didn't point out that the founders didn't have running water, either.

The mayor sat down at the table and waited to be served. I rolled my eyes and poured another cup of coffee and handed it to him with the carton of milk. I helped Grandma with the bagels and took a seat, too. Spencer was leaning up against the wall with his arms crossed. It was hard to focus when Spencer wasn't wearing a shirt. I would've thought I would've gotten used to it by now, but there was something about his barrel chest and washboard abs that prevented me from focusing on pretty much anything except for him.

"As you know, miners founded our beautiful town," the mayor said and took a sip of his coffee. "They were rough and ready and preferred dungarees over slacks. You know, I don't like dungarees. I think that you should make an effort to look your best. I don't know why young people continue to wear dungarees."

"That's very interesting, Mayor," my grandmother said. "Now as you were saying about Founders Day?"

I took a bite of my bagel and washed it down with some coffee.

"Yes, yes, Zelda," he said. "You're right. Time is of the essence. It's going to be a big day, and we need to get right down to it. As I was saying, the founders of our town were miners. As you know, they discovered gold in the mine in town, which has been closed for over one hundred years. You can see the outside of it, but the liability insurance was way too much for us to allow tourists to go inside. Anywho, the miners found their gold and made their money, some of which went to build this house. Isn't that right, Zelda?"

Zelda nodded with her mouth full.

"Then the gold died down, and it was like that show, *The Lottery Ruined My Life*. Lots of drama. But I guess we could talk about that another day. Anyway, there's a lot to be thankful for on our Founders Day, especially because it comes on the Fourth of July. Not only are we patriotic townspeople, but we're also patriotic Americans. You could say that today is the holiest of holy days."

"Hallelujah," Spencer said.

The mayor leaned forward. "Between you and me, I think that the Founders Day - July Fourth combination rivals Christmas and Easter for its holiness."

"I do like a picnic," my grandmother said. "I haven't been to one in years. I'm looking forward to today."

"It's going to be a humdinger, Zelda," the mayor said, excitedly. "A humdinger. I mean, if Gladie does what she's supposed to do."

I put my coffee cup down, and my head shot up. "What am I supposed to do?"

Since I had moved to Cannes, I was always supposed to be doing one thing or another. Usually, I either forgot about doing it or made a mess of it. I was terrible about responsibilities.

"Well, that's what I was talking to the Chief about," the mayor answered. "Last night I made a deal with the maniac dictator. You know, my spies had informed me that he was planning to desecrate our wonderful celebrations today. Desecrate, Gladie. Desecrate, Zelda. Desecrate. Can you imagine?"

If I had known what the word desecrate meant, I would've probably been able to imagine it, but it was way too early in the morning to learn new vocabulary words, and I was only half through with my cup of coffee.

"He won't do anything," Spencer said. "I'll make sure of that. Founders Day and July Fourth will go off without a hitch."

As he finished speaking, Spencer shot me a look. I knew what it meant. Nothing in Cannes went without a hitch, no matter how good Spencer was as a police chief.

"I appreciate law enforcement's cooperation, as usual," the mayor said. "But I'd like to hedge my bets. The maniac has agreed to a sit-down between the offending donkey stealers and himself. Zelda, you make the best coffee in town. Do you have any whole wheat toast? My doctor wants me to consume more whole grains. You know, whole grains prevent rectal cancer. I don't want rectal cancer. I like my rectum exactly how it is. I would hate for it to be abused."

Spencer thought that the mayor was an idiot. He pulled me out of the kitchen and told me that no good would come from us sitting down and talking to the maniac. But the mayor explained that the maniac dictator was going to drop all charges against Lucy, Bridget, and me, and that sounded great to me. I didn't mind talking to a crazy man if it meant that I wasn't going to have to share a communal toilet in jail.

That's how I wound up in the land of Fussia with my two best friends, my fiancé, and the mayor.

Spencer and I waited for Bridget and Lucy out front by the razor wire fence. Bridget had her baby strapped to her chest with a Scandinavian device that was supposed to aid in bonding. Lucy was wearing a peach-colored dress that went just below her knees and showed a little bit of cleavage.

"Harry said that he could finish this with two phone calls and a box of Cuban cigars, but I decided to go the civilized route," Lucy told me before we walked in. "But if this goes south, I'll give him a call, and he'll clear this up. Even if it's a little messy."

The maniac dictator came out and unlocked the gate. "Welcome to Fussia," he announced. "I will dispense with the usual necessary paperwork and the six-hundred-dollar visitor tax, because this is an international state diplomatic trip. But please note my exceptional generosity in this manner."

It was seven in the morning, but it was already hotter than hell. I didn't know how the maniac managed in his thick, wool uniform, laden with phony metals and ribbons, epaulets, and cap. But he was wearing it, despite sweating like crazy.

I was comfortable in my shorts and tank top. Fred and Julie were having a very casual wedding later, and I planned on wearing a light skirt and a no-sleeve frilly top. Even though it was going to be hot, there would be a nice breeze off of the lake, and I was actually looking forward to the afternoon. Now, I was being promised that the threat of prison was going to be off of me. So the day was looking pretty good, as far as I was concerned.

The maniac dictator had prepared for our visit. At the far side of the room was a large desk and a throne. Folding chairs, enough for all of us, were organized around the desk.

"Welcome to Fussia," he said. "Please look at some of the other notable personalities that have come to greet me and share diplomatic ties with me."

He passed around a series of highly Photoshopped photos. There was one of him with the Queen of England, another with Ronald Reagan, and two with Kanye West.

"Our plans for the post office are coming right along," he continued.

"We'll see about that," the mayor mumbled under his breath.

"And the bank," the maniac continued. "We have a lot of interest in our bank from a very nice family in Uzbekistan."

"Jesus, you can't make this shit up," Spencer whispered to me.

"This is a wonderful lesson for Jonathan about the decline and fall of democracy," Bridget said, happily.

"I've got Harry on speed dial," Lucy announced.

"You're dropping the charges, right?" I asked, proud of myself to stay on the subject.

"Yes," the maniac dictator said, surprising me. This was great news. I had been sure that there was going to be some kind of hitch and I was going to be tossed in jail or sent to Siberia or worse. "I have agreed with your mayor to drop all charges when Gladys Burger accepts her role as a member of my Cabinet."

"What did he say?" Spencer asked me.

"I think he wants me to do something in his kitchen," I said.

"Oh, darlin', I don't think it's that kind of cabinet," Lucy said.

The maniac dictator stood and walked to a utility closet, where he pulled out another wool uniform. This one looked a lot like his, but it didn't have metals or ribbons on it.

"My cabinet member. Congratulations, Gladys Burger. You've been named Minister of the Coin and my closest and only cabinet member."

"Are you kidding me?" Spencer said.

In the end, it was Spencer who convinced me to take the deal. It turned out that my term would only last for three days, during which I would go around town and sing the praises of the country of Fussia and hand out special coins with the maniac dictator's face on it.

"But I don't look good in green," I whined.

"It's three days, Pinky, and then you're in the clear."

"I don't think it's good for Jonathan to have a mother in prison," Bridget said. "Besides, there're far too few women in government. You would be a change for the positive. You could be the Hillary we never had."

Peer pressure. It's a bitch.

CHAPTER 11

Sometimes you get all the green lights. Sometimes you get all the red lights. Don't read too much into it, bubbeleh.

Lesson 135, Matchmaking advice from your Grandma Zelda

I was going to die. I was going to melt. I was going to ignite into flames. They were going to find a hot gelatinous mound, and it was going to be me.

I was going to be a hot gelatinous mound.

The uniform was worse than I thought. Not only was it heavy and hotter than hell, but it itched, too. And the cap was doing terrible things to my hair. And forget about the color. I looked like I was a corpse in the green.

"I'm going to be in Fred and Julie's wedding photos forever looking like this," I moaned, putting on the uniform in my bedroom about an hour after we left the meeting with the maniac dictator.

"The photos aren't going to come out, dolly," my grandmother told me, helping me put the uniform on. "Fred's cousin is going to take the pictures, but he's terrible with technology."

At least there was that. There would be no evidence. But I was still going to have to be seen by everyone in town dressed as a mini-me dictator. First, they saw me naked, and now they were going to see me like this. I didn't know which was worse.

I walked downstairs. Spencer was leaving for work. He was organizing the security for the day's events. I was going to the lake early, in order to help Ruth set up for the wedding. She wanted to get a good spot, but the lake was going to be packed with picnickers. In order to stake out a good vantage point for the fireworks, they had to get there early. Ruth was determined to get a prime spot by the shore, big enough for the entire wedding party.

"I used to think that I was attracted to women in uniform," Spencer said as he was about to leave the house. "But I might've been too hasty in that assessment."

"Thanks a lot. How are you going to explain this to your parents? Your mother's going to freak. Anybody's mother would freak. I'm going to freak."

"First of all, you're already freaking. Don't worry about my mom. We saw the marriage counselor, and you've been very good about not finding any dead people, so I think that you're swaying her to your side."

I gnawed at the inside of my cheek. It was a good thing

that Fanta didn't turn out to be a murderer. If she had been, I'd be an assistant dictator and a dead person finder. Spencer's mother Lily would have never gotten past that.

I blasted the air-conditioning in my Cutlass Supreme and took my hat off. But as I drove past Fussia, the dictator spotted me and waved down my car. I stopped and opened my window.

"Hello," I said.

"No, you say, 'Hello, my sovereign leader'," he corrected.

"Hello, my sovereign leader," I said and scratched at my collar.

"Why aren't you wearing your regulation Fussia Minister of the Coin cap?" he demanded.

"Well I was in the car, and…"

"No, no, Madame Minister. The cap stays on all the time, unless you're sleeping at night. When you eat, you wear it. When you go to the toilet, you wear it. If you break your end of our deal, I'm going to throw all of you donkey stealers in jail, including the little baby, and I'll make a big scene at the Founders Day celebration. Do you hear me?"

I put the hat back on. "Yes, my sovereign leader."

The lake was already packed with picnickers. The grills were lit and warming up, and there was an entire area dedicated to football fans who were complaining about the Chargers'

move to Los Angeles while they drank beer.

I found Ruth by the shore in a prime spot. She was yelling at a couple who were trying to take the spot for themselves.

"I don't care that you were here first," Ruth yelled at them. "My shirt is older than you. I was getting Social Security when your grandfather was still using pimple cream. Do you know what that means? That means that I was here before you. I was here a million times before you. I've been everywhere before you. Everywhere. So, I'm going to take this spot. You can walk a little further and do your picnic over there. I've got a wedding happening here. And no, I don't want any part of a wedding. I've got better things to do. I'd like to be in my shop, selling tea in the air conditioning. Instead, here I am under the sun, getting skin cancer, and forced to barbecue pig meat all damn day. So shut your piehole and stop your griping. You're going to get the hell out of here, or I'm going to take my Louisville Slugger to your ass. Do you understand me? Huh?" She took a breath and saw me. "Holy shit! Gladie, is that you? Did you get drafted?"

"It's a long story," I said, tugging at my collar. "Is there a problem here?"

The young father looked at me in horror. "Did you call the cops?" he asked Ruth. "What kind of person are you? The world doesn't belong to you, you know."

"I lived through the Depression and two terms of Ronald Reagan," Ruth snapped. "I know the world doesn't belong to me. But this spot does, so get the hell out, or I'll sic my friend the general on you."

The young father called Ruth all kinds of names, and Ruth gave it back to him as good as she got. Nobody could out-swear Ruth, as far as I knew.

"I'm not a general. I'm the Minister of the Coin of Fussia," I told her after the young couple left.

"I don't have time for your crap, girl. Help me set up for this cockamamie July Fourth Founders Day wedding."

I was dying to take off the uniform. It was sweltering under the sun while I set up chairs and tables and decorated them with crêpe paper and tulle. But Ruth told me she had heard that the maniac dictator had spies everywhere, and I didn't want to jeopardize the deal. So, I stayed in uniform.

"I only have to wear this for three days," I said more to myself than to Ruth. "I get to go back to myself for my wedding."

"Have you ever noticed that you get yourself into an enormous amount of trouble? I mean, like much more than your share."

"Shut up, Ruth. You have to barbecue an entire wedding, and you know that Julie is probably going to set the whole thing on fire, anyway."

"Joke's on you, Gladie. Julie's dress is made out of asbestos. I bought it on the dark web. It'll probably kill us all, but I don't relish the idea of burning alive."

We lugged the rest of the wedding supplies to our spot on the shore. Everything was plastic and nothing had sharp edges. Ruth had planned well. Still, I half expected the wedding to be a total disaster.

Still, if I was honest with myself, despite the sweltering heat and the fact that I was dressed like a dictator, I was tickled to death that I had made a match that was now getting married. Fred and Julie were a true love match. It took a lot of convincing to get them together, but once they were, they were a forever couple.

Fred had recently rented a small apartment for them over a pie shop in the historic district, and he and Julie had decorated it with some of Ruth's old furniture that she kept in storage. Now that they were getting married, they were already talking about having a family. They were truly happy.

And I had a part in that.

My grandmother showed up with Spencer, and Ruth's sisters were not far behind. Everyone helped with the decorations, and a couple hours later, our wedding setup didn't look half bad. Actually, it looked more like a Fourth of July picnic, but in my book, that was a hell of a lot better than a wedding, anyway. With the casual atmosphere, everyone was relaxed and ready to have a good time.

Unlike other weddings, we ate before the ceremony because Fred and Julie wanted to make their vows while the fireworks went off at the end of the evening. There were about thirty guests, mostly family. Fred's police colleagues were all on duty at the lake, but they stopped by in rotation to congratulate him and give him a gift. Spencer was attending, but he was in constant contact with his men on his cellphone and walkie talkie.

Fred was wearing a suit that fit well around his skinny frame, but it was six inches too short everywhere. The sleeves barely made it to his elbows, and his pants legs didn't reach his ankles. He was poorly dressed, but his face was ebullient and glowing. Julie was glowing, too, possibly because she was as hot as I was dressed in a gigantic asbestos wedding gown that made her look like she had been trapped in a taffeta tornado. The rest of the guests were dressed for a Fourth of July barbecue. Because the fashion choices were odd for a wedding, nobody commented about my uniform, even when I handed out the official Fussia coins and told them, "All hail the sovereign leader," as I had been instructed by the maniac dictator.

"The ribs need to be turned," my grandmother told Ruth at the grill.

Ruth pointed her fork at Grandma in a threatening manner. "Don't tell me what to do, old woman. I know what to do. You've never cooked a meal in your life."

"How's the tea shop, Ruth?" Grandma asked her, changing the subject.

Ruth turned the ribs. "What does that mean?" Ruth looked at my grandmother and squinted her eyes, as if she was trying to read something off Grandma's face. "What're you getting at, woman? Are you trying to bore into my brain and dig something out?"

My grandmother moved her purse to her other arm and

touched her hair, nonchalantly. "I don't bore into brains, Ruth. I'm just feeling something."

"Well, don't feel anything, Zelda. I don't want your feelings anywhere near me. Are you listening to me?"

"The ribs look good," my grandmother said, changing the subject, again.

"Okay fine. Tell me what you're feeling," Ruth said. "What are you hinting at? Is Tea Time doomed? Is it going to get flattened in an earthquake? A drive-by shooting by an apple orchard gang? What? What? Tell me, Zelda. You've always been the voice of doom, you know that? You're a dark cloud that follows everyone around."

"I'm seeing boredom," my grandmother said. "Boredom. Burnout. Ruth, I'm seeing you go on a vacation."

"Shut up."

Grandma threw her hands up. "I can't help what I see, Ruth. I just see it. I don't make this stuff up, you know. Just like I didn't make up the Bay of Pigs."

Ruth pointed at her. "I still blame you for that."

Grandma shrugged. "I see what I see. I feel what I feel."

She went to mingle with the people at the chips and dip table. Spencer was screaming at one of his cops on his phone. Fred turned on his boom box, and Queen started to play.

"You're burned out?" I asked Ruth. "This isn't going to change our latte relationship, is it?"

"I'm not burned out. Tea is my life. Tea Time is who I am. I'm not me if I'm not pouring tea. Burned out? I'll give you burned out."

"How're the ribs coming?" Spencer asked, coming to my side. He put his arm around my waist and then dropped it, quickly. "What's that uniform made of? It feels like sandpaper."

"I think it's made of sandpaper."

"I'm going to find you a Gatorade. You're wilting like lettuce. You want to sit down?" he asked, concerned.

"I'd like to sit down."

He helped me to a seat and mopped my face with a paper napkin. "I'd say it's not worth it, but it would suck to visit you in prison, Pinky. So, keep it up. You can do it. And the uniform is starting to turn me on. Perhaps it's the authority angle. Maybe after this is over, you could try the whole dominatrix thing."

"Gatorade."

He gave me the bottle, and I started chugging. "You won't believe what's going on here," Spencer said. "They've got a whole float-load of fireworks in the middle of the lake, but the fireworks guy didn't show up. There's no one to set them off."

I belched. "No way. What about Fred's wedding? They want to do their vows under the fireworks."

"There's going to be an uprising. Everyone's baking in this heat because they're waiting for the damned fireworks."

"What's going to happen?"

"The mayor is asking around to see if anyone else knows how to work the fireworks."

"Uh oh," I said, getting a bad feeling.

"Right?"

The Gatorade made me feel better. There was a lull in

the wedding celebrations, so I got up and walked around to other picnickers, handing them Fussia coins and telling them, "Hail to the sovereign leader." By that time, most of the townspeople had sucked down so many beers and had been under the hot sun for so long, that they didn't seem to think it was odd at all to be approached by me in a dictator's uniform.

Ahead, I was surprised to see Matilda walking with Fanta. Fanta looked pleased as punch, but Matilda looked like she was being held captive. She caught my eye, and she threw me a desperate look.

Without a word, I knew that Matilda was asking me to save her.

Just like my grandmother, I got a feeling. And just like my grandmother, I couldn't get rid of it, and I was pretty sure that my feeling was right on target.

"Hello Matilda. Hello, Fanta," I said. "Happy July Fourth Founders Day."

"Hello there, Gladie," Fanta said. "Beautiful day, right?"

"Beautiful," I agreed. "Where's Rockwell?"

"He had some last-minute business calls," Matilda explained. When Fanta turned her head, Matilda squeezed my arm. I nodded at her, and I hoped that she got the message: I was there for her. I would help her. And I also thought that we needed to do a little more snooping. But it would have to wait. Matilda and Fanta said their goodbyes and walked away.

With my coin supply given away, I went back to the wedding party. Ruth was sitting next to my grandmother, and they were eating potato salad and talking about seasickness and the power of ginger to help against nausea.

Spencer spotted me and brought me another Gatorade. "Did they find anybody for the fireworks?" I asked.

"No, and I heard something about the mayor's friend bringing in another load of fireworks in his BMW."

"Is that legal?"

"No. But I'm up to my eyeballs in arrests. I've had twenty-three public intoxications, sixteen indecent exposures, and a range of other misdemeanors. Three of my men are in the hospital from heat exhaustion, and I'm ready for this whole day to be over."

The afternoon passed into the evening. We finished off the barbecue and cut into the wedding cake, which was a Costco special and delicious.

With the sun down, I finally got some relief. The mayor arrived to officiate the ceremony, and the end was near. I was counting down to getting home and taking the uniform off.

"Don't worry about the fireworks, folks," the mayor announced. "They've gone off without a hitch since I've been mayor, and this year isn't going to be any different."

"You can't bring fireworks in a BMW," Spencer told him. "Don't you know how dangerous that is?"

"Now, now, Chief. Let's not be dramatic. I hate drama. Wedding guests of Cannes!" the mayor bellowed in his best Orson Welles impression. "Let us congregate by the caressing, beautiful blue waters for this amazing moment of the greatest love in the universe on the most beautiful spot of the world on the most patriotic day of the year," he announced.

"Not dramatic at all," I whispered to Spencer.

Ruth pushed the button on Fred's boom box, and the Wedding March began to play. We all took our places, and Julie walked up the sandy path toward her groom.

We could barely see the action because the sun had gone down and the fireworks hadn't gone off yet. When Julie reached Fred, the mayor paused as we waited for the fireworks to start. But they didn't. There's wasn't even a spark, so Julie and Fred couldn't say their vows.

"I thought Mel was going to get them going, but I guess he's having trouble," the mayor said, finally.

"Mel the arsonist, who just got out of prison?" Spencer asked and slapped his forehead.

"*Rehabilitated* arsonist," the mayor corrected.

There was a splashing noise, and a man walked out of the lake and up to our wedding party. He was holding a shotgun under his arm.

"Speak of the devil," the mayor said. "Hello, Mel."

"Congratulations on your wedding day," the arsonist called. "I couldn't get the fireworks going on the lake, but I've got an idea. This should do it."

He knelt down and aimed the shotgun at the float in the middle of the lake, which held the fireworks.

"Is he going to shoot the fireworks?" I asked Spencer. "Is that safe?"

"Only if you want World War III," Spencer said. He leapt at Mel the arsonist and fought him for his shotgun. In the dark, I couldn't make out who was winning, but there was a lot of grunting.

The mayor's cellphone rang, and he answered it. "Good news, everyone," he announced. "New fireworks are on the way. Do you see a white BMW? That's our fireworks. I told you the day wasn't a bust."

As Spencer battled for the shotgun against the arsonist, the BMW turned the corner into the parking lot, shining its lights on us. Just then, the shotgun went off and a shot flew through the air before Spencer took control of the gun.

Luckily no one was hit by the bullet. That is, except for the BMW.

CHAPTER 12

Did you know that dogs have three-hundred million olfactory receptors in their noses? A customs officer once told me that. I don't know what it means, but his dog found drugs in a septic tank, so I guess that dog had some kind of shtick. I haven't a clue how many olfactory receptors we have, bubbeleh, but we know how to sniff around, too. Sometimes we smell something bad but think nothing of it. But trust your nose. If something stinks in Denmark, there's probably a reason. Although, it might just be dog farts.

Lesson 79, Matchmaking advice from your Grandma Zelda

The shot went right into one of the car tires, throwing it out of control. The BMW drove onto the shore. It careened around picnickers, making them run screaming for their lives.

Instead of running, our wedding party froze in place, as

if we were watching a movie. The driver of the BMW totally lost control as it went into the lake at full speed.

Spencer held up the shotgun and shouted orders on his walkie talkie for his men to come quick. "Pinky, come get this," Spencer called.

"Me? You want me to hold a gun?" I asked.

"Pinky! There's a man drowning!"

I jumped into action and grabbed the weapon from Spencer. He ran into the lake to save the driver. It was hard to see what was going on because the car lights had turned off, but luckily, someone held up a blazing branch, which illuminated Spencer's heroism as he dove into the lake and pulled out the driver. The man held onto Spencer, thanking him for saving his life.

The other man with the blazing branch moved closer to the lake in order to see the action. Something about him made me nervous. I walked back to Fred and Julie, who were still waiting for the fireworks and their wedding vows.

"Maybe we should take cover," I told Fred, even though I didn't know why.

Then, I knew. As Spencer made it back to shore with the driver, the man's blazing log crackled and several sparks flew through the open windows of the BMW toward the pile of fireworks on the front seat.

Then, it was just a matter of time for Armageddon to begin. But one person's Armageddon was another person's happy accident.

When the first firework exploded through the BMW's

open window into the sky with a bright blue light, the mayor jumped into the wedding ceremony, just like Fred and Julie had wanted. "We've gathered here to join these two people," he began, practically screaming to be heard over the fireworks.

As he spoke, a second firework went off. This time the sky turned green. "Do you, Fred Lytton take Julie Fletcher as your lawfully wedded wife?" he shouted.

"Huh?" Fred asked.

A third firework went off. "Do you?" the mayor shouted, again.

"What?" Fred and Julie shouted in unison.

The third firework set off all of the other fireworks in the car. That's when the car exploded.

"Say I do! Say I do!" the mayor urged.

"What?" Fred and Julie yelled back.

"Say I do!" I screamed into their ears.

They said, "I do" just in time. A second later, the BMW's fireworks had found the fireworks on the float in the middle of the lake, and then Armageddon turned into the apocalypse.

"Run, Pinky!" Spencer yelled and grabbed me.

"Help Grandma!" I ordered in my new authoritarian voice. We ran as fast as my grandmother's legs could take her. But like Lot's wife, I couldn't help but look back to see the horror.

But there was no horror. Nobody was running for their lives. They were standing in place, watching the fireworks chaos. I stopped running and so did Grandma and Spencer.

"What the hell?" Spencer said. "What a crazy-ass town."

I guessed that Cannes had been through so many disasters that a few wild fireworks wasn't going to scare anybody. The picnickers watched the show finish, and then they packed up to go, as if it was just another July Fourth Founders Day.

Fred and Julie walked to their car hand in hand, euphoric and totally in love. As my grandmother would say, a good time was had by all. I gave my congratulations to them as they left. I had completed a match that ended in marriage and true love, and at that moment I felt completely satisfied, like my life had meaning after all.

I adjusted my dictator hat on my head and saw Fanta and Matilda walking nearby. I got an idea. I told my grandmother to keep Fanta busy for a while so that I could sneak Matilda away.

"Ruth, you help Grandma and drive her home." It was my new authoritarian voice, again. I guessed that the clothes really did make the woman. I was becoming a dictator. Ruth didn't like being dictated to, though. She was about to argue with me, probably to tell me that she didn't want to be involved in any of my cockamamie plans, but one look from my grandmother made her change her mind. Ruth had a loud bark, but she and my grandmother went way back. Even though Ruth complained about Grandma, she obviously respected and listened to her.

Spencer was busy as chief of police in the aftermath of the fireworks debacle. He was going to be busy for a while, so I had time to do what I thought I needed to do with Matilda. My grandmother got to work, quickly, distracting Fanta with her memories of fireworks on VE Day. As soon as my grandmother had distracted Fanta, I took Matilda's hand, and we ran to her car.

Matilda didn't seem surprised that I had stolen her away from Fanta. Instead, she looked relieved. We got in her Nissan Altima, and she started it up.

"Where're we going?" Matilda asked. "Scratch that. I know where we're going."

Aside from her education, her perfectionism, and her OCD, Matilda and I were exactly the same. We also seemed to read each other's minds, and we were always on the same page.

It didn't take long to arrive at Matilda's apartment complex. "How are we going to get into Fanta's apartment?" Matilda asked me.

"Don't worry. That's one of my skillsets."

It took me seconds to unlock Fanta's apartment. We walked inside and turned on our phone lights in order to see. I didn't know why I felt like we needed to snoop in Fanta's apartment, but something told me that there was more to the story than simply that her husband went on vacation. How did Rockwell know that Fanta wasn't lying to him? Sure, he had spoken to her husband, but something about that made me uncomfortable. Matilda had every confidence in Rockwell, but that didn't stop her from enthusiastically searching Fanta's apartment. She had the nosy gene, just like me.

There was no sign of the metal boxes in the living room.

We went into the bedroom, where there was a sad lack of a dead body. We weren't having much luck.

"You smell that?" I asked Matilda.

"Bleach. Lots of bleach. You know, Fanta doesn't strike me as the world's greatest housekeeper. That's an awful lot of bleach to use in a bedroom."

We stopped breathing and stared at each other, as if all of the answers to our questions could be found in each other's faces.

"We better hurry up," Matilda urged. "Fanta's going to get suspicious. We don't have a lot of time. Let's ransack the place, but do it neatly."

I found what we were looking for, even though we didn't know what we were looking for, in one of the nightstands. I pulled out Fanta's husband's wallet and opened it. His credit cards and ID were still in it, but there was no cash.

"You can't fly without an ID," Matilda pointed out.

"And if he drove, eventually he would've realized he didn't have his wallet, and she would've sent it to him."

If we were living in a movie, it would have been the perfect time for the scary music to play. But instead of scary music, we heard the front door open. Matilda and I froze and hugged each other in fear.

"Should we jump out the window?" Matilda whispered. It wasn't a bad idea.

"How many bones would we break? I'm getting married in three days."

"Probably just an ankle or a hand."

"Sounds good. Let's do it."

We went to the window, ready to jump out. It was definitely a better alternative to getting caught breaking and entering. But it was too late. Fanta had turned on the lights and walked into the bedroom, by the time we worked the latch on the window. She was furious. And soaking wet. I didn't know how that happened, but I was reasonably certain my grandmother had something to do with it.

"What are you doing in my home?" she demanded. She was spitting mad. Furious. Even ready to kill.

"Hi, Fanta. Your door was open, and I thought that I had left my pen here when I visited last," Matilda said.

I was impressed with Matilda's ability to think on her feet. I had been planning on either throwing something at Fanta, or running around her and out the door. But Matilda had thought up a good excuse on the spur of the moment. In my experience, though, making up stories rarely worked.

And in this case, it didn't look like it was working, either. Fanta hardly looked like a woman who was convinced that we were innocent pen-seekers.

"I didn't leave the door unlocked," Fanta barked. "I'm sure of that. And who breaks into an apartment to find a pen? Is it some kind of gold pen? You could've asked me for it at the lake. But you ditched me. You ditched me, and look what happened to me!"

"I didn't ditch you," Matilda said, still thinking on her feet. I had to hand it to her. She was still making up stories, despite all odds that Fanta would believe her. "I got lost in all of the chaos with the fireworks. I found Gladie, who needed a ride. As I was driving her home, I remembered that I had left my pen here. I love that pen. My grandmother gave it to me."

"I thought you didn't have any family. I thought they were all dead."

Drat. Matilda hadn't learned the art of stopping while you're ahead, but it was a good try. I had to hand it to her. She had potential in the snooping business.

Fanta raised her phone so that we could see it. "I've already called your husband to come pick up his crazy wife. I'm going to be pressing charges. Breaking and entering. And even if your friend here is some kind of military cop, it won't matter."

As if on cue, Matilda's husband walked in. He was worried and upset. He ran to Matilda and took her into his arms.

"Oh, my Matilda. It's so much worse than I imagined. I thought we had a deal. I thought you were going to get help. I love you, my sweetheart. I'm so worried about you."

"I was looking for my pen," Matilda said, but her heart wasn't in it. Her voice was weak and fearful.

"I'm pressing charges," Fanta announced to Rockwell. "This is beyond the pale."

"Please. Please, Fanta," Rockwell pleaded. "She doesn't know what she's doing. She's been having a hard time. Her whole life was transformed by marrying me, and it's been a very hard transition. She just needs a little help. She needs intensive therapy. I swear to you, Fanta, that this will never happen again."

Rockwell pushed Matilda out at arm's length and looked at her. "Right, my darling? It'll never happen again? We're going to get you help."

Matilda nodded, and a tear ran down her cheek. I wanted to defend her, but more than that, I wanted to run away. I was ashamed to watch such a private moment, a moment where a woman who was so much like me was hitting the lowest moment in her life. It was almost like she had become a non-person. Someone who couldn't trust herself and who other people couldn't trust. Now she would have to redo her whole life, even her whole psyche, in order to live her life again.

Miraculously, nobody blamed me for the break-in, and Spencer was never contacted about my illegal behavior. I gave Matilda a hug goodbye and left. My snooping was done. It was time to focus on my life and my transition to being a married woman. I hoped that I would be able to handle it better than Matilda had.

I woke up at six-thirty the next morning. Spencer was sound asleep, next to me. He had come home late after trying to clean up the Founders Day mess, which included an exploded car.

He had today, tomorrow, and Sunday off. Three days to relax and get married. After, we weren't planning on going on a honeymoon, at least not right away. Instead, we were going to just enjoy our new home, which we were moving into on Sunday after the wedding.

Today was the house's official done day. Spencer was going to show it off to me and his parents in the morning. He had planned the tour for days, and he was keeping it top secret, even though I had been in the house a million times while it was being rebuilt and redecorated.

I sat up in bed.

My uniform was draped over the chair in the corner of the room. I sighed. I didn't want to put it on again and hand out the coins of our sovereign leader, a.k.a. the maniac dictator. But a deal was a deal. Besides, I only had to wear it today and tomorrow and then I'd be free.

I thought about what he had said about having to wear it everywhere except for the bathroom and sleeping, but I figured I could eat breakfast in my grandmother's kitchen without him knowing about it.

Before I went downstairs to eat, I had something to do upstairs in the attic. The high school kid, Draco, who had been helping me organize in exchange for junk food, had fixed up the office in the attic. Everything they said about the younger generation was wrong. Just feed them preservatives, and they worked like beasts.

Upstairs, I was surprised to find Draco already at it in the attic. "I had a craving for Pop-Tarts, so I came right over," he explained. "I've got the last of the records inputted in the spreadsheets. I think you're ready for business. Everything is very organized."

Not only had he put the records into the computer, but he actually showed me how to use it, which meant a lot for his teaching abilities.

Draco had re-polished the old furniture that had been shoved into a corner of the attic, and he had decorated it so that the attic was now a beautiful sanctuary, in addition to being an office. I was impressed, and even more so, I was pleased to have a real office and a beautiful place to work.

"I love how you decorated," I told him. "The furniture looks perfect in here."

"A couple days ago, your grandmother hired a couple men to take out a bunch of the old stuff that was in the corner, and then the rest just fell into place. They're all antiques, and the two rugs are from Afghanistan. I think they're worth a fortune."

There were two desks with Tiffany lamps on them by the window. The rest of the room was filled with a sofa, various chairs, and the two rugs.

"I'm impressed, Draco. I think that there's a bag of Funyuns in the kitchen," I told him.

"Really? I've heard of them, but I never got a chance to eat one. Thank you, Gladie."

Draco's parents only allowed him to eat health food. As far as they knew, Draco had never eaten a French fry. But he had eaten more than his share of poison since he started to help me. My grandmother had a terrible lifelong habit of eating crappy food, and everyone who came in close contact with her adopted her way of eating.

"I'm glad you're here, Draco." I said. "I was wondering if you could do some research for me. A background check."

Draco perked up. "You mean like a private investigator? Like a spy?"

Yes, exactly like a private investigator and a spy. "No, nothing like that. I just need some information on a match. As much as you can give me."

"What sorts of things are you looking for?"

"Anything that stands out. Anything that shows that he's not perfect. Anything that would point to a reason why he would lie."

"Oh, this is going to be good," Draco said, rubbing his hands together.

Downstairs, my grandmother was already up and in the kitchen. The table was covered in a delicious spread of quiches, French toast, and everything that anyone could want for breakfast.

"What's all this?" I asked.

"It just arrived," my grandmother explained. "A gift for your wedding. I have a feeling we're going to eat really well until you get married, Gladie."

Spencer entered, wearing sweatpants and no shirt. He was singing. "Today we see our house. Today I give you the grand tour," he sang. He gave me a kiss on the lips and a kiss on Grandma's cheek.

"Zelda, I love the outfit," he said, sitting down and scooping eggs onto his plate. "What's the special occasion?"

My grandmother was wearing short pants, buttoned at the knee, a striped cotton shirt, and a baseball cap. It wasn't her usual style choice.

"I'm going to a baseball game today. I haven't seen a baseball game in person since my father took me when I was eight years old. He never took me again because I kept calling the plays before they happened. It caused quite a stir. I'm excited to go. I'm seeing a very nice team play. I think they're called the Daddies."

Spencer stopped chewing and looked up. "What? The Daddies? You mean the Padres? You're going to a Padres game?"

Spencer was obsessed with the San Diego Padres. If he could have married them instead of me, he would have without a second's hesitation.

"Yes, that's it," my grandmother said, pointing at him. "The Padres. Do you know that I matched the Padres' owner's daughter? She's very happy. She just had triplets. Unfortunately, the owner couldn't get me a regular seat. So, I have to sit with him and the general manager in a large room over home plate." She shrugged. "I guess it's better than nothing."

Spencer's mouth dropped open. "Zelda, are you telling me that you're going to the Padres game, and you're going to watch it in the owner's box? His suite? The owner's suite above home plate?"

"Yes, I think that's what he said."

"I want to go," Spencer said. "Please let me go with you, Zelda. Please. I'll do anything. I'll weed your lawn for the rest of my life. I'll hem your dresses. I'll bring home fried chicken every night. Anything. Zelda, anything."

"You know how to hem a dress?" I asked.

"But what about the house?" Grandma asked Spencer. "Aren't you giving a tour of the house to Gladie and your parents?"

Actually, I would have preferred that he went to the baseball game. I didn't want to take a tour of the house in front of my mother-in-law to be. I didn't want her to see me dressed as a dictator.

"I hear the owner's suite has all-you-can-eat hot dogs. I hear the players visit the suite after the game." Spencer was in a fugue state, talking to no one, deep in his fantasies about baseball owner suites.

"I'm sure your mother will understand. We can look at the house another day," I told him. "Like in five years. Five years from now would be a good time to invite her over. I think I'll be free in five years."

At the mention of his mother, Spencer snapped out of his reverie. His mom had a powerful effect on him. "No, I want her to see what I did. I want her to see our beautiful house. She'll be impressed, and it'll put her in a good mood for our wedding. You'll get another invitation to the owner's suite, right, Zelda?"

Zelda sipped her coffee and thought about it. "Eight-percent chance. He's got another daughter, and I've got a match in mind for her."

Spencer made a valiant effort not to be disappointed about the baseball game. The blow was softened because he was dying to show off his grand achievement. If I had had a normal mother, who wasn't in a prison farm for driving a mobile meth lab on her moped, I would have probably understood the need to impress one's mother. All I had to do was stay out of prison to impress my mother. That reminded me it was time to put my uniform on.

Spencer and I went back upstairs and got dressed. The uniform had taken on a nasty smell from my day in the heat at the lake. Oh, great. Now I looked like a maniac dictator, and I stank. I really knew how to impress the in-laws.

I put on earrings to see if that would spruce up my look, but it just made me look bizarre, so I took them off.

We went back downstairs just as a delivery man arrived with a tall box. "Delivery for Spencer Bolton from Dr. Tiffany's Love Happiness Factory," he announced. Spencer signed for the package, and the man slit it open with a box cutter.

"What the hell?" I said.

"What the hell?" Spencer said.

"What is it?" Grandma asked, walking into the room.

Draco walked down the stairs, probably to get his Funyuns. "You got a sex robot, Gladie? That's clutch. Really clutch." I didn't know what clutch meant, but Draco high-fived me on his way to the kitchen.

"It's a sex robot," I repeated.

"And it's clutch," my grandmother said.

CHAPTER 13

I'm a people person, dolly. But people never cease to shock the hell out of me. A match once told me that, "It's the known unknown." In other words, people are going to shock you, and you shouldn't be shocked that they shock you. You understand, bubbeleh? Don't be surprised that you're surprised.

Lesson 18, Matchmaking advice from your Grandma Zelda

We were the proud owners of a sex robot.

"It's a lease-to-own situation," Grandma said, reading the paperwork that came with the robot.

"It's a lease-to-own situation," Spencer repeated, smirking his little smirk. "We're leasing a sex robot."

"It's for you, Spencer," Grandma continued. "Not for Gladie. Oh, my. This is an interesting therapy strategy. I'm going into the kitchen to make sure that Draco finds the Funyuns."

She handed Spencer the paperwork, and he read through it. "Don't be angry, Pinky," he said.

"In general, or about your sex robot? What are you supposed to do with the sex robot?"

"I think everything," he said, reading. He finished and put the papers down. "Don't be angry."

"How about scared? Can I be scared?"

The sex robot was about five-foot-four and had a much better body than I had. Firmer. It whirred to life and stepped away from its box. "I am Farrah. How may I please you today?" it asked in a Marilyn Monroe breathy voice.

"Why did the therapist give you a sex aid?" I asked, trying to keep my cool.

"Don't be angry, but she suggests that I have sex with the robot and not you."

I flopped down on a nearby chair. "She wants you to have sex with the robot and not me," I repeated. "Is it the dictator uniform? Is that it?"

"I don't think so. You weren't wearing it when you met the therapist. As far as I can tell, her theory is that if we take sex out of the equation, we can just focus on our relationship."

"Without sex, our relationship is television, food, and you telling me to stay out of police business," I pointed out.

Spencer took me in his arms and kissed me. "Pinky, we're so much more than television, food, and you butting in where you don't belong. We're even so much more than sex. We're you and me. We're the happily ever after."

"I love you," the sex robot purred and nuzzled up to Spencer's back.

"I think I'm angry now," I said. "No, wait a minute. Let me think about it."

"You're my poo bear. Do you work out?" the robot continued.

"I've thought about it," I said. "Yes, I'm definitely angry."

"Oh, you're so strong!" the robot gushed.

"I'll find the off button," Spencer assured me.

"That better be the only button you find," I said, adjusting my military cap on my head.

He didn't find the off button. Spencer's sex robot followed us across the street, where Spencer's parents were waiting for the grand tour of their son's custom-made dream house.

Eight o'clock on the dot, and they were at the front the door, smiling wide as their perfect child waved at them. Their smiles dropped when they saw me. It was still blistering hot, and by the time I got across the street, I was already sweaty under my military uniform.

I waved brightly, and Lily grabbed onto her husband. "Did you join the military?" she asked me. "Are you going overseas? Don't worry, Spencer. Long-distance relationships are wonderful. Who cares if you don't see Gladie for six months at a time? It'll be good for your relationship."

I was tempted not to give her the bad news that I wasn't off to Afghanistan because she was suddenly so happy. Poor woman. The idea that I was off to Afghanistan put a smile on her face, but Spencer gave her the bad news. He explained that I only had to wear the uniform for another forty-eight hours in order not to go to jail for stealing a donkey when I was drunk. He shrugged. "See, Mom? Simple explanation."

"Oh my God," he whispered to me. "I'm thoroughly infected. You warped me, Pinky."

I kissed him on the lips, and his mother flinched. "I could say that my work here is done, but I'm assuming you still have a long way to go," I said.

"I want you. I want you so bad," the sex robot purred.

Spencer's mother stumbled backward, as if she was noticing the robot for the first time. "Who's your friend?" Spencer's father asked. "You should wear an outfit like that, Lily," he told his wife. "You would look good."

"It's the sex robot that Mom's therapist prescribed for us," Spencer said. "Thanks, Mom. It's a great wedding gift."

"The what robot?" she asked. Her eyes went wide, and her mouth kept dropping open. "The what?"

"Spencer is my dream man. I love you, Spencer," the robot said.

"Can we go inside?" I asked, definitely angry now. "I'm sweating balls in this outfit."

"It's not my fault," Spencer told me. "I didn't ask for the sex robot."

"I don't understand what's going on," Lily said. "I might be having a stroke."

"Don't say stroke in front of the robot. It could have unintentional consequences," James told her.

"Sweating balls," I said. "Sweating balls."

"All righty. Let's get this party started," Spencer said, jangling the house keys in his hand.

"I love to party," the robot announced. "Party with me, big boy."

"Isn't technology amazing?" Spencer's father asked.

Spencer stood with his back to the front door, and the robot cuddled up next to him. He cleared his throat and did his best to ignore the sex robot. "Ladies and gentlemen," he started. "I'm honored today to have the people I most love in the world, all except for my loser brother Peter, who's off saving the world and couldn't be here for my wedding. Anyway, I'm happy you're here to be the first to see the finished product of our new home, where we'll hopefully live forever."

"And it's not cursed anymore," I added. "It was cursed, but my grandmother's friend is a shaman, and he burned sage inside, so it's not cursed anymore. Money back guarantee."

"You don't say," Spencer's father said.

"It was never cursed," Spencer said.

"A man was murdered in it. A plane crashed on it."

"Two men were murdered in it," Spencer corrected. "And it's not cursed. Pinky, here's your key." He handed me the key on a pretty, gold keychain. I held it in my hand and studied it.

My very own key for my very own house. I felt giddy and excited, but at the same time I had a weird feeling of dread, like the five minutes before food poisoning hits. I tried to focus on the giddy and excited part instead of the dread part, and I smiled at him.

"Thank you, Spencer."

Holding his own key in his hand, Spencer began to describe the long process of turning a house that had been abandoned and the site of a plane crash into a stylish ultra-luxury, four-thousand-square-foot home.

"It's the largest house on the block, and it has a pool," he added and put his key into the lock. The door opened.

I hadn't been totally involved with the renovations and the decorating, but I had been there for every step along the way, and much to his credit, Spencer kept me in the loop and asked for my opinion on everything from door handles to the roof. More often than not, I told him I liked what he liked. So, the house was really his baby. It was his brainchild. I could never have thought to do the beautiful things he did to the house.

We walked inside behind Spencer and the sex robot. Spencer started by showing us the entranceway with the alarm console and the console for all of the automated functions of the house. "Bill Gates has nothing on this house," he insisted. "Bill Gates wishes he had this house."

The house had originally had five bedrooms, but Spencer turned it into only three, enlarging the master bedroom into a massive room and expanding the kitchen out. We visited the basement, which was a rare find in California. It used to house two panic rooms, but now there was a sauna and a workout room.

"We'll never have the excuse not to work out now," Spencer said, hugging me to him.

"Yay," I said, trying to drum up enthusiasm for never missing a day of exercise.

The house was beautiful, but the kitchen was a thing of wonder. And I mean, literally a thing of wonder because I didn't know how to cook, and there must've been fifty appliances in there.

"You'll like this, Pinky," Spencer said, excitedly touching a stainless-steel appliance on the counter. "It's a latte machine. You'll never have to go to Tea Time again. You'll have your latte with frothy steamed milk every morning right here in the kitchen. You won't even need to go outside, unless you want to go to the backyard."

"I'm never going to Tea Time again," I said, trying to smile. "Is it hot in here? I'm feeling a little hot."

"The house is entirely temperature regulated. Right now, we're at a cool seventy degrees. Isn't it fabulous, Mom?" Spencer asked

"I'm so proud of you, son," she gushed. "You're amazing. You've done beautiful work, and so generous to share it with Gladys. Not many men would spend so much money to pamper their wives to this extent. I mean who does this? Who spoils their woman this much?"

"And his sex robot," I added. "Don't forget how much he pampers his sex robot."

The passive aggressiveness or downright aggressiveness continued as the tour finished. Spencer and his father stayed inside to check out the automatic bagel slicer with the sex robot, while Lily and I went outside.

"Now that we have a moment alone, I just wanted to explain myself," Spencer's mother told me on the front lawn.

"That's not necessary," I said. I didn't want her to explain herself. I figured that I would get the raw end of the stick if she explained herself. I got the impression that her explaining herself meant insulting me.

"I think I need to," she insisted. "You don't understand what it's like for a mother. I have a very strong relationship with my children. We're connected on a very deep level. Emotional, psychological, and intellectual. You don't understand that because you don't have that in your life."

I smoothed out my dictator uniform. "I don't know what you think you know, but I understand about strong relationships with a mother. I happen to have a wonderful mother, who loves me very deeply. And I love her." Oh boy. I was so going to hell with all the lies I was telling. I hoped karma wasn't real because I was packing on the lies before my wedding. But I couldn't stop lying. It was the only way I knew how to win in this conversation. And besides, I was really good at lying.

"So, you don't have to explain your relationship to me, because one thing I know for certain is the love of a mother, and I can assure you that I'll bring that same kind of attachment and love to my relationship with your son," I said on a liar-liar-pants-on-fire roll. "As much as I understand how familial love works, don't worry because I'll take that knowledge and make my new family with Spencer be just as rewarding and loving as I've always had with my family."

As I spoke, I had to raise my voice because a large bus was coming down the street. It was a luxury charter bus, the kind used for sightseeing. "So, don't tell me I don't know about a loving mother, because I do!" I said, my voice rising above the roar of the bus's engine.

The bus came closer, and much to my surprise, parked on the street in front of us. The bus was white with a large green leaf painted on the side with *Senior Leaf* written next to it.

"What the hell is that?" Lily demanded. "What are you up to now, Gladie? Is this your new car? Does this have something to do with your uniform?"

"As God is my witness, I have no idea what this bus is. It's just a bus. Maybe it's lost."

But it wasn't just a bus, and it wasn't lost. The bus driver killed the engine, and the bus door opened.

Funnily enough, getting a sex robot in the mail wasn't my biggest surprise of the day. It turned out that it wasn't even close. You could have knocked me over with a feather when I saw who came out of the bus.

"Hello, Gladie. Am I in time for your wedding?"

"Mom? How did you break out of the prison farm?"

CHAPTER 14

Once you've made a match, it's not uncommon for one of them to get cold feet. Cold feet doesn't sound like a big megillah, bubbeleh. It sounds like you go to Target and buy some socks, and the cold feet are cured. Right? Of course, right. But sometimes, even Target socks can't warm cold feet. Sometimes, as a matchmaker, you have to massage them, yourself. Get down on your knees, grab those cold feet, and give them a big rub, dolly! Only you can do it.

Lesson 128, Matchmaking advice from your Grandma Zelda

My mother didn't look like herself. She looked respectable. She even looked conservative. My mom was wearing navy blue slacks, a white, button-down shirt, and flats. And she wasn't drunk.

She wasn't stoned.

"Mom? Is that you? What are you doing here? Did you

steal a bus and break out of the prison farm?"

It was the most logical explanation.

"Mom?" Spencer's mother asked. "Prison farm?"

"They bought me out," my mother explained.

"What do you mean, they bought you out?" I demanded.

"What do you mean, prison farm?" Spencer's mother demanded.

Spencer and his father walked out of the house and locked the sex robot inside. Spencer noticed the bus parked in front of his custom-made house. "Are you kidding me?" he asked. Then, he noticed my mother. "Are you kidding me?" he asked, louder.

"It turns out that if you have a marketable skill, they buy you out of the prison farm," Mom explained.

Spencer shook his head. "I don't get it. Who bought you out? What're you talking about?"

"Did you know that marijuana is legal?" my mother asked. Since she had been arrested for driving a mobile meth lab, she had gotten clean and sober and she was a new person. She had bright eyes, and actually seemed interested in the world around her. She had a long way to go to become mother of the year, but it was a relief to see her cogent and clean.

Although, it probably wasn't a good thing that she had broken out of prison and was driving a stolen luxury charter bus.

"I know that marijuana is legal," Spencer said.

"It is?" I asked.

"Everyone's doing it now, Gladie," my mother said, excitedly. "They've got clubs and stores, and even senior citizens are getting stoned."

I dreaded where this conversation was going.

"What the hell's going on?" Spencer's mother demanded.

"Do you smoke pot?" my mother asked her. "You look old, and old people are the best customers."

I put my hands on my hips. "Are you dealing drugs, Mom? Is that what we're talking about?"

"No, I've turned over a new leaf, Gladie. I'm not pushing, anymore. I'm *driving* them to get their drugs. There's a *Senior Leaf* store in San Diego. We drive the seniors from Cannes down to San Diego, and the old folks buy their week's supply. All with a scenic view of the Pacific Ocean and an extensive organic snack bar. Isn't that genius?"

It was sort of genius. It was the same idea as shipping seniors to the Indian casinos.

"They hired you to drive their bus, their pot bus?" Spencer asked, gesturing toward the giant green leaf on the side of the bus.

"They recruited me. It turns out that corporate America recruits employees from minimum security prisons. I've gone corporate. They said that since I already had experience, I would be perfect. It's the first time I've ever been recruited, Gladie, I have full benefits, including health insurance and a pension plan."

Health insurance and a pension plan? That was more

than I had ever gotten. "That's great, Mom," I said honestly. I was actually proud of her. In her roundabout way, she had wound up with a good, steady job.

"In what century and what reality and what universe is that great?" Spencer's mother shouted.

"Now, now Lily," Spencer's father said, calmly. "It's not our business. Besides, it's a nice bus. So, how does this outfit work, Mrs. Burger?"

My mother blinked, as if she was noticing him for the first time, or it might've been the fact that he called her Mrs. Burger and treated her with respect that surprised her.

"We pick them up and drive them to San Diego and back," she explained. "Each customer gets their own joint for free, just for riding, which they smoke on the way to the store."

"So you're getting a contact high every day. Perfect. Isn't there an agreement with the judge that you can't partake?" Spencer asked.

"Yes, don't worry about that. The driver sits in an airtight enclosure. It's a good set-up inside. You want to see?"

"Yes," Spencer's father said.

No," Spencer's mother said.

Spencer caught my eye, and the message was clear: Handle this. Clear this up.

"It was nice seeing you, Luann," Spencer told my mother. "Mom, Dad, time to come inside for brunch. I'm cooking for you in my amazing kitchen. That's part of the tour."

Since we had just eaten breakfast, I doubted that brunch

was part of the tour. Spencer was giving me time with my mom to smooth out any emergencies before they happened. Normally he was the one to smooth out emergencies, not me. This was a different strategy, but I went with it, since Spencer had to handle his own parents.

"I'm happy for you, Mom," I told her, once Spencer and his folks were back inside. "You like your new job?"

"I've only made one trip so far, but yes, it's perfect. They let me play whatever music I want in my little booth at the front. It's soundproof. We play old movies for the customers. You want to see?"

She pressed the button on her keychain, and the bus doors opened. We climbed in. My mother pressed another button, and the bus began to cool down. "They trained me for the job for three weeks at the farm. I even know how to fix it if it breaks. You believe that, Gladie? It's got every major gizmo and gadget. It can do anything. I know how to work it all."

The bus was very fancy. It had lavender mood lighting, and each chair had its own reclining position and television screen. It was like ultra-first-class in a fancy foreign airline. My mother wasn't lying about her booth. She showed me how it would protect her from smoke.

"And even if I wasn't in the booth, the bus has got this amazing Space X air filtration system."

I sat down in one of the chairs and reclined back. We got quiet, and I wondered if she wanted to ask me for something and that's why she had shown up. We didn't exactly have the greatest relationship, but I knew that whatever she asked me for, I was going to do. I didn't know why. She didn't deserve my help. She had been a terrible mother ever since my father had died. We had a miserable relationship. But I knew I would say yes, just like I always did. Perhaps it was my hope of having some kind of normal mother-daughter relationship that always made me help her in the end. But my mother had a perfect record of letting me down, and even though she had a plum job and she looked healthy for once, I figured there was a ninety-five percent chance that she would let me down now, and that helping her would just make me regret it.

"You didn't show up because all of a sudden I own a fancy house, did you? Because I'm not giving you any money. I don't have any. And I'm not giving you Spencer's money. And I'm not letting you live in our new fancy house, because it's Spencer's. He worked very hard on it, and he wants to live there with me and nobody else." Not even with a sex robot, I was hoping. "I'm not going to make him live with you, too."

There, I said it. It was sort of mean, but it turned out that it was easier to draw boundaries when it was for Spencer. Just like that, I had changed my life. I had put Spencer ahead of myself. I guessed that's what commitment and marriage were about. And I hadn't even said the vows yet. Something in me, something in my heart, had opened up and welcomed Spencer in, and I knew right then and there that it was forever.

"Don't worry, Gladie. I'm going to show you that I've changed. I got an apartment on Main Street, right above a shop, owned by a man dressed a lot like you. He's a little off-the-wall, but the rent is cheap. Zelda gave me some old furniture, and I set it up nice. It's a sweet little place. One bedroom and all mine. You can come visit anytime you want. I'll give you your own key, if you want."

"Wow, Mom. That's amazing." I didn't know how long this new mother with the job and apartment would last, but I never thought she would get this far, so I just enjoyed the moment.

"I'm getting married on Sunday," I told her. "You're welcome to attend if you want."

A tear slid down my mother's cheek. "Zelda already invited me. Thank you, Gladie. I can't wait to see you married. Your father would've been so happy."

My phone rang and I answered it, thankful for the interruption of our intimate moment, which was making me squirm in my seat. It was an unknown caller, and normally I wouldn't answer, but I wanted the distraction.

"Is this Gladie Burger?" a young man asked.

"Yes, but I don't do surveys, and I don't need new windows."

"Huh? What? No, this isn't a sales call. A friend of yours told me to call you. Do you know a woman named Matilda?"

"Yes." A cold chill went down my spine.

"Well she gave me a message for you. You want to hear it? She wrote it down on a napkin and smuggled it to me with twenty bucks."

"Smuggled?"

"Here's what she wrote: 'Gladie, help.' She added three exclamation marks. You want me to yell it?"

"No, I get the picture."

"There's more: 'Help me, please. I'm in an insane asylum. They're torturing me. I can't get in touch with Rockwell. Nobody to help. Get me out of here. I'm begging you.' That's all she said. There's some stuff here at the bottom, but it got kinda smeared in my pocket. Are we good here?"

"No, is this some kind of joke?"

"I don't think so. She was in pretty bad shape. They were sending her to room C. People come out of room C pretty messed up."

"And who are you?"

"Rather not say. I got a good job."

"At least tell me where she is."

He gave me the address, and I jotted it down on a Senior Leaf pad of paper that my mother gave me. I hung up the phone and immediately called Lucy.

"Lucy, can you go with me somewhere?"

"Did you find a dead body?"

"No, she's not dead yet."

"Oh, that's weird, because you had the dead person voice. Hold on a second. I'll be right back." I could hear her walk away and then a terrible retching sound. A few seconds later, she was back on the phone. "I'd love to come be your Ethel today, darlin', but I got some bad kind of food poisoning. I don't know what did it. Harry and I had the same thing for dinner last night, but I'm the one who's spilling my guts this morning. Will you forgive me?"

"Of course. Get better soon."

I didn't know what to do. Breaking Matilda out of a funny farm was definitely a two-person job. Lucy was throwing up, and Bridget was creating a super baby. That left one person. Me.

"What's the matter?" my mother asked. "Bad news?"

"Sort of. I need to break my friend out of a psych ward, but my friends are busy. I'm not sure how I can do it by myself."

"I don't have a Senior Leaf run today. I could do it. I could help," my mom offered.

"No."

"I'm good on my feet, and I have a lot of experience lying to officials."

She had a point. "I don't think it's a good idea," I said.

"Gladie, give me a chance. Let me prove myself to you. I'm not a screw-up anymore. I can help you break your friend out."

"No," I said, shaking my head. "No way. Impossible. There's no way that's going to happen. You just got out of prison. You used to drive a mobile meth lab on your moped. You showed up half-naked at my prom and tried to have sex with the varsity quarterback. You took me to see *Mission Impossible* and when you went out for popcorn, you never came back…for two days. There's no way you're going to go with me. Never. Not going to happen. Forget about it. No. No. No."

We decided it was better to take the bus than my Oldsmobile. It was more conspicuous, but it had more horsepower and lavender mood lighting, which I figured might come in handy for Matilda, since she had been tortured and medicated.

My mother hadn't lied about being a good driver. She was in complete command of the large bus all the way to the hospital. The hospital turned out to be a nondescript building in an industrial park. There was a razor wire chain-link fence all around it and a guard at the front gate.

My mother had brainstormed our break-in strategy, and it worked like a charm. She gave the guard at the gate three joints, and he waved us in.

"Marijuana is very popular," my mother noted. "It's like Barbra Streisand mixed with Oreos. Totally irresistible."

Mom parked the bus in front of the building, and miraculously nobody questioned why a charter bus was parked in the loading zone.

"How are you going to get in to see your friend? Are we going to bribe them with more joints?" my mother asked.

"I don't think so. They've got all kinds of pharmaceuticals in there, and I don't think they'll care about an ounce of Maui Wowie. Let me think a minute. I guess I didn't plan this out very well."

"Well, you look very official. Maybe they won't

question you. Maybe they'll think you're a general."

It wasn't the best plan, but it was the only plan we had. "Okay, let's go with that. Come on, let's go save Matilda."

We walked into the hospital and rang the bell at the main desk. The inside was more like a prison than any kind of hospital I'd ever seen. It was all *One Flew Over the Cuckoo's Nest* and not an ounce of *The Prince of Tides.* It wasn't a psychiatric hospital. It was a booby hatch.

There were loud buzzers going off, and the receptionist sat behind a security glass. I focused on being as sane as I could, because we were in the Gitmo of loony bins, and I was terrified that they were going to lock me up with the rest of the poor unfortunates who wound up in this shop of horrors.

I was surprised when my mother took the lead. "General Burger to see one of your patients," she told the receptionist. "This is a surprise inspection. We don't want any backtalk."

"General?" The woman asked. "What do you mean, general?"

My mother hit the wall hard and stomped her foot. "I told you, no backtalk. This is a surprise inspection."

"Not from the Portland office, again. Why can't Ellison leave us alone?"

"Because Ellison can't leave you alone," my mother insisted. "Ellison knows how to do his job. Ellison realizes that you guys aren't up to snuff and is just trying to make you better. So, you're going to buzz in the general immediately and let her get on with it. Or do you want us to do to you what

Ellison did last time?"

The woman flinched. "No, no, please not that. Okay, fine."

She gave us two badges and buzzed us in.

"Wow, Mom," I whispered as we went in the back. "That was impressive."

"Shhh, Gladie. Don't blow your cover."

Like a general, I didn't say a word. I remembered to stand up straight and pretend I was as official as I could. Maybe the whole dictator thing was a blessing. I was starting to understand why the maniac wanted to be a fascist leader. It was nice having people not question me. It was nice getting respect, even if the respect was from fear.

My mother gave the receptionist Matilda's name and ordered her to take us to her. We walked through the tiled hallways until we stopped at a room. The receptionist pressed a code, and the door opened. Inside, Matilda Dare was shackled to a table. An orderly was about to put an IV needle into her arm, and there was a suspicious looking IV bag full of what I assumed was crazy juice, ready to pump through her veins.

"What's this?" the orderly asked when we entered, although he didn't seem very interested.

"Ellison sent some kind of general," the receptionist told him.

"Those aren't standard-issue shackles," my mother said, angrily. "The general insists on standard-issue shackles. And she's still conscious? Do you know the added cost of every minute a patient remains conscious? You people have gone way off the rails. We're going to have to start fresh here. You'll be lucky to keep your jobs when we're done."

Wow, my mother was really good at this. I finally knew where I got my bullshit skills from. I shook my head and tsked. "This is worse than we thought," I complained, dropping my voice an octave so I sounded more like a general. "We need to remove the patient and get her to a secure location where we can really lock her down."

"Are you shitting me?" the man asked. "Do you have transfer orders?"

"Transfer orders? Transfer orders?" My mother shrieked. "We don't need no stinking transfer orders. Do you know who this general is? If you don't, you're in trouble. Remember Ellison."

Three minutes later we were carrying Matilda out and loading her onto the pot bus.

"Hurry, Mom, before they wonder why the general is riding around in a pot bus," I urged.

"Don't worry. This bus has Ludicrous Mode from Tesla. They won't know what hit them. Hold on to your seats."

I sat next to Matilda across from the driver's seat. My mother started the bus, and the lavender mood lighting came on and so did an old Cary Grant movie on the video screens. My mom turned the bus around and waved at the guard to open the gate. Luckily, he didn't stop us, and we drove out like a bat out of hell.

Once we were free of the place, Matilda rested her head on my shoulder and cried. "It was horrible, Gladie. Thank you so much for saving me. I didn't think I would get out of there."

"Why did Rockwell do this to you?" I asked.

"He didn't know what kind of place it was. It was supposed to be a nice psychiatric facility for me to work on my forgetfulness and OCD. But the minute I got there, they treated me like I was a psycho criminal. It was like *Silence of the Lambs.*"

"We have that movie if you want to see it," my mother said.

"Not necessary, but thanks, Mom," I said. "I'm taking you to my house, and you can hide there," I told Matilda.

"We need to reach Rockwell and let him know."

"We will in time," I said. Matilda was still under the impression that Rockwell was a good husband, even though he put her in a hellhole where they shackled her to the bed. I wanted to kick myself for doubting my grandmother. She had been right. Matilda needed to be unmatched on the double. But for now, she was still in denial. It would take some finessing on my part.

My mother parked the bus in front of my grandmother's house. "I'll see you at the wedding?"

"Sure," I said. "Thank you for your help."

We didn't hug goodbye because we weren't that kind of mother and daughter. But she dropped an extra key to her apartment in my hand. It was the most loving gesture she had ever shown me. Well, that and helping my friend break out of a lockdown facility.

When I opened the front door, my grandmother was

already there to give Matilda a big hug. "I'm so sorry, sweetheart," she told her. "This has never happened to me before. I wanted a life of love for you. I think my sight is wonky."

Matilda stared at her, as if she was trying to focus. "No need to apologize, Zelda. You were wonderful. You matched me with the love of my life. But everything has gotten muddled. I haven't been acting right. And Rockwell didn't know that that place was what it was. He thought it was more like a spa with therapists."

Grandma and I exchanged looks. Sometimes it took a while for women to accept the truth or even recognize the truth when they saw it. But we had time for her to realize the truth. My grandmother convinced Matilda not to contact Rockwell until after the wedding when she had fully recovered from her ordeal. It took some doing, but since Matilda was so exhausted and traumatized and hadn't been able to reach Rockwell before, she accepted my grandmother's advice to just sit tight in the house and recover.

CHAPTER 15

To thine own self be true. Shakespeare wrote that. Are you impressed that your Grandma Zelda knows Shakespeare? I've matched quite a few actors in my life, and I've picked up a couple things, bubbeleh. One of them is that actors are big pretenders. Let me tell you about pretending…it stinks for matchmaking. The worst kind of pretending is the kind where a match pretends so much that she's not honest about what she wants. "What do you want?" you'll ask her, and she'll respond, "Nothing." Feh. What a bunch of bull hockey. Dolly, the first step to love is being honest with yourself. What do you feel? What do you want?

Lesson 28, Matchmaking advice from your Grandma Zelda

The next morning, I woke up in Spencer's arms. We were lying like spoons. His strong muscular body was wrapped around me, making me feel safe and loved. I had gotten used to sleeping with him in my small bed. In our new house, our bed was a California King, and I wondered if with all of the added room, whether we would still sleep wrapped in each other's arms, or would he take his side and I take my mine.

I heard my grandmother walking down the stairs. The air conditioning was on full blast, which meant that our heatwave was still going strong. I loved this time of morning in my grandmother's house when I was cozy in my bed, and I knew that my grandmother was nearby, preparing our morning breakfast.

Happy. That's what I was. I was happy.

I realized, with a start, however, that it was Saturday, the day before my wedding. Holy crap. The old ball and chain was right around the corner. The till death do us part counter was about to start. I didn't have a great track record when it came to commitment, but here I was the day before the big Kahuna of all commitments. I had to hand it to me because I hadn't run away. I hadn't quit. I was actually going to see something through to the end. Either I had changed a lot in the past year, or Spencer was such a prize that I had to commit to him. In any case, I felt indescribably happy to know that in a little over twenty-four hours, I was going to be tied forever to Spencer.

I was about to turn around and give Spencer a dirty, day-before-the-wedding present, when something big and heavy plopped down on my bed.

"Hey there, little brother, you're not going to sleep through your stag party, are you?"

Spencer bolted up from bed. "Peter?" he asked.

It was his older brother, a superspy and hottie metrosexual. Spencer and Peter were freakishly linked and the definition of brotherly love. Peter was supposed to be off saving the world instead of attending our wedding, but here he was, surprising Spencer.

Spencer gave Peter a vise-like bear hug. There was a lot of testosterone in the room. Their hug turned quickly into wrestling, and the two behemoths took up most of the bed.

"I thought you were in the Mideast," Spencer said, punching Peter hard on his arm.

Peter punched him back. "And miss my little brother's wedding? No way. I want to see this happen. I want to witness the womanizing jerk get pinned down." He flopped backward on the bed, lying between Spencer and me and hugged us both to him. "Hello, sister-in-law," he said, kissing the top of my head. "Welcome to the family."

"She's not part of the family yet," Spencer reminded Peter.

"No, but she's going to be. Little brother, this is the smartest thing you've ever done. It's making me rethink my life, in fact. But there's not a lot of women out there like Gladie." He turned toward me and arched an eyebrow. "How about it, Gladie? If you want to change your mind and get the better Bolton boy, just say so. I'll make it happen."

"Oh no, you won't," Spencer growled. He rolled on top of Peter and started pounding him. They wrestled until they rolled off the bed, and then they wrestled on the floor. I took that as my cue to get up. I went to the bathroom, peed, splashed cold water on my face, and went downstairs.

In the kitchen, Lucy, Bridget and her baby, and my grandmother were already assembled. I assumed that Matilda was still asleep in the guest room, if she had managed to fall asleep. "Happy day-before-your-wedding-day," my friends announced.

"We wanted to make sure that you were okay after the christening," Bridget said. "Don't worry about the naked pictures. No one will remember them."

I had the feeling that everyone in town would remember my nudie pictures, pretty much forever, and that it would be written down in the official lore of Cannes for eternity. Nevertheless, I was overcome with the kindness of their gesture. There was nothing better than having good friends.

"I brought a gourmet breakfast," Lucy announced. "But I'm going to call that chef, because the food tastes off to me."

"It tastes great to me," Bridget said. "Maybe you're still recovering from your food poisoning. Zelda, is the food safe?"

"Totally safe, but I think that Lucy should probably get to a doctor soon. Or maybe just the pharmacy."

Lucy gasped. "Should I be afraid, Zelda?"

"No, Lucy dear. Everything will be fine in the end. Nothing to worry about at all."

Lucy fanned herself and giggled slightly. "Oh, thank goodness. You had me worried. For a minute, I thought there was something wrong with me."

My grandmother caught my eye. If it had been serious,

Grandma wouldn't have hesitated to tell Lucy, but there was definitely something wrong.

We sat at the table, drank coffee, and ate a variety of delicious breakfast pastries. We gossiped and talked about all the funny things that happened since I moved into town and we all became best friends.

Most of the misadventures weren't funny at the time, but now, looking back at it, we couldn't help but laugh. For instance, there was the time that Spencer broke Lucy's taillight and arrested me for it.

"I bet he was in love with you even then," Bridget said. "Even though he said you were a pain in the ass."

We talked about the cult that invaded the town, about the evil doctors at Westside Hospital, the airplane that crashed into my house, and of course, catching all the killers.

"It's a miracle you survived, Gladie," Lucy said. "I've never been happier in my life since I got you as a friend, no matter how dangerous it's been."

"Me, too," Bridget said.

I got up and went around the table, hugging my best friends. They had become more than just friends. They were my family. I was lucky to know that they would always be there for me, and I knew that I would be there for them, too.

Lucy dabbed at her eyes. "Damn it. I'm messing up my makeup. I don't know why I'm so emotional lately. I guess it's the wedding."

"I'm emotional, too," Bridget said, wiping her eyes under her glasses.

"It's an emotional time," Grandma said. "Love is the queen of emotions. And it's contagious."

I wondered if that was true about love. Was it catching? Was that why matchmaking was such a profitable business, because one love match sparked another?

Grandma passed a piece of paper across the table to me. "Bird made an appointment for you at Muffy & Dicks today, dolly. You're getting waxed and a deep conditioning treatment on your hair. I mean, the hair on your head. I don't think you'll have any other hair after they get done with you."

Ugh. Weddings were painful.

"Would you pick me up a honey baked ham while you're there?" Grandma asked. "I heard they sell humdingers."

Spencer walked in with Peter. They were both wearing jeans and Padres jerseys. Spencer's hair was mussed for a change, and he was giddy with the surprise of his older brother's visit. He looked five years younger and twenty times sexier.

"I'm stealing Spencer away for the day and pretty much all the evening," Peter announced. "I'll try to return him in relatively good shape. Oh, who am I kidding? He'll be in bad shape. But hopefully he won't have spinal fractures or brain damage. Although, how could you tell if he had brain damage?"

Spencer put Peter into a chokehold. Peter got out of it easily and threw Spencer down on the floor. They wrestled for another five minutes before they finally managed to leave.

"Boys," Grandma said, as if that said it all, and maybe it did.

"Good morning," Matilda said, meekly. She was

standing in the kitchen doorway, too timid to walk in without an invitation. Grandma put her arms around her and brought her into the room. I introduced her to my friends, and again, I was struck by how much I liked Matilda. She was a lot like me, but she had had a rough time.

And then there was her husband, Rockwell. It was still up in the air whether Rockwell was a good guy or a bad guy, but one thing I knew for certain: Rockwell was no Spencer.

"I'm lucky," I said, out loud. A heat crept up my face, and I was sure that I had turned crimson. I plopped down on my chair and stuffed a muffin in my face so that they wouldn't notice my blush.

Matilda seemed to notice my embarrassment and changed the subject. "I love this house," she said. "So much history. So cozy."

"Did you sleep?" my grandmother asked.

"I never sleep. Oh!" she exclaimed and checked the stove. "I turned it off," she said with a mix of relief and surprise. "I used it in the middle of the night and remembered to turn it off. That's great. I haven't had any episode since I've been here. Do you think the therapy worked?"

"No, I don't think the therapy did anything," I said.

"What kind of episodes?" Bridget asked.

"Forgetful episodes," Matilda explained. "But since I've been here, I've been on top of light switches, the refrigerator, and the stove. I wonder if I'm cured."

I had my own theory about Matilda's episodes, but I didn't have proof, yet.

"Sit down and have some breakfast," my grandmother urged her. "The coffeemaker's still hot. Drink a cup before it's too late."

"What do you mean, too late?" I asked.

All of a sudden, the refrigerator stopped making noise. The light over the stove turned off, and the coffeemaker clicked off, too.

"Too late," Grandma mumbled, taking a sip of her coffee.

"Did the electricity go off?" Lucy asked.

"Yes. We'll be fine for a few hours, but it's going to get hot later," Grandma said.

"It's going to last that long?" Bridget asked.

"Oh, yes," Grandma said.

"The town couldn't take the extra power use because of the heatwave," Bridget surmised. "It should go solar. Perhaps I should launch a renewable energy movement in Cannes."

I didn't ask the question I wanted answered. Tomorrow was my wedding. I hadn't been involved in the planning for it, but I was reasonably certain that we would need electricity.

Someone knocked on the front door. I moved to answer it, but my grandmother stopped me. "It's for Bridget," she explained.

Bridget left to answer it, and we finished breakfast. An hour later, my friends left. I got dressed in my dictator uniform and filled my pockets with official Fussia coins. The uniform was riper, and without the air conditioner, it was going to get worse.

"One last day of hail the sovereign leader," I reminded myself.

The body waxing wasn't as bad as I thought it was going to be. Luckily, the wax was already warm when the electricity went off. Melba the waxer woman used a new "painless" method, which wasn't painless at all, but at least it was fast. The deep conditioning treatment, however, was orgasmic. Melba massaged hot oil into my scalp, and I fell asleep. When I woke up, I was completely relaxed, and my hair was silky soft.

Melba was also a master butcher, it turned out, and when I left, she gave me a free rack of lamb. "It's the wedding special," she explained to me. "All brides get a rack of lamb with any waxing session."

Since the power was out, Muffy & Dicks was having a half-off meat sale before her stock went bad. I got Grandma's ham since it was already cooked, but I decided to gift Ruth the lamb because my grandmother's old refrigerator wouldn't keep it cold until the power came back on.

Next door, Tea Time was dead. Nobody wanted to drink a hot beverage in a stifling hot room. And it was definitely stifling hot. I slapped my butcher package on the bar and mopped the sweat off my forehead under my military cap.

"What's this?" she asked.

"A gift. You have a fancy freezer that stays cold, even when there's a power outage, right?"

"Seventy-two hours."

"Bon appétit. It's a rack of lamb."

"You want coffee? I can make you a cup of slow drip on my gas burner."

"No, thank you. I'm going home and sticking my head under the sink."

I dripped sweat onto the bar, and I wiped my brow with my sleeve.

"You're still wearing the fascist outfit? Have you defected to Fussia?" Ruth asked.

"No, but that reminds me," I said and tossed a handful of Fussia coins onto the bar. "Hail to our sovereign leader."

"Gladie, at some point you'll feel an irresistible urge to reflect on your life, but from me to you, when that happens, resist."

"I know. I try not to think too much about my life."

Ruth studied my face. After a moment, she scratched her nose. "You don't have a bad life, actually. As husbands go, the cop will probably be one of the better ones. And he looks at you like you're Princess Grace."

"Is that good?"

"Read a book, girl. Read a damned book. It's like you don't care a whit that you're a total ignoramus."

"Spencer's got me watching a lot of *Family Guy* and *The Simpsons*."

Ruth rolled her eyes. "Despite that, you've got a good man. And you own that beautiful house now. Although it's got some weird sex robot locked in it. When I walked by this morning, I could hear it trying to get out."

"It's on a lease. At some point, someone'll pick it up." At least I hoped someone would. I didn't know what Spencer had planned for the sex robot. We were moving tomorrow, and the robot was locked in our new house. The robot seemed very attached to Spencer, and I didn't want to have to fight it for my husband. It would win, hands down.

When I left Tea Time, I looked across the street at the two shops that were now the country of Fussia. The dictator wasn't outside, yelling at people. Instead, his country was quiet, but I didn't put it past him to be spying on me through the darkened windows to make sure that I was complying with our deal.

I walked home, sweating gallons through the heavy, wool uniform. With the electricity out, the whole town was quiet. The townspeople were probably soaking in cold tubs or lying on their beds, praying for a breeze.

The heatwave was getting worse. It was about five degrees hotter than it was yesterday. By the time I got home, I was already taking the uniform off, and as I walked in the door, I was quickly stripping down to my underwear and bra.

I found my grandmother in the kitchen. "We're all set for tomorrow," she said, handling a pile of paper. The wedding plans. They were more detailed than D-Day.

I sat next to her and took a deep breath. The house was warming up fast, but it was twenty degrees cooler than outside. "I'm so sorry, Grandma. I didn't help at all. I put the whole wedding on you."

"No, you didn't. I delegated. I know that you wanted a small wedding, but I turned it into the town's wedding. I didn't do a damned thing except to say no to the over the top stuff."

"Oh, please. It's going to be the most over the top wedding in history."

Grandma had a twinkle in her eye. "There might be a few surprises."

The truth was that I hadn't thought much about my wedding. I figured it would be a social obligation that I would have to get through and nothing more. It was the after-the-wedding part that I had focused on. Would marriage change my relationship with Spencer? Once I had committed to him in writing, would I want to escape, like I had escaped hundreds of jobs in my life?

Would I fail Spencer?

Would I want to fail Spencer?

Even though I was in my bra and panties, worrying was making me sweat even more. "I'm going to take a nap," I told her.

Grandma squeezed my hand. "No, dolly. It's time to deal with Matilda. It's time to take her home."

"Now?"

"Now."

CHAPTER 16

You have to kiss a lot of frogs before you get a prince. You've heard this bubbe-meise before. Right, dolly? I'll tell you a little story. When I was a young woman, men were all over me. They wouldn't leave me alone! I was a looker, you see, and I knew how to dress. The frogs and princes wanted me bad. One day, I was sitting at the Pietastic restaurant on Main Street where Saladz is now, and a real frog started to hit on me. "Hey, good lookin'," he said. Oy! Such a frog you've never seen in your life. "I'm busy," I spat back at him. He wouldn't take the hint. "What's a hot stuff cutie like you doing in a place like this?" he asked. It went on like that for a long time. The frog kept trying, and I kept pushing him away. You'll never guess who that frog turned out to be, bubbeleh. Don't guess. I'll tell you who he was. Your grandpa! I bet you didn't see that coming, did you? Yep, that frog turned out to be my frog. So, tell your matches not to hold out for a prince because sometimes a frog turns out to be a prince. And sometimes…a prince turns out to be a frog.

Lesson 7, Matchmaking advice from your Grandma Zelda

Matilda wasn't thrilled to be returning home. "I don't think Rockwell will make me go back to that place," she said hopefully, chewing on a fingernail.

"I'll tell him what a nightmare it was," I said. "You won't have to go back."

"I'm thinking clearer. I haven't had one episode all day. I feel sharp."

"We'll explain that to him."

I adjusted the air conditioning vents in the car to blast on my face. The sweat was finally starting to dry, and I dreaded getting out of the car and back into Matilda's furnace apartment. I brought a change of clothes with me, so that I could return the uniform on my way home after I dropped Matilda off. The thought of being free of the dictator uniform filled me with joy. At least the stress of that would be off me.

"It's been a long time since I've gone a whole day without an episode," Matilda continued. "I don't feel confused at all. My disorientation is completely gone."

I hoped the dictator didn't give me any grief about returning the uniform a couple hours early, but it was close enough. I had had enough. I had passed out all of the coins and told half of the town to hail the sovereign leader. My work for the land of Fussia was over, as far as I was concerned.

"When I was home, it was one thing after another,"

Matilda said. "I can't tell you how many times Rockwell caught the oven on or the lights. Even Fanta would catch it for me. Practically every time she came over, she found something crazy that I had done. In fact, when Rockwell wasn't there, she was the one to help me."

Matilda's voice drifted off. I snapped out of my selfish thoughts about clothes.

"Wait a second," I said. "What're you saying?"

"I don't know."

"But you're saying something."

"It's like it's at the outer edges of my brain, and I can't reach it."

I parked in front of Matilda's apartment building. As we walked inside, I put my arm around her. "When he sees the new you, it will all work out," I told her. "You're sharp. You're in control. Just have a discussion with him as his equal. You two will make this right together. Happiness is just around the corner."

I had no idea who was talking. I mean, the words were coming out of my mouth, but they sounded way too mature to be from me.

"I'm ready," Matilda said. "Whatever happens, I'll deal with it. For the first time in a long time, I feel like I can handle anything." She hugged me. "Thank you for everything. You're a great friend."

Since she didn't have her keys, Matilda knocked on the door, but Rockwell didn't answer. "Maybe he's out of town," she said.

"Don't worry. I can get us in."

I used my handy lock picks and opened the door. All of the windows were open for a change, but there was no breeze. "Are we in the right apartment?" I asked. It looked different, but I couldn't figure out why.

Matilda's mouth had dropped open. "This isn't my furniture. Some of it is, but most of it isn't. Hold on a second. I recognize that couch. And that coffee table. They're not mine, but I recognize them."

"I think Rockwell left the television on in the bedroom," I said. "I hear something."

Matilda's eyes grew wide, and she sucked in air. "We don't have a television in the bedroom," she hissed and marched to the bedroom, opened the door, and walked in.

"Oh my God!" Matilda shrieked. "Are you fucking joking? Is this a motherfucking joke? How dare you? How…oh, my God!"

I heard a crash as something hard hit the wall. Normally, I would have run in to see what was wrong, but something told me to give Matilda her privacy.

"Matilda, you're being irrational," I heard Rockwell say.

"Irrational?" Matilda shrieked. There was another loud crash against the wall. This time a woman screamed, and it wasn't Matilda.

As my grandmother would say: Oy vey.

Matilda ran out of the bedroom, and Rockwell was close on her heels. He was buck naked, and his weenie was flapping as he ran after his wife.

"You're supposed to be at the psychiatric facility," he said, wagging his finger at her. "Don't you want to get better, my love?"

"My… my… my?" she stuttered and exhaled in exasperation.

I wasn't totally sure what was going on, but Fanta came out of the bedroom after them wrapped in a sheet, and I figured it out. "You bitch! You broke my finger!" she screamed.

"They were naked," Matilda told me. "And they were doing it. Rockwell was on top. He told me that I have to be on top because he has a bad back. I guess his back isn't that bad!"

She picked up a knick-knack from the coffee table and threw it at Rockwell. He ducked before it could make contact.

"I want a divorce!" Matilda yelled.

Rockwell flinched. "It's nothing, my love. Don't you see how much I love you?" He embraced her. Matilda tried to push him away, but he was holding her in a death grip. "You're my soulmate. Fanta means nothing to me. We belong together."

I was frozen in place, unable to move, unable to say a word. Rockwell continued a long monologue about soulmates and how much they loved each other. He was very convincing, even though he was naked and the woman he had been naked with was standing two feet away, wrapped in a sheet with an afterglow on her cheeks.

I had no idea on what side Matilda was going to land. It was hard to throw away a man who claimed to love you. But she was thinking clearer now, and I hoped that extended to her marriage. I could have kicked myself for not listening to my grandmother from the beginning. I should have pulled Matilda out of her apartment and marriage the first moment that Grandma told me to. It was time to do my job and be responsible.

"Matilda, let's go," I said.

"Mind your own business," Rockwell growled.

Matilda managed to finally extricate herself from his embrace. "I'll take my clothes and leave," she said.

"What clothes?" Fanta asked.

"Be quiet," Rockwell ordered. His voice was steely cold, and it scared me.

"She doesn't have clothes here, anymore. You know that," Fanta insisted.

"You got rid of my clothes?" Matilda asked. She was eerily calm, as if the answers clicked into place for her, even if they were hideous and traumatic. "Come on, Gladie. Let's get out of here."

We walked toward the door, but Rockwell pulled Matilda back. "You're not going to leave me," he threatened. "You're crazy. Everyone knows that. You tried to kill me, throwing things at me. I'll see that you're put away forever if you try to divorce me. Do you understand? You better change your mind now, or your life will be hell."

Matilda yanked her arm away. "My life's already hell," she said, and we left her apartment.

We walked to my car without turning around once. I drove two blocks away and pulled the car to the side of the road.

“Are you okay?” I asked Matilda. “I mean, I know you’re not okay. But are you okay with not being okay?”

“He got rid of my clothes. He got rid of me. I guess I should be glad he didn’t chop me up into little pieces like Fanta did with her husband.”

“Yeah, I guess so.” Boy, marriage was a tough racket. I was trying not to take it to heart. After all, Spencer wasn’t Rockwell.

But I was a lot like Matilda.

Matilda got a glint in her eye, and I recognized it. The look. The murder look. I had been accused of getting it every time I stumbled over a dead person. “Fanta’s husband,” Matilda breathed, looking over my shoulder. I turned around, but there was no one there. “Gladie, we have to prove that Fanta killed her husband. We found his wallet, remember?”

“And the boxes. Don’t forget the boxes.”

“Yes, the boxes.”

We didn’t get back to my grandmother’s house until late. With her life in the toilet, Matilda was determined to prove that her husband’s mistress had murdered her husband. I was up for proving it, too. Because of the week’s distractions, I hadn’t had a chance to think about Fanta’s husband, but now with Matilda on the hunt, I wanted to get to the bottom of those boxes as fast as possible.

We drove to Cannes Smiley Auto Wrecking, but it was

closed. "Look at that," Matilda said, pointing to a small sign attached to the fence surrounding the business. "Cannes Smiley Auto Wrecking was sold. I'll bet you that Fanta sold it out from under her dead husband. Fanta is getting rid of her husband in more than one way."

We were at a dead end with Chris's death, but we were going to have to give the investigation a twenty-four-hour hiatus while I got married. "I'm going to divorce his ass Monday morning at nine o'clock sharp," she said, as we drove back through town.

The irony of a matchmaker enthusiastically supporting a match's divorce just before she was getting married wasn't lost on me. I wasn't exactly going by the book.

Cannes was in total darkness because of the power outage. I parked in front of Fussia and changed out of the uniform in the car. Wearing shorts and a tank top and carrying the uniform, I knocked on the fence, but the dictator didn't come out. I was relieved because I didn't want to see him. I draped the uniform and hat over the fence and finally went home.

I tossed and turned in my bed, but I couldn't sleep. The house was unbearably hot, and Spencer was still at his stag party, making my bed a lonely place. Or it could have been my impending wedding that was keeping me up. In only a few hours, I would be wearing my great-great-grandmother's wedding dress and walking down the aisle in front of the entire town to commit to Spencer until I died.

Yeah, it might have been the wedding that was keeping me up.

Downstairs, the front door opened, and I heard heavy footsteps on the floor. "Just a few more steps, little brother," I heard.

I got up and went downstairs. Peter was holding Spencer up. The love of my life was plastered and only half-conscious.

"Do you need help?" I asked Peter.

"I got this, little sister," he said and lugged Spencer upstairs. In my bedroom, Peter plopped Spencer onto the bed, and we worked to take off his shoes.

"She's so beautiful," Spencer moaned with his eyes closed.

"He's been going on like this for a while," Peter whispered to me. "Gladie this. Gladie that."

"Me?" I asked.

"Her hair says, 'I'm Gladie's hair!' It yells just like that," Spencer continued, talking into his pillow. I touched my hair. He was right. My hair had a mind of its own and probably a mouth, too.

"I love watching her. Not in a kinky stalker way. All right. All right. Yes, in a kinky stalker way. I love how she bites her lip when she's concentrating. And Peter, she blushes all the time. All I need to do is smile at her, and her face turns red. How sexy is that?"

Peter smiled at me, and I blushed.

We had managed to remove Spencer's shoes, but his clothes were more difficult. Spencer was a big man, and he was more or less dead weight in his current condition, lying on his stomach. Peter and I stood over him, but Spencer obviously wasn't aware of where he was or that I was in the room.

"When I'm not with her, I'm thinking about her," Spencer continued into his pillow. "Ever since the first moment I saw her on that telephone pole, I wanted to see more of her. And she makes me crazy! I love how she makes me crazy. Crazy with the murder mystery thing. No woman in the world has stumbled over more dead bodies than the woman I love. And I love her, bro. I love her. I ache with it. When she's in my arms, it's like the world's a good place, you know? And we both know the world's a miserable place, but not with Gladie in it. Not with my Pinky in this world. The world's a fucking utopia with my Pinky in it. I love my Pinky."

"He means me," I whispered to Peter.

"I know," he whispered back.

"My whole life," Spencer continued. "I'm going to spend my whole life with the most beautiful, wonderful woman on the planet. What did I do right in my life to get so lucky?"

My eyes filled with tears, and I choked up with emotion. Spencer often told me he loved me, but it was a gift to hear it this way, when he didn't know I was there to hear it.

"When I'm not with her, I want to be with her. When I'm with her, I never want to leave her. It's not just sex, bro, even though she has the finest ass. The. Finest. Ass. But it's more than bumping uglies. It's about her, Peter. It's about *her.*"

"She's special," Peter said, smiling at me.

"If anything happened to her, I would die. Bro, I can't let anything bad happen to her. I can't. It took so long to get her. Losing her would kill me."

"You won't lose her," Peter told him while looking at me. I nodded. Spencer wouldn't lose me. I was his forever.

CHAPTER 17

A matchmaker's goal is making a love match. The love is the happy ending. The marriage, the wedding are something different. A wedding can be the culmination of a true love match. It can also be the culmination of a woman's dream to have a big party and a pretty dress. So, we don't mess around with weddings. We don't push marriage. We push love. I'm not knocking marriage, bubbeleh. I'm not saying that weddings can't be wonderful. I'm not saying that at all. Emes, my hand to God, sometimes a wedding is the emblem of love. Such a great love that it must be shared with friends and family. When two people come together under the chuppah and they face each other, they become one in that very moment. The rabbi or the priest or the justice of the peace are just icing on the cake. The vows are secondary. The standing together is the main thing, dolly. It's the showing up. It's the being there for each other. It's the looking into each other's soul and claiming it, promising to honor, cherish, and protect that soul with all the love in your heart. When you find a match who will do that honestly and willingly…well, then, it's the happy ending of happy endings.

Lesson 136, Matchmaking advice from your Grandma Zelda

I woke up with a start and a hand over my eyes. "Don't look. Don't look," I heard my best friend Bridget tell me.

"What's going on?"

"It's your wedding day, and you and Spencer aren't allowed to see each other, or you'll have bad luck. I don't believe in the patriarchal mythology that binds a woman in servitude to a man for the rest of her life. And I definitely don't believe in hocus pocus wedding traditions. But this is so romantic! Don't peek!"

I heard Spencer struggling. "Ooph! Ugh!" The bed bounced up and down.

"Don't struggle, or I'll pound you one," a man said in a gruff voice and a thick New York accent.

"Listen to him, Spencer. I brought three of my guys with me. You don't have a chance in hell against them."

"Is that you, Uncle Harry?" I asked with Bridget's hands still plastered over my eyes.

"Hey there, Legs. Cute PJ's. Lucy says Spencer can't see you until the wedding, so that's what we're doing."

The bed bounced around, and I heard the unmistakable sound of knuckles against flesh. "Stop struggling!" another man shouted.

"Ooph! Ugh!" Spencer cried, again.

Crack! From the sounds, I could tell that punches were being thrown, willy-nilly. Spencer seemed to be giving as good as he got, even though he probably had the world's worst hangover.

"Sit on him! Sit on him! Stick a knee in his kidney!" one of Harry's goons ordered.

"Ooph! Ugh!" Spencer cried, again.

"Maybe you should just let him up," I suggested. "He won't peek. I don't think you have to fight him into submission."

"It's personal, now, Pinky," Spencer said. His voice was barely audible. Between the beating and the hangover, he was a shell of a man. I was secretly relieved. This way, he wouldn't be prettier than I was on my wedding day.

"Don't mess with that shit," another man yelled. "Uppercut the dude and do it fast."

Crack!

"Mazel tov!" Uncle Harry cheered. "Isn't that what your people say, Legs?"

"I'm not sure they say it under these circumstances," I replied.

"It's almost over," Bridget told me. "They're carrying him out of the room now."

"Did they knock him out?"

"No, he's just tied up and gagged. It's all good." The door clicked closed, and Bridget removed her hand. "It's your wedding day," she gushed. "I'm so excited."

"Where's baby Jonathan?"

"Home with Jackson. I'm part of the pre-prep patrol."

I sat up in bed.

"What's the pre-prep patrol? Is there a prep patrol?"

Bridget counted on her fingers. "First there's the pre-prep patrol to make sure you wash and eat, but that you don't eat too much. The pre-prep patrol is me and Zelda. Then comes the prep patrol. That's Bird and her employees to buff and polish you. Then, comes the moral support patrol. That's me, again, and Lucy. She's worried about sweating, so, she's coming at the last minute. Then, it's the words of wisdom patrol, which is Zelda. And then, we head off to the wedding area, and you come last in the limo."

"That's a lot of patrols. There's a limo?"

"I forgot about Dave. He's dressing you."

"Who's Dave?"

"Dave's Dry Cleaning and Tackle shop."

"Oh, that's right," I said, remembering. "Dave."

The morning went by in a haze. The windows were all open, but there wasn't a breath of fresh air to be had. It was like Cannes had been sealed into a sauna dome. But with all the heat, I wasn't uncomfortable. I wasn't sweating. Instead, even without much sleep, I felt totally refreshed.

Bridget gave me a box of old-fashioned lavender-scented body powder to use after my shower, and when I stepped out of the bathroom, there was a new silk robe waiting for me. Bridget kissed me on the cheek.

"I love you, Gladie," she said and wiped a tear from her eye under her glasses.

"I love you, too." I hugged her hard. "You're the best friend I've ever had."

We stood for a long time, embracing. There was something magical about being loved and cared for, and in that moment, I felt both so acutely that I didn't want to let the moment pass without relishing it a little longer. A little more intently.

Downstairs, my grandmother was waiting in the kitchen. This morning, there was no big spread. No feast brought in by Grandma's friends to celebrate my wedding. It was just Grandma, Bridget, and me having our regular breakfast.

My grandmother was dressed in her blue housecoat, and her plastic slip-on slippers that clacked on the linoleum floor as she walked. "I'll make the coffee, bubbeleh," she told me. "You put the bagels in. Matilda left early to go hunting, she said."

We made breakfast, just like we did every morning, except we used the gas oven instead of the toaster and the gas burner to make coffee the old-fashioned way. While the bagels were toasting, I took the orange juice, milk, and cream cheese out of the refrigerator. Bridget set the table. Then, we sat down and looked at each other. Grandma took my hand and brought it to her lips, kissing it, gently.

"My favorite granddaughter," she said.

"My favorite grandmother," I said and kissed her back.

It was a lovefest morning, and nothing could ruin the mood.

"Open this damned door! I can't stand here all day, you know! I haven't had cartilage in my knees since Carter was president. That's President Carter for your information, Gladie. You ignorant non-reader!" Ruth was at the back door, kicking it.

"Ruth is on the pre-prep patrol?" I asked my grandmother.

"In her way."

I opened the door. Ruth was carrying four to-go cups. "You didn't show up at Tea Time," she complained. "I thought you would want your latte. What's with you, girl?"

She looked honestly hurt that I hadn't visited her the morning of my wedding. "I'm sorry, Ruth. So much going on."

Ruth sputtered and coughed. "Too much going on to get the best latte in town?" She put the to-go cups down on the table. "It's not my normal latte. I couldn't do that without power, but it's better than anything Zelda can make."

"That's true," Grandma said, spreading cream cheese on her bagel.

Ruth sat down. "So, you didn't want old Ruth to be part of your wedding, is that it? I guess I'm not hipster enough for you." She shot a look at Bridget, who was wearing a conservative blue dress and her hoot-owl glasses.

"I'm not a hipster, Ruth," Bridget told her.

"Young people. Hunh," Ruth said.

She was upset. Hurt. I had hurt her feelings. I took a sip of the latte. "Delicious, Ruth. Even without electricity, you make the best coffee in town."

Ruth smoothed her shirt and adjusted her seat. "I could have told you that. To think you were going to get married without your coffee."

"I had a lapse in judgment. My doctor says I need more magnesium. It might be that."

"It's no wonder with the way you eat," Ruth sneered, more or less appeased by my excuse.

After breakfast, Bird showed up with her team, right on time. I didn't know who had organized my wedding, but it was being pulled off with military precision.

They set up in the kitchen, where they had given my grandmother her weekly beauty treatments for years when she was a shut-in. Bird dropped a box full of tools that looked like Medieval torture devices onto the table.

"No electricity," she said. "I had to drive to the Beauty Museum in San Bernardino and borrow hundred-year-old beauty implements. Zelda, I need to use the oven. I have to heat these cast iron tongs."

"Uh," I said.

"That damned dictator," Ruth complained.

I flinched. "What about him?" I asked, crossing my fingers that I wasn't in trouble, again.

"He sabotaged our electrical system. That's why we don't have power," Ruth said.

"Do you know that for sure?" Bridget asked.

Ruth squinted at her and frowned. "I may not be a hipster, but I do know a thing or two about the happenings in this town."

"I don't doubt it," Bird said, pulling the tongs out of the oven with oven mitts. "I heard he's a lunatic from Lake Havasu. He won a hundred thousand dollars with a scratch off, and he went downhill from there."

"I heard that the utility terrorism is just the beginning," the pedicurist announced. "I was doing Margie's nails this morning for the wedding, and she said the dictator has threatened all kinds of things."

"What kind of things?" I asked, thinking about my wedding.

"Margie said he's threatening 'mayhem.' That's bad," the pedicurist announced as she put my feet in a tub of water.

"This town *is* mayhem," Ruth grunted.

"These damned ancient hairstyling tools," Bird complained. "At least my diet is perfect for this power outage. Raw food diet. One of the good things about it is that I don't need electricity to eat." She dropped the tongs on the floor and swore in exasperation. When she leaned over to retrieve them, she farted. "But the diet isn't perfect," she added and farted again.

I was buffed and polished, and my hair looked like I was a fairy princess after Bird got done with me. After I thanked her, Bird left to get ready for the wedding herself. As she left, Lucy walked in. She was wearing a chenille robe, and she was carrying her dress in a garment bag.

"I'm thinking cool thoughts, darlin'," she said. "I refuse to sweat. Lucy Smythe does not sweat, do you hear me?"

"Absolutely."

The three of us went upstairs to my bedroom. Lucy and Bridget got dressed, but I was still waiting for Dave from Dave's Dry Cleaning and Tackle shop to arrive with my dress. Once Lucy was dressed, she gave me a light hug.

"You're going to be the belle of the ball, darlin'," she told me. "I can't say much more because I'll start crying and my makeup will be ruined. But this is good. You're doing the right thing. You're going to be very happy."

"I think so, too," Bridget said. "Spencer's a wonderful man, even if he refuses to implement my suggestions for changes to his holding cell."

My grandmother stood in the doorway, and Lucy and Bridget took that as their cue to leave. "We'll see you there," Lucy said, and they left.

"You look beautiful, Grandma," I told her.

She was wearing a tasteful white suit that fit her perfectly. "It's a little loose, but it'll do. I'm so happy to see you married today, dolly. It's going to be perfect."

"It is?"

"Oh, yes. It's going to be the ceremony that you want."

Downstairs, the door opened and closed. "Zelda, should I come up?" a man called.

"Yes, we're ready for you," she called back. "Here comes the dress," she told me and smiled. "Don't be afraid."

I was afraid. What if I didn't want to say yes to the dress? It was too late to back down, now.

Dave walked into the room, holding a large garment

bag. "Hardest thing I've ever done," he said. "The beading alone took me weeks to deal with."

"But it's done now, and it's perfect," my grandmother assured me.

Dave unzipped the gown and hung it on a portable rod. "I looked into it, Zelda," he said. "It's worth a fortune. The Met would love to have it in its collection."

The dress was an Edwardian ivory-colored gown with light blue beading and the most stunning lacework I had ever seen. "The tailor to the Czarina of Russia immigrated to the United States in 1901 and found himself in Cannes," Grandma explained. "My great-grandmother was at least sixty years old by then and a widow, but she knew a good thing when she saw it. He might have been a tailor, but he was her prince. He made the gown for her wedding with, as you can tell, a lot of love."

"It's exquisite," I breathed.

Dave took a deep breath and exhaled. "I'm so relieved," he said.

My grandmother shooed him out and closed the door. "Here we go." She helped me get into the dress, and I looked at myself in the mirror. It fit perfectly, just as my grandmother had promised.

"I'm beautiful," I said.

"Don't cry."

"I'm like an actress in a period movie. I'm like a princess."

"Like a czarina. Here, you'll need these." She gave me a pair of long, light blue gloves that went above my elbows.

"These I got new."

"Thank you," I croaked.

"Don't cry. We have some time before you can cry."

The limo drove my grandmother and me far up into the mountains, further than I had ever gone. The road wound up, first left, then right, and there was dense forest on either side of the road. The limo driver took it slow on the curves so that we wouldn't crash. Twenty-five minutes later, we arrived at the top of a mountain to a grassy plateau. A large, blue double-door was set up outside, blocking my view.

The driver opened my door and helped me out. My grandmother smoothed out my dress. My old match, Belinda Womble, handed me a bouquet. "Don't worry. They're not poisonous," she told me. Belinda had a love of poisonous flowers, which had gotten her into trouble a few months before.

"They're beautiful," I said.

"Don't cry yet," Grandma whispered.

The sound of violins filled the air. They were followed by more instruments and then a woman's beautiful voice, singing in Italian.

"It's Audra MacDonald singing with the Los Angeles Philharmonic," my grandmother informed me, taking my arm. "Esa-Pekka Salonen owed me one."

The double doors opened, and we walked forward, arm-in-arm, as Audra sang, and the L.A. Philharmonic played. We walked toward an elaborate canopy that was covered in ivy and flowers. The canopy was surrounded by a circle of chairs in rows. There wasn't an empty seat. The entire town had shown up. I recognized most of them, and I couldn't help but wave to many of them.

As I passed Remington, he winked at me and nodded. I felt myself blush immediately. Meryl waved at me, and Bird pointed at my hair and gave the okay signal with her fingers. Even Darth Vader had shown up.

But the guests didn't hold my attention. Not after I saw Spencer.

He was standing under the canopy with a very old rabbi. He wiped at his eyes, which were focused on me.

"No best man or maid of honor," Grandma told me, as we walked up the aisle. "I thought it would be better that way. The rabbi married your grandfather and me. It took some doing to track him down, but he was tickled pink to do the ceremony. Here we are."

My grandmother kissed me, and Spencer held out his hand for me. I took it.

"Are you kidding me?" he said, gently, as I took my place next to him.

That's when I started to cry.

Audra stopped singing, and the symphony stopped playing. Spencer kissed my gloved hands. I was having an out-of-body experience, like this wasn't happening to me but to another woman in a gorgeous dress, marrying a handsome man in an Armani suit.

"Pinky, look at me," Spencer said, quietly. We locked eyes. He searched my face, as if he was memorizing every plane and every angle. "You are my everything," he said, finally, not in planned vows but an impromptu declaration of his love for me before the wedding ceremony began in front of everyone.

Including his mother.

"I'll tell you a secret," he continued. "I don't deserve you. I don't deserve any part of you. If I have your heart, it's because I stole it, ruthlessly. I've known you for a year, and during that time, I've plotted and planned and done everything in my power to make you give me a chance. And to my great surprise and my infinite joy, you did. I've built you a house, and it's not enough. Everything I am and ever will be, I share with you, and it's not enough. I will love you until I grow old and turn to dust. But it won't be enough. How could I ever be enough when you are everything, and I am just a man?"

My tears streamed down my face, and he wiped them away with a handkerchief.

"So, here under the sky and in front of everyone, I give to you body and soul and let it be known that Spencer Bolton loves Gladys Burger and always will."

"I love you, too, Spencer," I declared and hugged him tight. "But don't call me Gladys," I whispered in his ear.

The rest of the ceremony went by in a cloud of hormones, and I didn't come to until Spencer kissed me and broke the glass under his foot. The L.A. Philharmonic played while we ate lunch, which had been brought in from San Diego. We sat at long tables. I sat next to Spencer. His mother was at my right hand, and Grandma and my mother were at Spencer's left.

"I'm so happy for you," my mother told me and dabbed at her eyes.

"I make good banana bread," Spencer's mother told me. "I'll send you a banana bread. Would you like that?"

"I love banana bread," I said.

"I'll send you one. And a sour cream cake, too."

"You're in," Peter mouthed in my direction and gave me the thumbs up.

Spencer and I ate for a few minutes, and then we made the rounds. The mayor was sitting next to Ruth, who looked like she wanted to stab him in the face with her fork. "Who the hell brings a donkey to a wedding?" she demanded.

"Dulcinea isn't at the wedding," the mayor insisted. "She's in a comfortably aerated trailer behind my rented truck in the parking area."

"Lunatic," Ruth said.

"You don't expect me to leave her unattended when there're donkey stealers in this town, do you?" he asked. "Besides, Gladie, I've taken it on myself to put the gifts in the back of my truck. Zelda had them out on a table, but I didn't think that was safe."

"My grandmother's antique tea set is with those gifts, and if something happens to it, I'll kill you," Ruth warned the mayor.

"You gave me your grandmother's antique tea set?" I asked her.

Ruth looked down at her food. "You can use it for coffee, too," she muttered.

"How's it going?" Harry asked at another table. "Your eye looks good. I thought you would have a shiner."

Spencer touched his side. "I think I have two broken ribs, but your hangover cure worked wonders."

"One ounce of Tabasco and a salami sandwich works every time," Harry said, happily. "Not grocery store salami. The good kind of salami from Chicago. The kind you dry for weeks, hanging from the ceiling. Legs, you look good enough to eat. Even better than a salami. By the way, Lucy and I gave you two a honeymoon cruise. The tickets are in an envelope in the moron mayor's truck."

"A cruise?" I asked. "I've never been on a cruise."

I hugged Harry, and I was surprised when he blushed. "It's nothing. A friend of a friend gave me the tickets, and I'm just passing it on. Nothing to make a big deal about. I think we gave you a toaster, too."

Most of the guests wanted to tell me what they had given us for our wedding. I had made out like a bandit, and I couldn't wait to get home and open the gifts.

"What're you doing about that dictator?" Meryl demanded when we stopped by her table. "I heard he was responsible for the power outage, and he's skipped town."

"I've got Margie on it," Spencer told her. "But if he's

skipped town, I'll hand it over to the FBI."

After we made our rounds, we sat back down. The champagne was flowing freely, and Bridget and Lucy had pushed their way next to me to tell me how gorgeous I was. Spencer and Peter were in deep conversation about the best way to kill a man with their bare hands and toasting each other with champagne. A waiter refilled their glasses. He looked familiar, but I couldn't place him, which wasn't new. I came in contact with a lot of people in my job, but I wasn't good at names and faces.

After a few hours, the party wound down. The symphony went back to Los Angeles, and it was time for Spencer and me to leave and move into our dream house. Spencer's father clinked his spoon against his glass and asked the crowd to be quiet so that the bride and groom could say a few words.

"You first, Spencer," I said.

"Okay," he said and then his eyes rolled back in his head, and he passed out onto his plate.

"Peter, what's wrong with Spencer?" his father asked.

"Don't worry," Peter said and then his eyes rolled back in his head, and he passed out onto his plate, too.

I froze in place, waiting for the domino effect of the rest of the guests to fall onto their plates, but it ended with Spencer and Peter.

"What's going on?" Spencer's mother demanded.

"Mayhem!" shouted the waiter.

That's when I recognized him. He wasn't in his usual

uniform, so he looked different, but it was him. It was the dictator.

With surprising speed and strength, he threw Spencer over his shoulder. “I roofied them!” he announced with glee and ran away with my husband.

CHAPTER 18

Easy come. Easy go. Pass it on, bubbeleh.

Lesson 138, Matchmaking advice from your Grandma Zelda

"What's with this town?" Spencer's father asked, as we watched Spencer fade into the distance on the shoulder of his lunatic kidnapper.

"I think it's called small-town charm," Lucy said.

"I think it's called the Bermuda Triangle of crazy," Spencer's mother said.

"I think it's called the deterioration of labor rights and civil responsibility," Bridget said.

Remington was the first to jump into action, running after Spencer and the dictator.

"He's taking my truck!" the mayor yelled. "My Dulcinea!"

"My grandmother's antique tea set!" Ruth yelled.

It was a free-for-all. A good portion of the wedding party ran after Spencer to save him on what is supposed to be the happiest day of his life. Another portion of the guests ran after their wedding gifts. And another portion ran for no particular reason.

In hindsight, it would have been a much better outcome if they had all let Remington handle it on his own. But we didn't let him handle it on his own. The dictator stole the mayor's truck, and before Remington could get to his car and chase after Spencer, the mayor stole Remington's car.

"That's an official police vehicle!" Remington shouted.

"Don't worry, Dulcinea! Daddy's coming for you!" the mayor yelled and peeled out in the direction of his stolen truck.

Ruth jumped into her car and drove after them.

It was mayhem. One car after another peeled out and drove after Spencer and his kidnapper at a high speed.

"My husband! I've been married for three hours!" I moaned.

A Nissan Altima stopped in front of me, and the window opened. It was Matilda. She had managed to get her car back, and I wondered how the rest of her hunting had gone. "I'll go after him," she announced. "I've got your back, Gladie!"

"What about me? Aren't you going to take me?" I called, but she was already gone. "My husband's been kidnapped!" I yelled and stomped my foot on the dirt parking area.

"Come with me!" my mother yelled. She had Grandma,

Spencer's mother Lily, and Bridget with her.

"I'll get him," Uncle Harry announced. "Come on, Lucy." They hopped into his Bentley and drove away.

"What about me? What about me?" I moaned.

My mother grabbed my hand. "Come on. I'll take you."

Grandma, Bridget, Lily, and I followed her to the pot bus. "Rev up this marijuana behemoth, and let's get my baby boy," Lily demanded.

"I'll show you how it's done," my mother announced and started the motor. As soon as the engine turned over, she peeled out of the parking area and hit the winding path like a maniac.

"How's Peter?" I asked Lily.

"Okay. He's coming around a little. James is with him. Can you make this go faster, Luann?"

I sat in the first row of seats and held on tight. The lavender mood lighting wasn't reducing the stress level. Ahead of us, car after car was running off the road into the forests. My mother wasn't kidding about knowing how to drive the bus. She took each hairpin turn like a professional racecar driver.

As we reached the top of a steep hill, I saw Uncle Harry ahead of us, chasing after Matilda, who was chasing after Ruth, who was chasing after the mayor, who was chasing after the dictator. My mother put her foot on the gas and sped up.

"So, this is how I die," Lily said. "Gladie, before we die, I want you to know that I'm happy to have you as my daughter-in-law. I'm lucky to have you. Had you, I mean."

"This isn't how you die," my grandmother told her. "I

know how you die, and this isn't it."

"Ohhhhh!" we yelled in unison, as my mother took another turn, and we were thrown to the right.

"This is very exciting," Bridget said. "It's like an action movie with an all-female cast of heroes. If we live through this, I'm going to write to all of the major Hollywood studios and remind them of the sad lack of good parts for women."

"We're heading into town," I said. "We survived the mountain!"

"Hold on tight, dolly," Grandma said.

"Uh oh, Bridget said. "That doesn't sound good."

"The madman is heading for the Historic District," my mother announced.

"Don't let him out of your sight," I urged her.

"Don't worry. He's easy to spot. There are two cop cars heading right for him."

Sure enough, Spencer's police force had gotten word of his kidnapping and were zeroing in on the mayor's truck. The bus's height was great for seeing ahead of us.

"Look, they've got him cornered," Spencer's mother said.

"No, he's turning onto Zelda's street," Bridget said.

There was a squeal of rubber, and the truck turned just in time to miss the squad cars. "Holy cow, the donkey," Bridget said, pointing.

The well-aerated donkey trailer's hitch freed itself from the truck, and it rolled off the street into a front yard. The mayor braked hard, and tried to turn, presumably to get to his beloved donkey, but Ruth was right behind him and rammed him hard.

"Holy cow, it's the demolition derby," my mother said. We were approaching the scene fast.

"The cars are hooked together," Spencer's mother said, aghast. "Their bumpers are locked together. They're heading for your house, Zelda."

"What are the odds?" Bridget said. "I hope they don't hurt your house, Zelda."

Matilda was a better driver, and she swerved out of the way, but so did the police cars. Just then a Burger Boy eighteen-wheeler turned onto the street.

"Holy smokes, even I didn't see that one coming," my grandmother said.

Then, it happened. The dictator swerved out of the way of the truck, but he overcompensated and flew onto the sidewalk.

"This isn't happening," I said.

"What? What isn't happening?" Spencer's mother asked.

"That," I said, pointing.

She followed my finger to her baby's dream home, custom-made for his new bride, the biggest house on the street, and it had a pool.

The cursed house.

The mayor's truck was the first to hit it. The maniac dictator had turned so sharply that the truck hit the house right through the front door, as if it was dropping by to visit.

One of the cop cars almost collided head-on with the

mayor in Remington's stolen car, which was attached to Ruth's car, but the cop car managed to miss it. "And there goes another one!" Bridget yelled, as it slammed into the side of the house.

"I think that was my cedar walk-in closet," I said.

The Burger Boy truck's brakes squealed, and smoke billowed out from under it. My mother slowed the bus down. "Uh oh," she said.

The truck started to jackknife. The mayor and Ruth swerved around it, and they jumped the sidewalk like a flying train of expensive cars and landed through the other side of my new house.

"That was the kitchen. It had a double-sized refrigerator," I said.

"It's like the house is a magnet," Bridget exclaimed. "Every car is irresistibly attracted to it. It's like an episode of the *X-Files.*"

The Burger Boy truck jackknifed and sideswiped the other cop car with it, tossing it like it was a puck in a hockey game.

"It's like bugs drawn to a bug light. Zap! Zap! Zap!" my mother yelled.

Matilda's car screeched loudly as she tried to get around the truck, but it was no use. She went over the sidewalk, too.

"Matilda missed the house," I said hopefully. "Nope. Nope. She got the back corner. That's Spencer's man cave."

"Maybe the basement is intact," Spencer's mother said, hopefully.

The truck went over on its side, landing on the front yard. Uncle Harry hit it and kept going into the house. "And there's the master bedroom," I noted.

The back of the truck broke open and tons of French fries flew out, like it was raining delicious, salty carbohydrates. My mother stopped the bus, parking it in front of my grandmother's house.

"Zelda, your house is fine," she assured her. The bus was fine, too. We piled out and looked across the street.

"I love you. You're so sexy," someone said.

"Who said that?" Bridget asked.

"I'm going to please you all night," the voice said, again.

From the rubble of my custom-made house, the sex robot emerged, holding Spencer, who was struggling against her. "Let me down! My house! My house!"

"You make me hot," the robot told him. Spencer pushed away from the robot and dropped to the ground.

"My house," he moaned. "How is this possible?"

A fire truck and two ambulances raced down the street toward our dream home. Miraculously, the mayor, Ruth, Matilda, the two cops, Uncle Harry, Lucy, and the Burger Boy truck driver all escaped unharmed. They stumbled out of the house, looking confused.

"What happened?" the mayor asked.

"I'll tell you what happened," Ruth growled and hit him with her clutch purse. "You braked for your stupid donkey, that's what happened."

I walked across the street to Spencer. "Are you all right?"

I asked him.

He kissed me. "Our house is gone."

"No, it's not," I assured him, rubbing his back. "It's just a little damaged. The bones are still there. It's still intact."

We looked across the street at our custom-made dream house. Six cars had crashed through it, a Burger Boy truck was lying on the front lawn, and it was covered in French fries. But it still looked like a house. The roof was intact and some of the walls were still upright.

"I guess you're right," Spencer said. "We can renovate, I guess."

As we stood across the street, there was a loud creaking noise, and our dream house's roof caved in, landing with a huge crash.

"My television," Spencer moaned. "My beautiful television."

"That house is cursed," Uncle Harry announced. "There's no other explanation."

Spencer held me in his arms. "Pinky, one minute the house was there, and then it wasn't. There. Not there. There. NOT THERE. What happened? What happened?"

"The maniac dictator drugged you and kidnapped you and Dulcinea. The rest sort of just happened."

"I'm going to kill him," Spencer said.

"Don't. If you do, he'll make you wear the uniform."

Spencer dealt with the first responders. There were going to be a million reports to write. My mother offered to drive everyone home in her pot bus.

"The wedding was beautiful," I said.

"I told you it would be perfect," my grandmother said.

"I'm sorry I missed it," Matilda said. "But I had a profitable morning. Oh! I'll be right back."

Matilda walked across the street.

"It really was a beautiful wedding," I told Grandma, as we watched Matilda circumvent the army of law enforcement and first responders and walk around to the back of what used to be my house.

"The pictures are going to come out great," my grandmother told me.

After a couple of minutes, Matilda walked back toward us, and she was carrying a metal box. "A box," I breathed. "One of Fanta's boxes. How did she get it?"

"Matilda has a gift," Grandma said. "Not our gift. A different one. A powerful one. She doesn't know about it, yet, though."

"I've been busy this morning," Matilda said, reaching us. "I went back to the car smashing place. Look what I found."

She opened the box and showed it to me. "What's that?" I asked.

"Is it alive?" Grandma asked.

"No," Matilda said. "It's dead. It used to be part of Fanta's husband, Chris. It's his nose. A small, English nose."

"What happened to his face?" my grandmother asked.

"That's what I asked Fanta," Matilda said and showed us the text messages on her phone. Matilda had threatened Fanta with ratting her out to the police. Fanta insisted that Chris was alive. After a few more of Matilda's texts, Fanta stopped insisting that Chris was alive and moved on to saying that she was innocent. Then, nothing.

"We've got her right where we want her," Matilda told me.

"We?"

"Don't you want to find justice for Chris?"

I didn't know Chris, but I was sorry that he had been chopped up into little pieces. And then there was my buttinski nature that wouldn't allow me to mind my own business. So, I guess I did want to find justice for Chris. But now wasn't a good time. My house had just been pulverized, and my new husband was probably going to need a Xanax IV drip.

"Don't you want to stick it to Fanta?" Matilda continued. "Don't you want to put her in prison for the rest of her life so that Rockwell never sees her naked, again?"

Matilda wanted that. She wanted that real bad, as far as I could tell.

"I feel responsible," Grandma said. "I made a bad match. I'll help you stick it to Fanta."

"You will?" I asked, surprised. "But you do love. You don't do murder."

My grandmother shrugged. "Maybe you're contagious."

Matilda's phone dinged. "She texted me again."

I read the text message. Fanta wanted to meet at the

mine. She was going to tell Matilda everything in exchange for the nose.

"Let's go," Grandma said. She walked up the driveway and opened the driver's door of my Oldsmobile Cutlass Supreme. "I'll drive," she announced.

I didn't have time to change out of my museum-quality wedding dress. Matilda was itching to get to the mine, and Grandma insisted that it was now or never.

"I have a feeling that never would be the better option," I said.

My grandmother drove us past the emergency vehicles toward the mine. "I'm a good driver," she said, running through a stop sign. "I don't know why they took away my license."

The old gold mine was the birthplace of Cannes. Gold was discovered there in the late 1900s, but it dried up quickly. It was now considered a historical landmark, but it was closed to the public because it wasn't safe.

Matilda pointed at a Toyota Camry. "That's her car. Park there."

My grandmother parked next to it, and I pocketed the keys. "You realize this is a trap, right?" I said.

"Of course it's a trap," Matilda said. "But we can take her. I'll go for her knees while you karate chop her neck."

"I don't know how to karate chop."

"I'll bite her," Grandma offered, happily. "I've got great choppers."

"You stay at the car, Grandma. Let Matilda and me handle this."

"No, Dolly. I'm supposed to go in the mine with you. It's my destiny."

"What does that mean?" I asked, alarmed.

"C'mon, let's get this bitch," Matilda said and marched toward the entrance of the mine.

"Stay behind me, Grandma," I told her.

Matilda turned the light on her phone, and I held on to my grandmother as we made our way deep into the mine over a rocky and uneven dirt path. My poor dress.

"Dave will clean it," my grandmother said, as if she had read my mind.

"Stop right there," we heard as we reached the inner recesses of the gold mine. It wasn't Fanta. It was a man, his voice steely and cold.

"Rockwell," Matilda said. "I knew you were going to help your murderous girlfriend."

Fanta stepped out from behind Rockwell. She didn't look like a confident, scheming killer. She looked scared. She looked like she didn't want to be there any more than I did.

"You can't protect her," I said. "We have proof of what she did."

"About that, we need it back," Rockwell said.

Matilda waved her hands in front of her. "Wait a second. Wait a second. It's you. You helped her kill Chris," she accused Rockwell.

"It was him," Fanta announced. "It was all him."

CHAPTER 19

Welcome to Zelda's Matchmaking, dolly! I'm so glad that you said yes and moved in with me. You have the gift, bubbeleh. As you know, you come from a long line of matchmakers, and you're the next in line. You're going to make beautiful love matches. Now, I have to warn you that there's a learning curve to this business, but I know that within a year, you'll be the queen of love. I've written this short book of matchmaking advice for you, but you don't need it. You've got the instinct, and my helpful hints aren't going to make a difference. But here are my little lessons. Take them or leave them. I love you, dolly. Don't forget…you have the gift. You can do this. With me or without me.

Lesson 1, Matchmaking advice from your Grandma Zelda

"I thought you were the perfect match. I'm so sorry that I was wrong," my grandmother told Rockwell.

"What're you talking about? We were the perfect match," he said.

"Ha!" Matilda barked.

"She was a gift. Perfect for our plans," he said.

"Not my plans," Fanta said. "I was fine the way we were."

"Shut up," Rockwell growled.

"I know what the plan was," Matilda said. "You gaslighted me so that you could get rid of me and be with your mistress."

"You figured out about the gaslighting?" Fanta asked.

"As soon as Gladie saved me and took me to Zelda's, I realized that I wasn't having any more episodes," Matilda said. "Then, I thought about it. All the times that Fanta came over, walked into the kitchen, and announced that I had left the oven on. You were in it together."

She was right. They had gaslighted her, but something was missing. Why would they kill Fanta's husband, but gaslight Matilda? If they wanted to be together, why didn't they just get divorced and marry each other? Why all the drama?

"You think you know so much," Rockwell sneered. "You were a pawn. A cog in the works. It was perfect. You still have no idea what was really going on."

"But Chris found out," Fanta said. "He wanted in on it."

"On what?" I asked.

"I know," Grandma said. "I don't understand why I didn't see it before. Rockwell's great aunt Liberty died. That must be it. She was a weird one, rich, and she had a thing about marriage. Am I right, Rockwell? She left you money in her will, but you had to be married? That would explain everything."

"Five years. I had to stay married for five years," Rockwell explained. "That bitch. Do you know how hard I have to bust my ass, making a living in sales? I'm on the road all the time. Do you know how many doors I've had slammed in my face? Do you know what that does to a man?"

"Turns him into murderer?" I asked. "That's what it does?"

"I didn't want to kill Chris," Rockwell insisted. "He made me do it."

"He found out about our affair, and he was blackmailing us," Fanta said. "He wanted a piece of the action. He was stirring up trouble."

"I get it, now," I said. "You two were already having an affair when Rockwell married Matilda. But Fanta was already married to Chris before that. Rockwell's rich old aunt dies and leaves him a bunch of money, but he has to get married and stay married for five years. He couldn't marry Fanta because there wasn't time for her to get divorced and marry him. So, he goes to my grandmother and gets matched on the double. Within a week, he was kosher. Married and ready to inherit."

"You're good at this," Fanta said.

"She has the gift," Grandma said. "And this isn't her first time. She has a lot of experience with murders."

"The gaslighting was simple," I continued. "Put Matilda away so that you're still officially married, but you don't actually have to live with her. When you killed Chris, that was just gravy and allowed you to finally be able to live with Fanta. Pretty simple. Usually, murderers are a lot more complicated."

"I think it's pretty complicated," Matilda said.

Grandma rubbed her temple. "Me, too. Love is so much simpler than murder."

"Well, this'll be simple," Rockwell said and pulled out a crowbar from behind his back. "I'm going beat you to death. Your bodies won't be found for years."

"Rockwell, sweetie, maybe we can do this a different way," Fanta said, much to her credit. "We could hop in the car and drive away. Somewhere where they won't find us."

"That sounds like a good plan to me," I said.

"I'll never stop looking for you. I'll bring you to justice if it's the last thing I do," Matilda threatened. Rookie mistake. Never tell a killer with a crowbar that you're going to hunt him down. Now Rockwell was determined to bash our brains in.

He raised the crowbar over his head. "This is too much for me," Fanta cried and ran for it. I guessed in her book, killing three unarmed women was a tad worse than chopping up her husband.

"Come back!" Rockwell called. "I'm doing this for you!"

The moment he was distracted, Matilda leaped for him and tried to get the crowbar away. But he was much too strong for her. He threw her off of him, and she lost her balance. She flew backward and hit her head hard on the wall of the mine.

"Gladie, help," Grandma moaned. I turned around to find her clutching at her chest with both hands and sinking to the ground. I helped her down gently, holding her in my lap. Even in the darkened mine, I could see that her face was ashen and scrunched up in pain.

"Is it another heart event?" I asked. She moaned and doubled over in agony. "Help! Call 911! Get help for my grandmother!"

But Rockwell wasn't going to help us. He was still determined to silence us forever. He raised the crowbar over his head and ran at us at full speed.

But the mine was dark, and the ground was rocky and uneven.

And sometimes, justice is swift and fair.

Rockwell tripped. As he fell to the ground, he swung his arms, trying to regain his balance. But he swung too wildly, and the crowbar caught a piece of his skull. Rockwell was unconscious before he hit the ground.

I turned my attention back to my grandmother. Her head had slumped back, and she was grabbing my hand.

"I'll get help," I told her.

"No. I need to talk to you first."

"But Grandma. Is it your heart? Let me call for help."

She shook her head and squeezed my hand. "I don't have much time. Nobody can help now. This is what's supposed to happen. This is where I say goodbye and leave this earth."

I choked up and started to cry. "No, Grandma. No. It's just a heart event. You're going to be fine."

"No, bubbeleh. This is my end of the road. This is

where I die. I've known it for a long time. But I need to talk to you before I go, and we don't have a lot of time."

"But Grandma..."

"Listen to me closely. I won't be able to say it again. You must remember my words and take them seriously. Gladie, you have the gift. Don't look at me like that. This is important. This is the only thing that's important. You have the gift. You have the third eye. You're more talented than I ever was."

"No, I don't have the gift. I don't see things like you do."

"Because you don't believe in yourself, dolly. You think you're a quitter, a loser. But you're not. You're a wonderful woman, who will be great someday. You'll match this whole town and beyond. You'll guide people before they make mistakes. You'll save people from bad choices. You have the gift, but you need a push. You need me to give you a gift of the gift."

"But Grandma..."

She shushed me and urged me to bring my face closer to hers. "The time for talking is over," she said. "I have just enough time to do what I need to do."

She cupped my face with her hands and closed her eyes. Suddenly, I felt heat course through my body. My eyes closed, and I saw a bright, white light in my mind's eye. It was the gift, and it traveled through me, settling in my soul.

I was bombarded with vision after vision. Some were of events that happened years before I was born. I saw my father as a young boy, stealing bubble gum from the Mini-Mart. I saw my great-grandmother wearing my wedding dress for the first time. Then, the visions moved to the present, and I saw Lucy pregnant with a baby girl named Laura growing inside her. I saw Spencer showing me the deed to our dream house with my name on it, which he had changed the day before we were married. I saw Peter falling in love with a mysterious woman in San Francisco and going on a wild adventure. I saw me living in Grandma's house, which was now my house forever. Then, I went far into the future, and I saw Spencer old and gray and still very handsome, sitting with me on the couch and kissing me behind my ear.

My eyes opened. "I see, now, Grandma. I see so much. Thank you for this gift. Grandma? Grandma?"

My grandmother lay lifeless in my arms. Her body was just the shell of where she had once lived. I checked her breathing and listened for a heartbeat. There was nothing. The woman who had shown me more love than any other family member or friend was gone.

I was alone, now. Rudderless.

How could I continue on without my Grandma guiding me?

"Why did you do this if you knew it would kill you?" I asked, crying. Rolling sobs wracked my body. I couldn't see because of the tears, and my wails echoed off the walls of the mine. "Why? Why? Why?" I screamed.

I wasn't ready to lose my grandmother. I wasn't prepared to mourn so deeply and for so long. The joy I had felt only hours before was gone and replaced now with a crushing despondence.

After a few minutes, my sobs quieted to simple crying, and I smoothed out Grandma's hair and adjusted her suit. "You were the greatest gift in my life," I told her dead body. "I didn't need anything more than you could give me."

I hugged her to me and tried to memorize this, our last moment together on the earth. In Jewish tradition, the next day she would be buried, and my grandmother would be gone from my life forever.

But even through my grief, I knew inside me that I would go on, that I would continue her business. I even knew that Spencer and I would live in her house and love each other, and I would make matches, just as she predicted, even if part of my heart could never be whole again.

I kissed Grandma's forehead. "I'll love you forever, Grandma."

Matilda moaned and crawled toward me. "What happened?"

"Rockwell fell and hit his head with the crowbar. And my grandmother had a heart attack."

My tears flowed, again. It was hard to accept that my grandmother, who was so full of life, was lying dead in my arms.

"She died?" Matilda asked and began to cry.

"Yes. She was such a wonderful woman. I loved her so

much."

"She was a wonderful woman," Matilda agreed. "I'm so sorry."

We sat with my grandmother for a long moment. With each minute, the grandmother I knew was further away. Her body was unresponsive and growing cooler. My tears flowed steadily.

Matilda reached out and touched my grandmother's face, cupping her cheek. "Don't go away, Zelda," she said.

Grandma's body shuddered, and all of a sudden, she drew breath.

"What the hell's going on?" I asked.

Matilda looked at her hand. "Did I do that?"

"I think you did."

"Should I touch her, again?"

"No! It might work in the reverse."

Grandma opened her eyes. "What happened? This isn't heaven, is it? I thought there would be more windows in heaven."

I hugged her tight. "Grandma, Grandma, you're back! You came back!"

Grandma sat up. "This wasn't how it was supposed to happen. I'm supposed to be dead."

"I'm sorry, Zelda," Matilda said. "I touched you."

"You touched me?" Grandma asked her. "She touched me?" she asked me.

"She touched you," I told her. "You were deader than a doornail, and then you were alive again. Your heart had stopped beating. You had stopped breathing. Now you're breathing. Now your heart is beating. How do you feel? You had a heart attack."

"I know I had a heart attack. I had a massive heart attack that was supposed to kill me, dolly."

"It killed you temporarily," Matilda pointed out.

Grandma touched her chest. "I feel fine. Never better. It's like I got… what do they call it with a computer?"

"Rebooted?"

"Yes, I've been rebooted. I feel seventy years old again."

Matilda studied her hand. "My hand never did that before."

"You've never touched a dead person, before," I told her, sure of myself. "But you're going to touch a lot more." Matilda's eyes grew wide in fear. "Don't worry. Not in Cannes. You're going to move."

"I am?"

"You should buy a cowboy hat," Grandma told her.

EPILOGUE

We think of life as a series of milestones, of happy events and tragic ones. But it's the spaces in the middle that make up the living parts of life. A dinner here. A sunset there. These are the building blocks. If you focus on only the big and the bigger, you'll miss what's in front of you. Focus on the mundane and the everyday to create a life of love. Love is never more than a step away.

Lesson 1, Heart Advice from Gladie Burger

ONE MONTH LATER

We moved the entertainment center with the giant television into my grandmother's old room. It was one of the few things that we managed to salvage from the house across the street. We got the couch and two recliners, too, which Spencer was thrilled about, but his beloved refrigerator bit the dust.

We stood back and looked at the redecorated bedroom.

"Are you happy with our new bedroom?" I asked him.

"I'm happy for more room," he said, pulling me in close to him. "Now, I can make love to you here and there and there and there and there. We could try some acrobatics, now, see how far back your legs can go."

"You're five years old."

Spencer smirked his little smirk and rubbed his pelvis against me. "Really? Is this five years old? Huh? I don't think so."

"Is what five years old? I don't feel anything."

"Oh, Pinky. You wound me. You know it's the Guinness Book of World Records giant anaconda, biggest shlong that ever existed."

"Oh, I know that, do I? If I knew that, I must have forgotten it."

Spencer lifted me in his arms and tossed me onto our bed. He nestled his body between my legs and rested his weight on his forearms. "You're sure you're happy here?" I asked him. "You're not too disappointed that we're not in the dream house?"

"You mean the cursed house?"

"Maybe it's not cursed," I said.

"It's cursed."

"We could renovate it, if you want."

"It's cursed. We'll get the insurance money and sell the shambles. Let someone else handle the curse."

"It's better to hold onto it. In two years, a successful artist will buy it for three times the price we paid for it."

"Wow, I like the new Pinky. The all-seeing Pinky."

"Not all-seeing. Just a-lot-seeing. Hey, is that your anaconda, or your service revolver?"

"My anaconda is my service revolver, hot stuff."

"We're going to need to cool it, Mr. service revolver. Grandma is downstairs, waiting for us to take her to the cruise ship terminal in Long Beach."

Spencer waggled his eyebrows. "Four months alone, just you and me."

"You, me, and the entire town. Business has been booming."

"But at night, it'll be just you and me."

Matilda had been staying with us, but she moved away last week, after a distant cousin left her a house and business in New Mexico. So, now, it really was just going to be Spencer and me.

"How long are you going to make us wait?" Ruth yelled from the bottom of the stairs. "We're old, you know. You're taking up some of our last minutes on this planet. But take your time, by all means. Think about yourselves. Don't bother with other people. Who cares about society?"

"I was upset about abandoning my latte habit for four months, but she's making it easier," I told Spencer.

"Zelda and Ruth on a four-month vacation together. That's called the nuclear option."

Downstairs, Spencer gathered the suitcases and packed up his car. Ruth searched through her purse a tenth time before she was satisfied that she had remembered their tickets and passports.

"It's not easy leaving Tea Time for four months," she said, getting into the backseat of Spencer's car. "What if Julie burns the place down?"

"Bridget will handle it," I told her. Bridget was taking over Tea Time while Ruth and Zelda traveled. They had already planned on a six-week glamping trip after the cruise.

"How about you, Zelda?" Spencer asked. "Are you worried about being in retirement and leaving Cannes to Gladie?"

"I'm not retired, sweetie. I'm semi-retired. And Gladie has the gift. She won't let me down."

For the first time in my life, I believed her. Spencer backed out of the driveway, and we started on the road to Long Bcach. My cellphone rang. It was Lucy.

"If I get a stretch mark, I will kill not get finished killing Harry," she said.

"You won't get a stretch mark," I lied. "How are you feeling?"

"The good news is that I've thrown up three times today. I can fit into my skinny pants."

"Has Harry recovered?"

"He was speaking in full sentences for a while, but someone mentioned diapers and he went back to gibberish." She told me to tell Grandma and Ruth bon voyage, and she hung up.

On the way out of town, we passed the pot bus, and I waved at my mother. We still didn't have the world's best mother-daughter relationship, but she had come a long way. She invited me for lunch next week.

Fanta had made a deal to rat out Rockwell for a reduced sentence. The last I heard, he was sharing a cell with the dictator. The mayor personally asked for the harshest sentence for the dictator because he had kidnapped his donkey. He was so upset about Dulcinea that he moved her to a donkey sanctuary in Colorado.

"I'm glad to get out of this town," Ruth said, as we turned onto the freeway. "Crazy-ass town. I don't know why I didn't leave earlier."

"Because you love it," Grandma said.

"Well, besides that."

Ruth was right about our crazy-ass town, but Grandma was right, too, about loving it. I couldn't imagine living anywhere else. It's where I found my love and found my home.

And where I found myself.

THE END

The next book in the Matchmaker Mysteries is *Ship of Ghouls. Keep reading for a preview!*

And don't forget to sign up for the newsletter for new releases and special deals: http://www.elisesax.com/mailing-list.php

elise sax

SHIP OF GHOULS EXCERPT

CHAPTER 1

At some point, we all get in a rut. If your relationship is all about the same old, same old, force it onto a new path. Go on a road trip! Or better yet, go on a cruise. Cruise ships have an all-you-can-eat midnight buffet. All you can eat crab legs might not get you out of a rut, but at least you'll have a belly full of crab legs.
Lesson 2, Heart Advice from
Gladie Burger

For some reason, Spencer always made the bed. It was one of the good things about being married, and there were a lot of good things about being married, it turned out.

It had been almost two months since we said "I do" and

our dream house disintegrated in a huge post-wedding pile-up. I didn't want Spencer to know it, but I was relieved that our dream house was now Pompeii, post-volcano. I loved my grandmother's house, which for me was home and the only home I'd ever known. It was true that we didn't have a refrigerator just for champagne or a giant island in the kitchen with an inlaid computer monitor, not to mention a workout room and a sauna, but my grandmother's house was a beautiful Victorian home, full of history and happy memories.

Cozy.

Spencer didn't seem to be too sad about the demise of our custom-made home, either. Occasionally when he would go to work, he would pause at his car, look wistfully across the street at the rubble of our house, and sigh. But otherwise, he seemed happy in our newlywed home.

I explained to him that we weren't going to get hit, financially. The rubble of our house would get sold, and we would turn a good profit. I was sure of it.

I had seen it.

That's right, I had the gift.

The gift didn't turn out to be an all-seeing eye. I couldn't tell when every little thing was going to happen or read minds, but I always knew when to wear a sweater or bring an umbrella. It was also helping me make matches left and right. I had turned into a dynamo matchmaker. A whiz. I could do no wrong in the love business.

For instance, I knew that Molly Evans should be with Jake Robbins. It wasn't an obvious match. She was six-foot-two and a librarian, and he was a five-foot-four boxer, but I knew that they would make each other happy, and that's what I was going to tell them at an early morning match greet I had set up.

"What're you doing?" Spencer asked pulling me back into bed. "Where are you going?"

"Molly and Jake are coming to meet each other this morning, and I need to dress professionally."

"You mean you have to brush your teeth? Come on, we've got time."

Since we had gotten married, we had fallen into a morning routine. Spencer woke me up at the crack of dawn, and we'd jump all over each other like newlyweds until around six-thirty. Then, we would take a communal shower and possibly do some more down and dirty monkey sex while the water was still hot. After we were clean, Spencer would make the bed, and we would go downstairs and eat breakfast.

My grandmother was still on her cruise with Ruth, and it was just Spencer and me in the house, outside of matchmaking hours. It had taken a little while to get used to not having Grandma there, but not too long. At first it was like Spencer and I were playing house, that it wasn't really our home and that we were just pretending to be adults. But that ended fast.

We quickly adapted to our new roles as grownups with our own house. I got used to being the "wife," and Spencer seemed to be born to be the "husband." We had traded bedrooms with my grandmother, and we finally had enough space for Spencer's clothes. Our morning routine just sort of happened organically. Without discussion between us, we fell into a rhythm.

I had to admit that there was little in my life that gave me more joy than eating a bagel and drinking a cup of coffee with Spencer at seven o'clock every morning. But this morning I had a lot to do, and I couldn't let Molly and Jake down. I didn't have time for our normal routine.

"Would you be upset if we skipped the morning bed noogy?" I asked Spencer.

Spencer shot me his best hurt puppy look. "No noogy? Why? Why?"

"Molly and Jake are going to be here right on time, and they're going to get right down to the match greet. Then, Jake is going to have a flat tire, and Molly's going to give him a ride. That's when they'll fall in love. So you see, I'm on a tight schedule. It has to happen on time."

Spencer arched an eyebrow. "Okay. You know, it's hard to argue with your wife when she's a witch."

"I'm not a witch. I just have the gift."

"Okay. Okay, Glinda. No bed noogy. But we'll give the shower noogy a bigger punch today. I've been meaning to try out the soap dish."

I couldn't lie. I was as intrigued as I was scared about the soap dish remark. "Deal," I said.

Spencer turned on the shower, and we walked inside. As much as possible, he was very good about letting me have the spot under the showerhead. I took in his nakedness and sucked air between my teeth. Spencer was very impressive naked. Even more impressive than he was dressed in his fancy clothes. He had washboard abs and muscles everywhere. And then there was his face, which on a scale of one to ten was a number so high that only Stephen Hawking could have counted to it.

Even without a fancy workout room at home, Spencer was diligent about exercising at the police station every day. The only exercise I got was sex with Spencer and minimal walking to get coffee. I placed my palm on his chest with my fingers splayed. "You're in such good shape. I can't compete."

Spencer wrapped his arms around me and pulled me in close. He already had a big erection and he ground it against my belly. "Don't change anything about you, Pinky. You've got exactly the right biological and physical makeup. It's like Frankenstein created you in the lab just for me."

“Just for you?” I croaked. “Exactly right biological and physical makeup?”

He palmed my breast with one hand and squeezed my ass with his other hand. "See? Perfect. Fleshy, yet firm. You’re beautiful, Pinky. And more than that, you’re the sexiest woman I have ever had the pleasure to be with. Strike that. The sexiest woman that I could've ever conjured in my imagination."

I swallowed with difficulty. "Wow, you do foreplay good."

"You like it? I've been playing around with it for a while and thought I would try it out this morning. Now let's get this party going. How about you turn around and bend over?"

"In the shower? What if I drown?"

He smirked his normal little smirk. "Don't worry. I

know CPR. If you drown, I'll bring you back to life."

"Yeah, like I believe that. You're not going to give me CPR if you haven't finished yet, if you know what I mean."

Spencer scratched his chin. "You have a point, Pinky. I guess I'll just lift you up against the tile and do you like that."

"Do me?"

Spencer shrugged and smirked his little smirk, again. "Don't shoot me, Pinky. I haven't worked out the rest of my foreplay speech. How's 'making love'? Or 'fucking your guts out'? I like 'fucking'. There's a certain poetry to it."

"Sure. Let's go with that."

With the words out of the way, Spencer's hands were all over me. He caressed his way down the front of my body and slipped a finger inside me. He was getting me ready, but the joke was on him. I had been ready since I had woken up in bed in his arms.

Spencer was ready, too. He looked like he could chop wood with his penis. He picked me up, and I wrapped my legs around him. He backed me up against the tile wall and entered me.

"Oh," I moaned. It felt really good. Normally we did a lot more foreplay, including tongues and everything that nature provided. But today Spencer was all about getting it done before my appointment.

He was thoughtful like that.

Anyway, I didn't need a lot of lips and tongues. By the time that he thrust three times inside me, I felt the familiar rush of pleasure through my body as it rose to orgasm.

Geez, I loved orgasms. They were even better than chocolate.

Thirty minutes later, we were downstairs in the kitchen. Spencer was dressed for work in a tailored Armani suit, his hair perfectly coiffed, and his beard was scruffy and barely visible. I was wearing black pants and a blue top. That was fancy for me.

I put on the coffee, and Spencer sliced the bagels and tossed them into the toaster.

“Orange juice?" he asked. One of the changes that Spencer had implemented was no more bottled orange juice. He insisted on making it fresh every morning.

"Sure," I said. He squeezed the orange juice, and I cracked eggs into a pan.

When the food was ready, we sat down at the table and faced each other. Spencer smirked his little smirk, and I blushed. "Love that," he said. "Love that I can make my wife blush. And I plan on making you blush every second we're on our honeymoon." He checked his watch. “Countdown, Pinky. I can smell the sea air already. Just a few more hours before we leave town and sail the high seas of love.” He broke into the Love Boat theme, singing off key.

We had been given a honeymoon cruise as a wedding gift from my best friend Lucy and her husband Harry. Spencer and I had been planning all the things that we were going to do on the cruise, and none of them involved shuffleboard or hanging out on the Lido deck with Captain Stubbing.

Most of our plans entailed new ways to get naked together and pushing the boundaries of lovemaking. I had secretly bought new racy négligées, one outfit for each night, and I had them delivered to my other best friend Bridget's house so that it would remain a surprise for Spencer. I was going to pick them up from her at Tea Time after the match greet.

After Spencer left to go to work, the match greet happened exactly as I had foreseen. Jake got a flat tire, and Molly gave him a ride. They had hit it off at the house, but I knew that they would fall in love in Molly's Honda Fit. It was one of the easiest matches I'd ever done.

With another love match made, I walked to Tea Time, which was my favorite place for coffee. I had a deal with Ruth Fletcher, who owned the tea shop, to give me free lattes for a year. But Ruth was away on an around the world cruise with my grandmother, and she had left Bridget in charge while she was gone.

Tea Time was housed in the center of the historic district. It used to be a saloon, and there were still a few bullet holes in the wall. Bridget was a bookkeeper and she just had a baby, but running the tea shop turned out to be a natural fit.

The social interaction was a relief for her. No longer isolated in her house with the baby, she was now around people all day long. She brought baby Jonathan with her, and he got a lot of attention from the customers.

I walked into the shop. A group of customers were cooing over baby Jonathan, who was perched on the bar in a baby seat. When he was born, Bridget didn't allow anyone to talk to him in baby talk because she thought it would stunt his cerebral cortex. But these days she was giving into it, and I had caught her on more than one occasion calling him her “baby waby.”

Bridget waved me over to the bar. I gave Jonathan a kiss on his forehead. "Latte?" Bridget asked, even though I never got anything else to drink. She put her hand over her mouth. "Are you picking up the you-know-whats?" she asked me in her best spy voice.

I nodded.

"Normally, I don't condone women wearing stuff like this to objectify their bodies and make men want them as objects,” Bridget said. “But boy, you got some racy, pretty stuff. Sizzle hot!"

I hadn’t tried the lingerie on yet, and a little bubble of worry popped inside me. Would I have the nerve to get that down and dirty with Spencer? What if I looked ridiculous in the sexy outfits?

"I put them in bags so you can carry them easier," Bridget explained, putting three large bags on the counter. She made the latte and sat down with me at a table with baby Jonathan on her lap.

"Have you heard from Ruth, lately?" I asked.

"Are you kidding? It's been nonstop. She calls at least twice a day, even though the charges for telephone calls are crazy on that boat. She micromanages everything. When I bought too much Lapsang Souchong, I thought she was going to have a stroke. I won't make that mistake again. And you know what, Gladie? I think something happened on that cruise. Ruth doesn't seem quite herself. I mean, she's still ornery as hell, but she seems a little different to me."

"I'm Skyping with her and my grandmother in about an hour."

"They discovered Skype?"

"Spencer introduced it to them. But this will be the first time they're placing a call. I'll let you know how it goes." I took a sip of the latte. It was good, but it wasn't quite as good as Ruth's.

"Are you all packed for the cruise, besides the dirty stuff?" Bridget asked.

"Spencer is packed. But I haven't started. I bought three new dresses because they make you dress fancy for dinner." I gnawed on the inside of my cheek. I hadn't done a lot of fancy stuff in my life. I was much more a jeans and t-shirt kind of girl.

Bridget put her hand on mine. "It's going to be wonderful, Gladie. You'll be beautiful, all glammed up, and it's going to be the perfect honeymoon. Even though I don't believe in honeymoons."

I tried to see what the cruise would be like. I was seeing excitement and adventure, but the rest was blurry. I was okay with that. A vacation was a vacation, and I had never been on a real one with Spencer before. I hugged Bridget goodbye and went home. I quickly packed my things, and threw my toiletries into a grocery bag. It took me two minutes to pack completely.

"There. That wasn't so bad," I said, looking

appreciatively at my packed suitcase. It was time for the Skype call with my grandmother and Ruth, so I went upstairs to the attic office where my laptop was. As I stepped into my office, I smiled. It was a beautiful sanctuary, filled with antiques and light. Spencer was jealous of my space, and he hinted more than once that he wanted a man cave. I told him that was ridiculous because the whole house was his man cave, but I had secretly planned to have the little room off of the parlor turned into his man cave while we were away on the cruise. It was my wedding gift to him, I mean, besides the hoochie mama underpants.

I turned on my laptop just as the Skype app dinged. I pushed the button and waved at Grandma and Ruth. "Back up a little," I urged. "I'm only seeing cheeks. You have to back up so I can see all of you."

"It's this damn technology. It's the dehumanization of our species. Not that we didn't deserve it," Ruth grumbled as she and Grandma rearranged themselves. It took a good five minutes before they could see me and I could see them.

"You look beautiful, dolly," Grandma said with a smile.

"What are you wearing?" I asked.

"It's called a muumuu. You like it?"

"Of course she doesn't like it, Zelda," Ruth spat. "You look like you're wearing a circus tent. A circus tent made of fifteen colors. Nobody likes it."

"I never realized how comfortable baggy clothes are, dolly. My whole body's breathing. Even my tuchus is breathing. Such a great invention. They wear muumuus here in Fiji."

"Fiji," I breathed. "That sounds like heaven."

"If you call mosquitoes heaven, then yes, it's heaven," Ruth complained. I didn't know what Bridget was talking about. Ruth seemed exactly the same to me.

"Are you all ready for your cruise?" Grandma asked me.

"I just packed. And I matched Molly with Jake."

Grandma clapped her hands together and smiled. "Perfect. What a wonderful love match they are. Good work, Gladie. You've got the gift."

Didn't I know it. I had the gift and how. I could do no wrong.

It was sort of disorienting.

"How's the rest of the cruise?" I asked. "I hear that they have midnight buffets."

"People eating like pigs," Ruth said. "Pigs. They can't get enough. They shovel it in morning, noon, and night. I've never seen anything like it. I don't know how these people don't explode with all the food in their systems. They don't even chew. They just swallow. I saw a man swallow an entire slice of cheesecake, and then he asked for another one. Revolting. I'm not seasick, but I still want to throw up."

"Ruth's a little upset because her friend got off the cruise early," Grandma explained.

"I'm not upset. And you know that I don't have any friends, Zelda."

"What friend?" I asked.

"A man kind of friend," my grandmother said.

"Oh, really? A man friend?"

"Knock that smile off your face, girl," Ruth snapped at

me. "You think no man would be interested in me? I'll have you know that I have to fend off advances every day."

"But she didn't fend off this advance," Grandma explained. “Rudolph Varian. A dentist, now retired. He got off early because he's doing a cross-country trip of America, instead."

"That's more of my style," Ruth said, earnestly. “You know, the Grand Canyon, New Mexico, the St. Louis arch. There's a lot to see in our country. We don't have to go to Timbuktu for a little dose of travel and adventure."

Grandma patted Ruth on her back. "There. There. We’ll find him, again. We won't let him get too far."

"So, you're going to call the cruise short?" I asked.

"We're talking about it, dolly."

"Spencer and I leave in a couple hours," I said. "I still don't know where we’re going. Harry's keeping it a surprise. I can't get a reading on it.”

"We're not machines, bubbeleh. We have the third eye, but the third eye doesn't see everything."

“Third eye, my Aunt Fanny,” Ruth said. “She didn’t warn me off the clams, and we know how that turned out."

Grandma shrugged her shoulders. “No one bats a thousand, Ruth. Have a nice time on your cruise, dolly. Take lots of pictures.”

“And don't make a pig of yourself like the rest of them,” Ruth insisted. “Wait until you see the pigs at the troughs. Disgusting. Gross. I don't know why people on cruises are allowed to live. Consume consume consume. All they do is try to get as much food in them as possible. It's nauseating. It's repulsive. It's a crime against nature."

"Don't worry, Ruth," my grandmother said. "We'll find him. We'll chase him down and find him."

Since Spencer was leaving his car behind at the station, I went to pick him up from work. He was only working a half day, just enough time to give last-minute orders to his people. I walked into the station, and Fred, the desk sergeant, greeted me. "Hello, Underwear Girl," he said. "Gee, you sure do look pretty today."

"Thanks, Fred. How's Julie?"

"Oh, she's fine. She's out of the hospital. It turned out that they could save her toe. It's a miracle, really. I was sure that toe was a goner."

He mentioned something about a bagel slicer incident, but I didn't have time to get into details. "Tell her hi for me. And I'm glad about the toe."

Fred buzzed me in back, and I walked down the hall to Spencer's office. I stopped just outside because he was giving orders to his two detectives, Remington and Margie, and I wanted to give them their privacy.

"No problem, boss," I heard Remington say. "I got you, Mr. OG."

"I've got the schedule done," Margie said. "And I moved my needlepoint group meetings until after you get back. So, I'll give my total devotion to the security of the town, chief."

"That's what I want to hear," Spencer said.

Everything was going to plan. I hadn't found a dead person in over a month. The town hadn't been invaded by any cults or crazy people. I was doing a whiz-bang matchmaking job. And Spencer's police force was almost competent. It looked like smooth sailing for our trip.

Peeking in, I got a little thrill watching Spencer give commands. I liked that he was a good police chief and was devoted to his work. I also liked knowing what he looked like naked. Spencer caught my eye, and as if he knew what I was thinking, he gave me his little smirk and waggled his eyebrows like Groucho Marx.

Oh, yes. He looked good naked.

As soon as Spencer was done, I drove us home and parked my Oldsmobile Cutlass Supreme in the driveway. Lucy and her husband Harry arrived soon after to take us to the cruise terminal in Long Beach.

"We still don't know where we're going," I told Lucy as Harry and Spencer lugged the suitcases to Harry's Bentley.

"Harry won't tell me," Lucy said. "He did say something about not making eye contact with the crew. I don't know what that means." Lucy pulled me aside and whispered, "Tell me the truth. Do I look fat? Do I look fat? How fat do I look? Don't lie to me. I mean, don't lie to me unless you think I need to be lied to. Do I need to be lied to? Am I that fat?"

"No," I said, truthfully. "You don't even look pregnant. I wish my stomach was as flat as yours. You don't have an ounce of cellulite anywhere on your body. Your face is aging in reverse. You're Benjamin Button in a peach organza dress and designer shoes."

Lucy exhaled, as if she had been holding her breath, and kissed me on the cheek. "You're the best friend a woman could ever have."

We piled into the Bentley. Harry started it up, and Frank Sinatra began to sing on his fancy stereo system.

"Now, this isn't your normal kind of cruise," Harry explained, as he drove out of town. "But you don't want any of that froufrou pansy stuff. This is a real man's cruise."

What the hell did that mean? A real man's cruise? I wasn't a real man. I wasn't even a part-time, so-so man. Spencer took my hand and brought it to his lips. I reminded myself to sit back and relax. I was on my honeymoon with the man I love. And what could go wrong on a cruise?

Grab your copy of *Ship of Ghouls* today!

ABOUT THE AUTHOR

Elise Sax writes hilarious happy endings. She worked as a journalist, mostly in Paris, France for many years but always wanted to write fiction. Finally, she decided to go for her dream and write a novel. She was thrilled when *An Affair to Dismember*, the first in the *Matchmaker Mysteries* series, was sold at auction.

Elise is an overwhelmed single mother of two boys in Southern California. She's an avid traveler, a swing dancer, an occasional piano player, and an online shopping junkie.

Friend her on Facebook: facebook.com/ei.sax.9
Send her an email: elisesax@gmail.com
You can also visit her website: elisesax.com
And sign up for her newsletter to know about new releases and sales: elisesax.com/mailing-list.php